Internal Enchantment

By Helen Harper

BOOK TWO OF

THE FIREBRAND SERIES

BOOK COVER DESIGN BY YOCLA DESIGNS

For David and his endless supply of lockdown memes

Chapter One

The vamp came out of nowhere. One minute I was strolling down Beak Street, enjoying the night air in those joyous moments before dawn when the world seems to hold its breath, and the next I was sprawled on the pavement with a flapping, cackling body on top of me. It happened so quickly that for a moment or two I genuinely didn't know what had hit me. I didn't have time to panic which, I suppose, was some sort of progress on my part.

'Gotcha!' The vampire leered, his white fangs bared. 'You ain't so tough.'

I shoved my palms upwards, forcing him off me, and leapt to my feet. 'You do realise what the penalty is for assaulting a police officer?' I glared. 'What do you think you're doing?'

He swayed from side to side, his feet stumbling as he sought to maintain his balance. Then he frowned and gazed down at the pavement, silently suggesting it was the ground's fault that he couldn't stand upright. 'Council should do something about that,' he declared loudly, pointing down at an invisible spot.

I hissed in irritation. The guy was three sheets to the wind. I could smell the cloud of stale alcohol enveloping his body, and his eyes were glazed and unfocused. Whatever he'd been drinking, it was clearly strong stuff. But that wasn't an excuse for his behaviour. This was the third time in as many weeks that I'd been jumped by a supe, and I was getting mightily fed up with it.

While I believed that neither werewolf, nor vampire,

4

nor any other manner of supernatural being who lived in this part of London would dare to harm me, it seemed to be a growing sport to see who could take me by surprise. It was apparently the latest challenge in the supernatural world, like planking or that ice-bucket thing for humans. At least those pastimes had willing participants. As far I was concerned, this was the sort of regular experience I could do without. It wasn't news that I was neither as strong as a wolf nor as fast as a vampire.

'Are you on your own?' I demanded. 'Or do you have buddies nearby who are enjoying the show?' I was fed up with my position as an entertaining spectacle for supes.

'Buddies?' he blinked at me. 'Yesh. I have many buddies.' He waved his arms around as if he could conjure up hordes of fanged friends from the shadows. When no-one appeared and there were no muffled guffaws from any hidden spectators, his bottom lip jutted out. 'I dunno where they are,' he confided, his brow creasing. 'Mebbe they went home.' Then his confusion cleared and he jabbed a finger at me. 'But I got you! I got you! I got the detective!'

Unbelievable. I rolled my eyes. I'd had enough. It hadn't taken me long to discover that I had very little sense of humour where this sort of high jinks was concerned. It was time to put a stop to this shit.

I reached into my pocket and pulled out a cable tie. In one swift movement, I snapped it round the vamp's wrists. It took him a moment to register what had happened, then he stared down at his bound hands and frowned. 'Hey!'

'These are magic ties,' I told him, aware that he had the ability to yank himself free in less time than it would take me to toss my head. 'If you break them, you'll be automatically cursed.' I was lying through my teeth.

Magic didn't exist – not in the sense that I was describing, anyway. 'In fact, the last guy who snapped them off ended up covered in suppurating boils. I've never seen pus like it in my life.' I shook my head. 'The colour,' I whispered. 'And the *smell*.'

The vamp blanched. 'You … you … you can't do this to me! You can't lock me up or arrest me. It's not allowed. You're a human.'

I probably wasn't human at all, but he didn't need to know that. 'You'd be surprised what I'm allowed to do,' I remarked mildly. 'But don't worry. I won't stick you in a jail cell.'

He stared at me. 'What will you do then?'

'We'll pay your boss a little visit.' For the first time since he'd jumped me, I smiled. 'Together.'

'Lord Horvath?' The vamp's eyes widened.

'He *is* your boss, right?'

'Uh…'

'And he'll be holding court at Heart as we speak, right?'

'Um…'

'And he'll rip your head off for bothering me.' I paused. 'Right?'

The vampire's jaw worked uselessly. I grinned and patted his shoulder. 'Come on then, sir,' I said with a cheerful twang. 'Let's go.'

The vamp gazed at me for a moment then twisted round, running off in the opposite direction. I folded my arms and watched. He staggered left then right, then smacked into a lamp post and bounced off it, falling backwards into a dirty puddle at the side of the road.

I tutted loudly and strolled over to him. 'Well,' I said, looking down at him, 'that wasn't very clever, was it?'

He groaned. I reached down, hauled him up to his feet and patted his back. 'Come on.'

'What – what did you do to me?'

Nothing. 'I'm with Supe Squad,' I told him. 'In fact, as far as you're concerned, I *am* Supe Squad.' As the only detective in the department, that part was true. 'There are all sorts of … tools at my disposal.'

He sniffed and hung his head. 'I don't wanna get in trouble.'

'Perhaps you should have thought of that before you attacked me.' I patted him again and steered him along the street. 'Come on. I don't have all night.'

This time he acquiesced, although he clearly wasn't happy about it. 'I didn't mean anything,' he mumbled. 'I wasn't attacking you. I only wanted to surprise you.'

'Yeah, yeah.' He stumbled against me, veering off course. I set him right again and continued. 'What's your name?'

The vampire hesitated just long enough. 'Joe.'

I sighed. I wasn't expecting him to tell me his real name because supes rarely did – and it wasn't because of stubborn criminality. Their names could be used against them by someone more dominant. In theory, anyone with the right kind of power could compel a supe to do their bidding once they had their name. In practice, very few supes were capable of such a feat, and it wasn't possible to compel anyone to do something that went against their true self. For example, you couldn't force someone to commit murder unless that murder was something deep down they already wanted to do. By now, every supernatural being in London knew that I possessed compulsion abilities – but, like everyone else, I still had considerable limits.

'If you say so.' I looked 'Joe' over. Vampires age differently. While they certainly aren't immortal, their life spans are around double the length of a typical human's. Joe appeared to be in his early twenties but he could have been twice that age for all I could tell.

For all that, there was something about his demeanour – and his actions – that suggested youth. He possessed the same glowing good looks that most vamps achieve after they are turned, when their features are enhanced and nature works to boost their predatory abilities. His hair was blond and shiny, and his eyes were an alluring cornflower blue. However, he still retained a callow immaturity that was clear despite his lack of sobriety and his pretty vamp-boy facade.

'You were turned this year, right?' I asked.

Joe pouted. 'No. I've been a vampire for three years.' He held up four fingers. 'Three. Years.'

'Uh huh.' I hid my grin. 'And why were you chosen to be turned? Lots of people petition to be changed. Why were you one of the lucky ones?'

'Because,' Joe declared, 'I am amazing.' Thus far, evidence for that assertion was sorely lacking.

I rubbed my chin. 'I wonder,' I said casually, 'if Lord Horvath will still think you're amazing when I haul your drunk arse in front of him and tell him what you did to me.'

Joe's steps faltered. 'You don't have to tell him everything,' he mumbled. 'You could leave out the part where I knocked you down.'

I wasn't going to tell Lord Horvath a damned thing. I didn't need Lukas to protect me, and running to him would only make me look weak. But that was something else Joe didn't need to know.

'I won't be able to help myself.' I let out a loud, melodramatic sigh. 'Whenever I see him, he makes me forget myself. I think it's his black eyes. They're so mesmerising. Just one flash of those dazzling peepers and I want to tell him all my inner secrets. I can't explain it.'

Joe swallowed. 'He's very busy. Lord Horvath has a

lot going on, so he probably won't want to be bothered.'

I pretended to consider this. 'I think he enjoys being bothered by me,' I said slowly. I tapped my mouth thoughtfully. 'And didn't he tell all his vampires that I was to be respected? I reckon he quite likes me.' I cast Joe a curious glance. 'I wonder what punishment he'll mete out for what you've done. Will it hurt?'

The vampire paled further. 'Don't take me to him. Don't tell him what I've done.'

I shook my head. 'Joe, I'm only doing my job. I have to keep the streets safe. You assaulted me. What happens if you assault someone else and they're seriously hurt?'

'I won't! I wouldn't do that! I'm sorry!' He turned pleading eyes on me. 'I'll do anything. Just don't tell Lord Horvath what I've done. Please.'

'You'll do anything?' I asked slowly.

He bobbed his head up and down frantically. 'Anything!'

I gazed at him. He was still very drunk, and there was a good chance he wouldn't remember any of this the next day. I shouldn't have been taking advantage of someone in that sort of inebriated state. But Joe had come to me, not the other way around.

'The thing is, Joe,' I said, 'I need someone on the inside. Someone in the know who can give me the scoop on vamp matters. Not gossip. I need someone who can give me the real good stuff.'

'Like – like an informer?' His blue eyes went wide

He wasn't as daft as he was acting. 'Yeah. Just like that.'

'If Lord Horvath found out I was passing on secrets…'

'They don't have to be confidential matters,' I said quickly. 'I'm not asking you to betray your own kind. I only want to know what's going on from time to time.

You seem like the kind of person who pays attention and has the inside track.'

Joe pulled back his shoulders. 'I am. I am definitely that kind of person.'

'So?' I enquired. 'Do we have a deal?'

He wrinkled his nose. 'Maybe. I'll have to think about it.'

'There's no time to think, Joe. It's either yes or no. You have to decide now.'

He hesitated.

'Or we can head straight to Heart and talk to Lord Horvath about what you…'

'I'll do it,' he interrupted.

I smiled. Perfect. 'Once a week. We'll meet under the large oak in Trinity Square right after dusk every Wednesday evening, and you'll tell me what you know. In return, I'll keep quiet about what you did to me.'

'Once a week?' His voice was incredulous. 'And right after dusk? I've got better things to do at that time than hang around with a policewoman!'

I remained calm. 'That's what it will be to begin with. Then we'll see how things go.'

'I can't… I won't…' Joe's shoulders sagged. 'Alright.'

I dug out my phone and turned the camera onto record. 'Say it to video, Joe. I'm sure you're honourable, but you might forget your promise. I need to record it, just in case.' I leaned towards him. 'Evidence protects us both.'

A more sober Joe might have refused but his judgment was already compromised. 'Fine.' He looked at the lens. 'I will meet you every Wednesday night and tell you what's happening with the vampires. If I do that, you won't tell Lord Horvath that I attacked you.'

'Good lad.'

He held up his wrists. 'Will you take these off now?'

I pulled out a penknife and swiftly cut through the plastic. 'There. Job done. No nasty oozing boils for you.'

Joe shuddered. 'Can I go now?' He was almost meek about it.

'Go on, then. But if you don't show up on Wednesday,' I waved the phone, 'I'll release the video.'

'I'll be there.' He shuffled his feet. 'I'm sorry if I hurt you.'

I held my sympathy at bay. I wasn't hurt – but I could have been. 'So you should be.' I nodded at him. 'See you soon, Joe.'

He bowed his head and, a moment later, scarpered off down the street. Halfway down, he collided with a parked car and I winced at the thud. That looked more painful than his encounter with the lamp post. I watched as he picked himself up and took off again, weaving this way and that. Then I spoke again. 'You can come out now.'

There was a faint chuckle from the shadows at my side. 'You knew I was here?'

I shrugged. 'I guessed.'

Lukas stepped forward, peeling himself away from the darkness. 'It's good to see you again, D'Artagnan.'

'Likewise, Lord Horvath.' I inclined my head.

A small smile curved his lips. 'Is my presence making you forget yourself?' he asked softly. 'Are my black eyes mesmerising you right now?'

'I'm weak at the knees,' I said drily. 'And far too flustered to think straight.'

He laughed, then he looked down the street where Joe had disappeared. 'I'm beginning to think it was a mistake turning that one. Young vampires often lose their heads for a while, but I expected better of him.'

'Are you upset that I'm forcing him to inform on

you?'

Lukas waved a hand dismissively. 'He's hardly privy to state secrets. You can play your little games with him if you so desperately want to. You should know, however, that if there's anything you want to know, you only have to ask me.' He bared his teeth. 'Sometimes I might even give you a truthful answer.'

I smiled. 'It's useful to get information from a variety of sources.'

'If you say so, D'Artagnan.' He moved closer. 'Did he hurt you?'

My back felt bruised from where I'd fallen but I'd survive. 'Not really.'

Lukas's eyes glittered. 'He shouldn't have done that.'

'No,' I agreed. 'He shouldn't have. But you can't punish him for it. You're not supposed to know what happened.'

'Hmm.' He gazed at me for another long moment. 'You don't have the crossbow with you.'

'Whatever Joe did, he didn't deserve a silver bolt through his heart.' I'd been practising with the weapon, but I wasn't much better than I'd been four weeks ago.

'No,' Lukas murmured, 'but it won't always be a drunk vampire on a dare who comes at you. You should be able to defend yourself properly.'

'I'm working on it.'

'Work harder.' He folded his arms. 'You might think you're immortal, D'Artagnan, but there are always loopholes – and we don't know for sure what you are yet. You might not always resurrect. It would … pain me if something happened to you.'

I met his gaze. Nothing was likely to happen to me. Not given what I'd been up to in the last month or so. 'Do you know what I've been doing lately? Supe Squad is supposed to be more involved in your affairs, but I spend most of my time directing lost tourists.'

'That's not a bad thing.'

I stood my ground. 'It's not what I'm here for.'

Lukas licked his lips. 'Are you telling me that you wish there was more crime so that you can justify Supe Squad's existence?'

'No, I'm telling you that when a crime is committed I should know about it so that I can help out. That was the agreement. I wouldn't have to force vamps like Joe to spy for me if you and the clans were more open.'

His eyes sharpened. 'Do you also have wolves informing on their kind?'

'That would be telling,' I said primly. 'I'm not the bad guy, Lukas. I'm not your adversary.'

'I'm glad to hear it.' He tilted his head, and I had the strange sensation that there was something else he wanted to say. Something he wanted to ask. In the end though, he simply nodded at me. 'Stay safe, D'Artagnan.'

'Back at you, Lord Horvath,' I returned.

And before I'd finished my sentence, Lukas had melted away into the night.

Chapter Two

I strolled into the Supe Squad office early the next afternoon. From what I could tell, a heated – and rather loud – discussion was taking place in the small meeting room reserved for general queries from the public. I paused outside the door and listened, then I knocked and entered.

Fred, for once properly attired in his uniform, was sitting opposite a well-dressed couple in their late forties. He sprang up as I entered, relief written all over his face. 'This is DC Bellamy,' he said, by way of introduction. 'She's the lead detective here at Supe Squad.'

I was the *only* detective here at Supe Squad. Not that anyone cared about semantics.

'You're a *real* detective?' the man asked, doubt colouring his tone as he looked me up and down.

'It's about time,' the woman snapped. 'This is a serious matter. We need more than a low-grade police officer dealing with our case.'

I raised an eyebrow at Fred. He implored me silently with his puppy-dog eyes and started to explain. 'This is Patrick and Vivienne Clarke. They wish to put in a complaint about some werewolves.' He held out his notepad but I made no move to take it.

Mrs Clarke huffed. 'This is about far more than making a complaint! These wolves need to be dealt with. They're terrorising us! What they've done to our family is beyond the pale!'

I offered my most professional smile. 'I'm so very

sorry to hear of your troubles. You're very fortunate that you have PC Hackert to help you. He's incredibly efficient and more than capable.'

Fred sent me an imploring look that I pretended not to see. Fred needed to learn to step up to the plate – and the only way he'd do that was if I empowered him to take control. While it was clear that the Clarkes were not the easiest of people to deal with, it was rare that any member of the public wandered in off the street with a happy smile. People like the Clarkes were combative because reaching the point where you had to make an official complaint to the police was unbelievably stressful. When you added the supernatural into the mix, tensions were only heightened further.

'PC Hackert will listen very carefully to everything you have to say,' I reassured them. 'Once we have all the relevant details, we'll work together to solve your problem. You're in very capable hands.'

Fred blanched.

'The only problem around here is those wolves.' Mr Clarke's cheeks were turning purple with rage. 'They should be rounded up and thrown into a damn zoo!'

'A zoo would be too good for them,' his wife chimed in, her hand reaching for his. Emotions certainly were running high.

Fred swallowed and raised his chin. 'I understand this is a difficult situation for you both—'

'I'll say!' Mrs Clarke interrupted.

'However,' he continued, his tone growing firmer, 'we treat all species with respect – and that includes werewolves. If your son had come to us, he would have received the same treatment as anyone else.'

'If that were true, you'd have done something when they kidnapped him the first time around!'

Okay. My gaze flitted from husband to wife. Now I

was interested.

'We investigated at the time,' Fred said gently. 'He became a werewolf of his own free will.'

Ah. Now the Clarkes' attitude was starting to make more sense.

'Our boy would never have chosen that path if he hadn't been coerced,' Mr Clarke mumbled. His chest was rising and falling rapidly as he struggled to control his emotions. However, Fred's growing confidence, as well as his words, was having the desired effect and the couple were calming down. Atta boy. I knew he had it in him.

'I'll leave you to complete the interview,' I said. 'PC Hackert will ensure no stone is left unturned.' I left them to it. By the time I'd closed the door, the Clarkes' voices were already more muted and reasonable.

Liza's head appeared at the far end of the corridor where the main office was located. 'Are they still there?' she whispered.

I nodded. She pulled a face and ducked back into the office for safety. I headed in after her.

'Those guys are nuts,' she told me in a hushed tone. She waved a file at me. 'They used to be in and out of here all the time. Harassment. Kidnapping. Murder. They even suggested that Clan Carr was some sort of weird sex cult.'

'This is all to do with their son?'

Liza nodded. 'Julian. The day he turned eighteen, he made an official petition to all four werewolf clans.'

'He wanted to be a wolf?'

'Yep. He probably couldn't wait to get away from his folks.'

I wandered over to the kettle, checked it for water and flicked it on to boil. 'Coffee?' I asked.

Liza declined. 'I've got juice, thanks. I'll take a biscuit, though.'

I grinned and grabbed one, tossing it in her direction. She caught it deftly in one hand.

'So Julian Clarke's petition was accepted?'

'After three years of trying. The Clarkes' single-minded focus was him, and his single-minded focus was to become a werewolf. Tony investigated it at the time and Lady Carr allowed an interview. It was all above board and legal. The Clarkes just couldn't accept what their son had become. From what I know, Julian Clarke did well for himself. He made rank within twelve months, and was on his way to becoming epsilon.'

The four werewolf clans are built on a very specific hierarchy. Non-ranking wolves, who end up doing the more mundane tasks required by a clan, are called iotas. They are considered to be pups and are typically young and inexperienced, or not very skilled.

Each werewolf clan is permitted to turn a small number of willing humans each year and there are strict procedures in place to avoid unnecessary … accidents. It usually only takes two or three bites for those humans to become pups. Their numbers are strictly capped by the government, which is a source of considerable rancour amongst the wolves since it takes time to settle into what is essentially an entirely new species. To achieve rank and gain promotion, a wolf must challenge another wolf during the full moon.

The lowest rank is made up of zetas, followed by epsilons, gammas, deltas, selsas and betas. At the very top are the alphas – and each clan only has one alpha. Six weeks in, and I was still getting to grips with the system. It helped that most werewolves wore arm tags to identify their place in the hierarchy, but even so there was a lot to wrap my poor head around.

I spooned a teaspoon of instant coffee into the cleanest mug I could find. 'So where does murder come into it?'

'Pardon?'

The kettle started to judder. I turned it off and poured out the hot water. 'You said that his parents made murder allegations.'

'Ah.' Liza grimaced. 'Unfortunately, Julian met an untimely end.'

I paused, holding the kettle in mid-air. 'Go on.'

'It wasn't anything to do with the werewolves,' she told me. 'It was a hit and run. He went out to celebrate making rank, but he was mowed down before he got to the pub. The driver was never caught.'

I winced. 'But the Clarkes still alleged he was murdered?'

Liza read from the file. '"If Julian hadn't been forced into becoming a werewolf, then he wouldn't have been out on Bartholomew Street and wouldn't have been killed."' She paused. 'Their words, not mine. They also suggested that the werewolves killed him and used the accident to cover up his death.'

'Was there anything in the pathology report to suggest foul play?'

'He was hit by a car. It was messy, but there's nothing else there.'

I sighed. So the Clarkes had effectively lost their son twice, firstly to the werewolves and secondly to a speeding car. I felt a brief surge of sympathy for them.

'He was killed last year,' Liza said. 'Just over twelve months ago, in fact.'

That made sense. The first anniversary of his death had probably hit them hard and they still wanted someone to blame. I sipped my coffee. People's lives could be so shambolic. Unfortunately, I included myself in that statement.

'Did you come across anything useful last night?'

Liza asked, changing the subject.

'I procured another not-so-confidential informant,' I said, explaining what had happened with Joe.

Liza's brow creased with confusion. 'He won't be much of an informant if Lord Horvath knows about him.'

'The vamps aren't criminals and we're not trying to uncover any illegal activity. We just want a closer eye on what's going on. Joe will be perfect. We get a steady stream of information, and Lukas is forced to keep us in the loop. He won't feel threatened by anything we work on because he knows where all our information is coming from.' I took another sip. 'The Lord of all vampires is not particularly keen on Supernatural Squad. If he thinks he's controlling us, he'll be more amenable in the long run.' I grinned. 'It's all part of my master plan.'

'If you say so.' She eyed me. 'How many other people are on a first-name basis with Lord Horvath?'

I took a sudden interest in the contents of my mug. 'He's a friendly guy.'

'Sure. The Lord of all vampires is a real sweetheart.' She smirked. 'With cheekbones to die for. Has he asked you out on a date yet?'

I started to choke. 'Don't be ridiculous. Our relationship is purely professional.'

'It's coming, Emma. Any day now. He'll make it sound like it's a business meeting but, when he suggests you have a meeting over dinner, you'll know it's really a date.'

'It's barely been a month since my boyfriend tried to kill me,' I reminded her. 'The last thing I want or need right now is romance.'

Liza's smile grew. 'I'm not talking about romance. I bet Lord Horvath is the shag to beat all shags. You can't pretend to me that you've not thought about it.'

I could feel my cheeks heating up even though, no, I

hadn't thought about it. Not much anyway. And I seriously doubted I was Lukas's type.

Fortunately, Fred took that moment to join us. He stomped into the room, heaved himself over to the sofa by the far wall and flopped down. 'Man.' He blew air out loudly. 'That was hard work.'

'You handled them very well,' I told him, glad of the interruption.

He pouted. 'You could have stayed and helped.'

'I didn't need to,' I said simply. 'You had it under control.'

He twitched. 'It was nothing. I just did what any police officer would have done.'

I shook my head. 'Let's make an agreement right now to stop being so damned British. You did a great job with the Clarkes, Fred. You calmed them down, subtly pointed out their racism without being confrontational, and remained professional at all times. Own up to your success.'

He considered this for a moment. 'You're right. I was pretty fucking marvellous.'

'Amen.'

Liza smiled.

'Unfortunately,' Fred continued, 'we do need to look into their complaint. It's kind of weird.'

Something about that word always put me on edge. 'Go on.'

'The Clarkes arranged to have their son's body exhumed.'

'Ew.' Liza made a face. 'Why would they do that?'

'Let me guess,' I said. 'They're still looking for proof that Julian was killed by a werewolf.'

'Not quite,' Fred said. 'They decided that they'd been lied to all along, and Julian was never turned into a werewolf at all.'

I raised my eyes heavenward. 'A judge agreed to allow his body to be exhumed for that?'

'The Clarkes are rather ... dogged in their persistence.'

'Tell me something I don't know.'

'Alright then, I will.' Fred glanced at me. 'When they dug up Julian's grave, there was no body in there.'

I blinked. Of all the possible scenarios, that one hadn't crossed my mind. 'Did the funeral parlour mess up?'

'Nope. It was an open casket. The body of Julian Clarke was definitely buried twelve months ago, but it's not there now. The coffin was extracted but no body was found.'

I scratched my head. 'Uh...'

Fred nodded. 'That was my reaction, too.'

I swallowed. It was, without doubt, one of the creepiest things I'd ever heard. Fred and I exchanged horrified glances. Liza simply unwrapped the biscuit I'd tossed to her and started to munch on it. 'We should get the caramel ones next time,' she said.

I stared at her.

'What?' she asked through a mouthful of crumbs.

'It doesn't bother you that a corpse has gone missing from its own grave?' Fred asked.

'I try not to think about things like that too much,' she said. 'Although that's why I'm going to be cremated. It's written in my will.' She took another large bite of her biscuit.

'Liza,' I said faintly, 'can you explain that?'

'If you're cremated, Emma,' she said, 'you can't be eaten. Obviously.'

Nausea stirred in the pit of my belly. 'Eaten?'

'By a ghoul.' She wiped a few stray crumbs from the corner of her mouth. Then she realised Fred and I were still staring at her. 'Oh. I forget that the two of you are quite new to Supernatural Squad. It's just what happens. It's pretty icky but it's the circle of life.' She shrugged. 'What else did you think ghouls feed on?'

I couldn't say it was something I'd ever thought about. In my five weeks at Supernatural Squad, I was sure I'd not met any ghouls, although I was aware of their existence. Supes who weren't either vamps or wolves were classed as Others; ghouls fell into that category, together with gremlins, pixies and various other supernatural beings. 'Ghouls eat corpses?'

'Yep.' She licked her fingers. 'They burrow down to the coffins and munch away to their heart's content.'

Fred was pale. 'You're expecting me to tell the Clarkes that their son was eaten?'

'This is why it doesn't get talked about much,' Liza said. 'People get very sensitive about this sort of thing.'

It didn't take much to imagine why.

'They're not breaking any laws. It's legal to eat a corpse. Well,' she amended, 'it is if you're a ghoul. They can't eat anything else.'

She'd been right the first time: it wasn't the sort of thing I wanted to think about too much. 'We should look into it anyway,' I said. 'To be sure.' I looked at Fred. 'Where was Julian buried?'

He checked his notes. 'St Erbin's.' My heart sank. 'It's on the edge of Soho, not far from Piccadilly Circus.'

'I know where it is.' My insides tightened. St Erbin's Church was where I'd been killed. The first time. There were only three people – or possibly four – who knew it had happened, and that I'd risen from the dead in a ball of fire twelve hours after my death. None of those people were in this room.

I still felt shaky about the whole thing, and visiting the scene of my first murder again was very low on my list of priorities. Unfortunately, it didn't look like I'd have much choice. I shuddered. 'Liza, can you note down everything you know about ghouls? Fred, can you come up with a list of all the ghouls who live in London?'

The pair of them nodded. Fred, in particular, looked relieved that I was taking the lead. 'What about the Clarkes?' he asked. 'Should I call them back?'

'From what we know about them, they'll need absolute proof that werewolves weren't involved. Let's hang fire on that for now.'

He exhaled. 'Good plan.'

I forced a smile. It was still early afternoon and the sun was shining. I supposed there was no time like the present to revisit the scene of my own death and investigate a grisly case of corpse-munching at the same time. I liked my job, I told myself. Honest.

Chapter Three

I hadn't died once. I'd been killed twice – and on both occasions by the same person. He was dead now so, in theory, I had nothing to fear.

I'd stared at myself in the mirror every day for the last month, checking hopefully for signs of natural ageing. I didn't want die, but I didn't want to be immortal either. In my ideal world, I'd be nothing more than perfectly normal – but rising from the dead wasn't normal.

Lukas knew about it and, even though he'd been a vampire for a good fifty years or so, he'd never heard of anyone like me. Neither had Dr Laura Hawes, the pathologist at Fitzwilliam Manor Hospital, who'd been the first person to witness my resurrection. My boss, Detective Superintendent Lucinda Barnes, was also aware of what had happened. And the good Reverend William Knight of St Erbin's Church probably knew too.

Reverend Knight had seen me before my first death – and after it. He might not have appreciated the ins and outs of my situation but he was aware of enough to be cautious. I reckoned that was why he ran inside and barred the church door when he saw me approaching from the other side of the street. Either that, or he was terrified of my winning personality and winsome ways.

I pushed open the rusty iron gate and walked along the short path, pointedly avoiding looking at the spot where I'd died. When I reached the heavy church door, I knocked politely. There wasn't any answer. The vicar could pretend to be out all he wanted but I'd seen him. He knew that I'd seen him. And I knew that he knew.

'Reverend Knight,' I called. 'It's DC Bellamy. I'm with the police.'

I waited for a beat or two. Still nothing. Last time we'd spoken, the reverend had convinced himself that my first death, which took place in this very graveyard, had been faked. He'd allowed himself to believe that it was some sort of clever ploy cooked up by the police, and I hadn't disabused him of that notion. Unfortunately, he'd now had enough time to think about that version of events and had clearly decided, quite rightly, that it couldn't be true.

I tried again. 'Last time we met I was just a trainee, but I'm a fully qualified detective now. You're going to have to talk to me sooner or later.'

Silence. I drew in a breath.

'I understand you have some questions about me,' I called. 'I'll tell you everything I know, if you want. It's not very much.' I hesitated. 'I'm here on police business, Reverend. My visit has got nothing to do with what happened here last month.'

I was beginning to think I'd have to give up and come back on another occasion when there was a rattle from the other side of the door. It opened a fraction, then Reverend Knight seemed to gain confidence. He swung the door open wide, jumped out and thrust a wooden crucifix towards me with a sharp yell. I remained where I was. He slammed the crucifix against my chest. Unfortunately for him, I didn't writhe, or scream, or spontaneously combust.

'Begone demon!' he shouted.

'Good afternoon,' I said politely.

His hand trembled. 'Begone!'

'I'm not a demon, Reverend. Or a vampire. I'm a

detective investigating a possible crime and—'

'Leave this place immediately.'

He was very, very scared. I felt sorry for him, but I couldn't walk away. This was my job. 'I'm afraid I can't do that.'

'I'll call the police.'

'Reverend Knight,' I sighed, 'I *am* the police. But if you want to call someone else, that's fine. I'm happy to wait.'

His eyes searched my face, then his shoulders sagged and he withdrew the crucifix. 'I thought this would work,' he said. 'Maybe you're not evil.'

'It's been my experience so far that we all have a capacity for evil. I would certainly never profess to being good. I instinctively distrust anyone who is confident enough to boast about themselves in such a way.'

'You died. You didn't fake your death for some police operation. I've thought about it and thought about it. And then I thought about it some more. You were dead. You *passed away*.'

I didn't flinch. 'Yes.'

'You shouldn't be alive.'

I raised my shoulders. 'Probably not. But I am. I can assure you that it wasn't my doing. I'm as surprised about it as you are.'

Knight gripped the crucifix in one hand and raised his other hand towards me. He poked me with his index finger. 'Solid flesh,' he muttered to himself.

'I bleed too,' I said cheerfully. 'And not just monthly. If you cut me, I'll have a wound like anyone else. In fact, apart from the whole resurrection thing, I'm exactly like you.'

'You are *not* like me at all.'

'You didn't tell anyone else about me, did you?' I asked gently. 'You didn't report me to the church authorities.'

He started. 'How did you know that?'

'Because they'd have come here asking questions if you had.'

He swallowed and looked at his feet. 'Yeah,' he mumbled. 'They would do that.' He sniffed. 'I thought about informing them. I also realised they might think I was crazy or, worse, a big fat failure. It's bad enough that you were killed in front of my own church.' He shrugged helplessly. 'I made such a big deal about coming here. I *asked* for this posting. I was so sure that I could make a go of it. I know supes don't get on with the church as a rule, but I was convinced that with the right person in place, genuine inroads could be made. We could start a conversation.' He sighed. 'It's not working out that way.'

I might not be religious but I understood exactly what he meant. I'd thought much the same during my detective training. I'd been convinced that I'd be a super-duper investigator who would solve complex crimes through my dedication, hard work and clever ideas. It took me a while to realise that, no matter what grandiose ideas I had about myself, harsh reality would not match up to my imagination. And I wasn't as capable as I wanted to be. Not yet, anyway. It had been a hard lesson.

'This is just a suggestion,' I said, 'but perhaps all the signs you've posted outside the gate, which are trying to stop people from joining the supes, aren't a good idea.'

He raised his head and met my eyes. 'Part of my role is to counsel members of the public and prevent them from approaching any supernatural being,' he said bleakly.

'Have you had any success?'

Knight's expression was resigned. 'None.'

I offered him a sympathetic smile. 'People follow their hearts. You can't change that.'

'But that's exactly what I'm supposed to do,' he protested.

I put my hands in my pockets. 'Do you remember the man I was here with last time? The vampire?'

'Yes.' His tone was wary.

'It just so happens that he's Lord Horvath.'

Reverend Knight stumbled. His hand reached out to grip the door frame and steady himself. 'Seriously?'

'Yep.'

He shook his head in dismay. 'How could I not have known that?'

'If it makes you feel any better,' I told him, 'it took me a while to realise who he was, too. Anyway, I could speak to him and ask him to chat to you about a way forward. Maybe you could come to some sort of arrangement that would help you both.' I doubted very much that Lukas would be pleased with my suggestion, but he couldn't pretend that St Erbin's Church wasn't here. Perhaps some good could come out of it.

'Why would you do that?' Knight asked, his eyes narrowing. 'What do you want in return?'

'I'm not asking for anything in return. If you don't want me to—'

'No!' He released his hold on the door frame and straightened up. 'If you could arrange a meeting, I'd be very grateful.'

'I can't promise anything,' I said. 'But I will try.' I smiled, glad that we were on a better footing. 'Now, I have a few questions for you about another matter.'

Knight frowned 'I thought you didn't want anything in return.'

'I don't. I would be asking these questions regardless. I'm investigating a complaint made by a member of the public, and you can help.'

He knitted his fingers together. I knew that he was

secretly pleased to help. At the end of the day, we all want to be useful. 'Go on, then.'

I drew in a breath. 'What do you know about ghouls?'

Reverend Knight recoiled. 'Why are you asking about them?' he whispered.

I knew from the look on his face that he knew exactly why I was asking about them. 'An attempt was made recently to exhume a body from one of the graves here.'

Knight shrank further into himself. 'Yes. Julian Clarke. Poor boy.'

'Did you preside over his funeral?'

'No. That was my predecessor.'

'But,' I pressed, 'you have no reason to think that Julian's body wasn't in the coffin when it was buried?'

'No.' He spoke so quietly I could barely hear him. 'The Clarkes were very … vocal when they realised his coffin was empty. I tried to stop them from going ahead with the exhumation. The graveyard has had problems with ghouls for decades, centuries probably. I'm not supposed to tell people about it unless they specifically ask. If the ghouls can't feed here, they'll move elsewhere. It's the church's thinking that it's better to confine them to one area. Bodies are mere vessels, after all. It's the souls inside those vessels that concern us.'

I had the sense that he was parroting what he'd been told, but it certainly wasn't my place to question his beliefs or the church's practices. 'How do the ghouls operate?'

Knight threw me a baleful look. 'You're in Supe Squad. And you must be a supe yourself. Don't you already know all this?'

'I'm new,' I said, splaying out my hands. 'I don't really know anything at all. Educate me, Reverend. Don't leave anything out.'

He sighed distractedly. 'There's not much to tell. As far as I'm aware, there is only a handful of ghouls in London. They reside underground between Soho and Lisson Grove, along with the other supes who aren't vampire or werewolf. They feed on corpses. Typically, one ghoul requires a minimum of one corpse per annum to survive. They dig into the earth, burrow underneath a new coffin and...' His voice trailed off.

'Dine?'

Knight nodded. 'You know when they've been because there's always a small pile of earth like a molehill.' He swallowed, his Adam's apple bobbing nervously. 'It's happened twice since I started here.' He looked ashamed.

'Have you ever seen a ghoul?'

'No. Frankly, I don't know what I'd do if I did.'

I didn't blame him. Nothing about the ghouls' actions was easy or simple. 'Can you show me Julian Clarke's grave?' I asked.

Knight pointed. 'It's this way.'

My gaze followed his finger and I exhaled in relief. Julian Clarke had been buried on the opposite side of the graveyard to where I'd been killed so I wouldn't have to go near that spot. As much as I'd come to terms with my murder at the hands of my own boyfriend, there was a lingering trauma that I had no desire to confront yet. 'Lead the way.'

We picked our way along the path. 'When a body is exhumed,' Knight told me, 'a temporary tent is erected to protect the scene. Nobody wants to go strolling past on their lunch break and be confronted with a corpse rising out of the ground. Death is the final taboo for a lot of people – we don't like thinking about it, or talking about it.' He glanced at me. 'I'm not talking about the grieving process, you understand. Even in my line of work, death itself is a difficult concept.' He paused. 'Which brings us full circle back to you.'

'I can't explain what happened to me,' I said honestly. 'I don't know why it happened and I certainly don't understand how.'

'How long—?' He shook his head, unable to complete the sentence.

'How long was I dead for?' I asked. 'Twelve hours. And, no, I don't remember anything about it. It's a blank space.'

Reverend Knight absorbed this. I was expecting more questions but he appeared to be as reluctant to discuss my experiences as I was. Thankful for small mercies, I followed him in silence until we reached the gaping hole where Julian Clarke had supposedly been laid to rest.

'There's not much to see, I'm afraid,' Knight told me. 'His coffin was removed from the scene for further examination. I can give you the details of the coroner's office that took charge of it.'

I nodded my thanks and gazed around. Julian Clarke's headstone was ornate, with not only his birth and death dates inscribed but also some intricately carved flowers, trumpeting angels and a short quotation: *The vengeance of the innocent knows no bounds.* No doubt that was his parents' doing.

'They visited his grave every week, you know,' Knight told me. 'The Clarkes. There were always fresh flowers.'

I knelt down, peering into the hole to look for signs of burrowing. All I could see was dark, squelchy-looking mud and a few small, forlorn puddles. But then it could have been many months since a ghoul had been here. 'The Clarkes are blaming the werewolves for what happened to their son. Did you tell them about the ghouls and their … proclivities?'

'They didn't want to hear it. I did try.'

Hmm. The Clarkes were focused on the wolves as the source of all their woes to the point where nothing else mattered. I bit my lip and stood up, sliding my phone out of my pocket. 'Hi, Fred,' I said when he picked up. 'It's Emma.'

'I was about to call you. Uh ... someone's here to see you.'

I frowned. 'Is this another member of the public who you don't want to deal with?'

'No. Not exactly, anyway. It's a supe. He only wants you.'

I brightened considerably. Even though Supe Squad had recently been given the all clear to deal with more supernatural crime, we hadn't had any supes themselves coming in to make a report. This could be the turning of the tide. I beamed. 'I'll be back as soon as I can. Twenty minutes tops.'

'Great.' Fred sounded relieved. 'I've been looking up the ghouls. There's not many of them, and I think I've tracked them all down.'

'Even better. Well done.'

'It was nothing.'

'Fred...' I warned. 'Remember what I said before. Take the praise.'

There was a smile in his voice. 'Then you're welcome. I thought that I'd go and knock on a few doors and speak to them.' He paused. 'If that's alright with you.'

Normally, it would have been but I had the gnawing feeling that there were more pressing concerns to worry about. 'Later. Forget what I said before. Right now, I need you to locate the Clarkes. Make sure they don't do anything stupid.'

'Stupid?'

'They really dislike the werewolves, Fred.'

'Oh.' Then, '*Ohhh*. I'll track them down straight away.'

'Thank you.' I hung up and glanced at Reverend Knight. 'I've got to go. If you see any evidence of ghoul action, could you get in touch?' I dug out a business card and handed it to him.

'Okay. I can do that.' He looked at me.

'I haven't forgotten about Lord Horvath,' I said. 'I'll speak to him as soon as I can.'

Knight exhaled. 'Great. Thanks.'

I nodded at him and walked out of the graveyard, managing to act nonchalantly. I was still not looking at the spot of my first death. Go me.

Chapter Four

I parked Tallulah directly outside the Supe Squad building and jumped out. The tiny purple Mini was in better condition than when I'd inherited her. She now had all her windows intact and she was considerably cleaner. She'd even had a proper service and MOT.

I wasn't sure it made much difference to the car herself. I was beginning to think that she genuinely did have a mind of her own and that she was still miffed that I wasn't Tony, her previous owner. At odd moments her brakes would feel loose and, when it had been raining last week, her windscreen wipers had resolutely refused to work. The mechanic I'd spoken to assured me that she was in good nick, and that I was imagining things, but I still wasn't convinced.

Out of deference to Tony's memory, I'd keep her around for a while yet but she was living on borrowed time. All the same, I gave her bonnet a pat as I passed it. I didn't want Tallulah to know what I was thinking. Five weeks into my tenure at Supe Squad and I was treating an ancient car that belonged in the scrappers' yard as if it were an actual person. Goodness only knew what might happen if I hung around for five years.

I waved at Max, the friendly bellman who worked at the hotel next door, and opened the main door to Supe Squad. Then I gaped. Instinct made me fling my arms up in front of my face, though it wouldn't have done me any good. Not when there was a satyr five feet in front of me, pointing a loaded crossbow at my head.

'Boom,' he said gently. His long ears, which pointed upwards and were covered with soft golden down, quivered.

I glared at Kennedy. I'd seen him around a few times since our first meeting in a werewolf bar when I'd been tracking down Tony's killer. While I genuinely liked the alcoholic satyr, I didn't appreciate being greeted by him in this manner. Especially when it was on my own turf. 'What the hell do you think you're doing?'

He gave me a congenial smile. 'Proving a point.'

I dropped my hands and balled them into fists. 'What sort of fucking point?'

'The sort that tells you that you might end up getting yourself killed if you don't do more to protect yourself.'

Unbelievable. 'Lukas sent you, didn't he?'

'If by Lukas you mean Lord Horvath, then yes,' Kennedy replied.

I ran an irritated hand through my hair. 'You're the supe who's here to see me?'

'I am.' He continued to grin.

'You're not making a crime report?'

'I am not.' His grin grew. 'I'm here to teach you a few new skills.'

I rolled my eyes. 'I appreciate the thought, but I don't have time for this.'

He raised an eyebrow. 'You don't have time to learn how to keep yourself safe? DC Bellamy, I expected better from you.' He lowered the crossbow. 'Come here, Emma.'

The back of my neck prickled. 'You can try and use my real name to compel me all you want, *Lee Oswald*,' I snapped, using his real name in return. 'It won't work.'

Kennedy's expression didn't alter. 'I was merely testing out a theory. You know, it's not smart to give away all your secrets. You don't know that you can trust me.'

'No,' I said flatly. 'But I trust *me*. Thank you for the offer of tuition, but I'll manage.'

'While one might successfully argue that success in battles is to break your enemy without fighting, I've been told not to take no for an answer.'

I ground my teeth. 'Look, Kennedy, I—'

'I cleared your schedule for the next hour,' Liza called out from behind the satyr. 'He's all yours.'

I counted to ten in my head. Then I told myself that the path of least resistance was often the best one to take – and I did need some help with using the crossbow. Although whether that help should come from a whiskey sodden satyr with a penchant for philosophy remained open to question.

'Fine,' I snapped. 'But one hour only. I've got things to do.'

Kennedy reached into his leather jacket and took out a silver monogrammed hip flask. He unscrewed the lid and took a long swig. 'Excellent,' he said. 'This will be fun.'

***

Kennedy had already cleared a space on the third floor in the room where all Supe Squad's ancient weapons were housed. He'd even hauled a dummy up the stairs and set it in the centre of the room to use for target practice. I stared round as he handed me the crossbow.

'Show me what you can do.'

I sighed but I did as he asked, checking the crossbow over and making sure the safety was off and it was cocked. I raised it up and squinted at the target.

'Wait,' Kennedy said.

'What?'

'Your angle is all wrong. If you shoot now, that bolt

will smash through the window, fly out into the street and quite possibly kill someone by accident. I don't suppose that will go down well with all your cop buddies.'

'How can you tell the angle from where you're standing?'

'I've been doing this a long time. You might be surprised.'

I grunted; very little surprised me these days. I adjusted the crossbow and squinted again.

'Wait.'

'The angle's wrong again?' I asked.

'No,' he said. 'It's not the angle. You won't hit the dummy – but you won't accidentally kill any innocent passers-by, either.' He slowly circled round me. Exasperated, I started to lower the bow. Kennedy shook his head. 'Don't move,' he instructed. 'Hold that position.'

'Is this really necessary?'

'Shh. You talk too much.'

That wasn't remotely true, but arguing wouldn't improve my position, so I did as he said and kept my mouth shut. Anything to get this over and done with as quickly as possible.

'How often do you work out, DC Bellamy?'

What did that have to do with anything? 'I go running a few times a week,' I said. 'I don't have time for much else.'

'Weights?'

'No.'

'Hmm.' Kennedy scratched his chin and continued circling. 'Interesting.'

'What? What's interesting?'

'Have you been practising with the crossbow?'

I shrugged. 'I've been trying to, but I haven't had a whole lot of time.'

'Have you been practising with *this* crossbow?'

I glanced down at it. 'No. The one I've been using is a different colour.' My eyes narrowed. 'Why? What's wrong with this one?'

'Nothing at all.'

'Kennedy...'

He gave me a wry grin. 'It weighs almost ten kilograms. That's pretty heavy for a crossbow and you're rather petite, if you don't mind me saying so. You've held it level for several moments without even thinking about it. You're stronger than you look.'

Puzzled, I looked at the crossbow again. It didn't feel heavy at all. My eyes travelled along its length then I paused. I glanced at the empty spot on the weapon-laden wall where the crossbow must have been hanging, and an odd chill ran through me.

I'd held this bow before. When I'd first discovered this room, this was the first crossbow I'd tried. I'd barely been able to hold it upright for more than a few seconds and I'd quickly abandoned it for a lighter version. I gave my biceps a doubtful frown.

'Is everything alright?' Kennedy enquired.

'Fine.' I shook myself. 'Absolutely fine.'

He watched me for a moment longer then apparently decided to forego further mention of my weight-lifting capacity. 'I assume you've heard of the ten-thousand-hour theory?'

'Sure. Spend ten thousand hours practising something and you'll be an expert. The last thing I have is ten thousand hours to spare.'

'It's not about the time,' Kennedy said. 'It's about the focus. You shouldn't fear the person who has practised ten thousand kicks, you should fear the person who's practised one kick ten thousand times.'

'Who said that?' I asked. 'Sun Tzu?'

Kennedy smiled. 'Bruce Lee.' He looked me up and down critically. 'Usually, we'd spend the first few weeks just practising loading and cocking.'

'Weeks?' I half-screeched.

He took the bow from me and uncocked it. 'I said usually. We need to get you prepped and able to defend yourself in far less time than that. I'll still focus on the basics, but it will be up to you to put in those ten thousand hours. You'll never become truly skilled otherwise.'

I calculated in my head. Ten thousand hours was more than four hundred days and I certainly didn't have that sort of time to spend on crossbow training. I understood Kennedy's meaning, however; if I was ever going to rely on using a crossbow, something that a Supe Squad detective was entitled to do, then I had to work at it.

'Okay.' I turned the bow towards the floor, planted my foot in the stirrup, pulled on the string and cocked it again.

Kennedy nodded approvingly and I tried not to feel too pleased with myself. After all, I'd taught myself to get this far.

'Using your bare hands like that is the fastest way. For true accuracy, you should re-cock the bow every time you shoot it, although it's not technically necessary. When you're being attacked, that might not always be easy to pull off but it's a good basis to work from.'

I gave my fingers a mournful look. My skin would end up ripped to shreds. 'Can I get a pair of gloves?'

'Do you usually wear gloves?'

'No.'

'Then no, you can't. You'll develop calluses quickly enough.' He pulled a stopwatch from his pocket. 'Try it again. I'll time you.'

Oh goody.

***

Kennedy and I spent more than an hour practising. He didn't allow me to shoot any bolts; all we did was cock and uncock, load and unload, over and over and over again. By the time we were done, my arms were aching and the skin on my fingers was raw, but I could see my progress. It was more satisfying than I'd expected.

'What time does your shift usually start?' he asked when he finally indicated that I could put the crossbow away and relax.

'About two,' I said. 'But no-one's really checking.' With supernaturals, most of my work was done once night had fallen.

'Good,' he said. 'I'll meet you here at midday tomorrow. That'll give us two clear hours to continue.'

I met his eyes. 'Thank you for this, Kennedy.'

'I'm happy to help.'

'Are you?' I asked baldly. 'What's in it for you?'

He smiled. 'You're going to be around here for a while, so it'll good if you're not trigger happy. A well-fired crossbow bolt is one of the few things that will halt any supe in their tracks. It will be better for all of us if that bolt is intentional. I don't believe in happy accidents.'

I grunted agreement.

'For now,' he continued, 'don't touch the crossbow unless I'm here. I don't want you picking up any bad habits.'

'I thought you wanted me to practise a lot.'

'I do,' he said. 'But there's a world of difference between good practice and bad practice. Until we can be assured of the latter, you should leave it well alone.' He checked his watch. 'And speaking of practice, my drinking arm is beginning to seize up. I'd better get going and make sure it gets properly oiled.'

'Kennedy,' I started, wanting to suggest that he lay off the alcohol but not sure how to go about it without offending him. 'Maybe—'

The door to the weapons room burst open and Liza appeared, my phone clutched in her hand. 'You left this downstairs,' she said breathlessly. 'Fred's been calling.'

I took it from her. Kennedy took advantage of the opportunity to avoid an awkward lecture and left with a brief wave while I answered. 'Fred?'

'Emma, thank goodness. You need to get here. Everything's about to go tits up.'

The first tingles of dread uncoiled in the pit of my stomach. 'Where is here? What's going on?'

'I'm in the car. You were right – Patrick Clarke has it in for the werewolves. I managed to track him to his house, but he left in his own car about twenty minutes ago. I've been following him and I think he's heading towards Lisson Grove. He has a look on his face that spells trouble and,' Fred's voice dropped, 'I think he's armed.'

My shoulders tightened. 'Damn it. I'm on my way.'

I snapped my fingers at Liza. 'Get onto Clan Carr. Tell them that a human is on his way who might attack them but I'll try and intercept him. They are *not* to make a move against him.'

She bit her lip. 'I'll do it now.'

We exchanged grim glances. And then I ran for the door.

Chapter Five

Thanks to Inner London's one-way system and heavy traffic, I could run faster from the Supe Squad building than I could drive. I ignored Tallulah and sprinted down the street towards Lisson Grove. It was just as well that I rarely wore anything on my feet these days that wasn't a pair of cushioned trainers.

The last thing any of us needed was for Patrick Clarke to attack the wolves of Clan Carr under the misguided belief that they were responsible for both his son's death and the loss of his body. We'd just had a full moon so, in theory, all the werewolves would be in full control of their animals and able to show restraint. But they would still defend themselves if they were provoked, and that might spell further disaster for the Clarkes – not to mention human–supernatural relations.

I wove in and out of the pedestrians, narrowly avoiding a woman with a pram. Most of the people on the streets were tourists and more than one of them took out a phone to video my dash. A few even tried to follow me but none of them could keep up.

When I reached the crossroads, I turned left and calculated the fastest way to get to the Clan Carr stronghold. I'd never been inside it, but I knew exactly where it was. Over the last few weeks, I'd spent time mapping out all the main supe points of interest and now I was benefiting from that hard work. I knew that there was a narrow snicket not far ahead where I could cut down and avoid the worst of the traffic. It would mean crossing a busy road before I entered the Lisson Grove area but it would be worth it.

I leapt over a large puddle and spun into the

alleyway. A startled cat eyeing up a bird sprang out of the way as I thundered past. The wind was whipping at my hair and my feet were pounding the ground beneath me. I didn't tend to push myself this hard when I was out running in the mornings, but I still wasn't out of breath. Adrenaline – and the fear of what might be about to happen a few streets ahead – continued to spur me on.

I emerged from the snicket onto a wide pavement. Spotting a break in the traffic, I barely slowed before I tried to cross over. As I did so, a car that was trying to pass before the lights changed to red speeded up.

The driver slammed on his horn. I heard the screeching of brakes and the squeal of tyres. I turned my head and realised that he wouldn't be able to stop in time. I was about to get flattened.

I didn't have time to think. I jumped up into the air, my unconscious desire for survival taking over. The car came to a juddering halt while I spun upwards – and landed feet first on its bonnet.

I blinked. How in hell had I managed that? I swung my eyes to the driver, who was staring at me white-faced. Then, as his shock gave way to fury, he started to shout and shake his fist. I grinned, gave him a wave, leapt off and started running again.

My heart was hammering against my chest. I sucked in air, aware of how close I'd come to ending up as a bloodied pancake. I ducked my head and put on a final spurt. Within seconds, I'd rounded the corner onto the Carrs' street.

I'd been fast, but not fast enough. From the look of the crowd gathered outside the Carrs' mansion and the sound of loud shouting, Julian Clarke's father was already there. 'You murdered my son!' he yelled. 'You stole his body!'

'Fuck off, mate,' one of the younger Carr

werewolves said. He advanced on Clarke, raising his fists and baring his teeth in a snarl that made his intentions clear. Fred, who was there too, tried to bar his approach and calm things down but, neither the wolves nor Clarke paid him any attention.

I sprinted up just as the door to the Carr stronghold opened and Lady Carr stepped out. She looked less like a werewolf alpha than a well-dressed woman on her way out for lunch with the ladies.

Her fragile, bird-like features and small frame completely belied what I knew of her. Lady Carr was as tough as they came. I hoped she could also prove to be diplomatic and understanding when it came to a grieving father.

The crowd of werewolves, which had to be at least thirty strong by now, parted to allow her to stride forward. 'Mr Clarke,' she said icily, 'why are you here *again*?'

'My son!' he bellowed. His voice turned more guttural and anguished. 'My son!'

I winced at his obvious pain. It didn't excuse what he was doing but it did offer a reason.

'We have been through this, Mr Clarke. Your son became a werewolf of his own volition. The law was followed to the letter. He died because of a tragic accident. We feel his loss as greatly as you do but—'

Her choice of words couldn't have been worse. I elbowed my way through the crowd and reached Mr Clarke's side as his face suffused with red and he started to shake from head to toe. 'You lying bitch! You could never feel what I feel. You could never understand!' He reached into his pocket and, as Fred had feared, drew out a gun.

To her credit Lady Carr didn't blink. There wasn't reason to panic – yet. I'd been doing my homework and I knew that a gun was potentially less lethal to a werewolf than a crossbow. A typical lead bullet can be expunged from a wolf's body with ease, and the wolves' healing abilities mean that the damage will be superficial. Of course, it's possible to cast silver bullets that might do the trick, but that is a difficult process that is rarely successful. They are difficult to make, expensive to buy and wholly illegal. Even if an assailant manages to procure some, the bullets have to penetrate deep enough into a werewolf's flesh to allow the silver to work against their blood. Exit wounds are no good: the bullet must remain within the wolf's body to cause harm. That's one of the reasons why crossbows are more useful. Surprisingly, a silver crossbow bolt, with its cunning snags built into the tip, is far more difficult to yank out than a bullet and the damage it can cause is usually far more catastrophic.

Unfortunately, Mr Clarke had been thinking about his revenge for some time. He waved the gun menacingly. 'One hundred percent pure silver,' he snarled. 'Tried and tested. I've been practising. If this won't stop you dead, nothing will.'

I drew in a breath and stepped between Clarke and Lady Carr. Fred goggled at me – and so did most of the wolves. A silver bullet could kill a human just the same as a lead bullet.

'Mr Clarke,' I said sternly. 'Drop the weapon immediately.'

'Armed police are on their way,' Fred said quietly.

I nodded to acknowledge that I'd heard him. Mr Clarke, however, didn't hear me.

'I'll kill you!' he shouted at Lady Carr. 'I'm going to do to you what you did to my son. And then I'll desecrate your body, just like you desecrated his!'

'I have no idea what you're talking about,' Lady Carr

said. 'DC Bellamy, I suggest you deal with this creature before I do. I imagine your methods will be less messy than mine.'

I held up my palms, all but forcing Clarke to look at me instead of Carr. 'I can't begin to understand how you are feeling,' I said softly. 'I've experienced loss, but the pain of losing your own child is beyond my comprehension. However, none of this is the Carrs' fault. None of it is the werewolves' fault.'

'They stole him!' He gazed at me, agony etched into every line of his face. 'They couldn't let him rest in peace. They had to dig into his grave.' He raised his head to stare at Lady Carr again. 'Where is he? What have you done with my son?'

'I don't understand the question,' she said. 'We returned his body to you, as requested after his death, although it is not our usual practice to do so.'

'And then you stole him back!'

'Step away, Lady Carr,' I said. 'Let me talk to Mr Clarke on his own.'

'I'm not sure that's wise.'

'Step away.'

She sighed but did as she was told, gesturing to her other wolves to fall back with her. I turned my back on them and faced Clarke. I needed him to listen to reason without the added pressure of the werewolves he so despised crowding him.

'Mr Clarke,' I said gently. 'It was not the wolves who took Julian's body. It's not their way. The most likely explanation is that it was a ghoul.'

His eyes snapped to mine. 'What?'

'Julian wasn't targeted because of who he was or what he'd become,' I said, trying to explain while not inflaming matters further. 'It was simply a case of being in the wrong place at the wrong time. We believe that a ghoul took him from his grave.'

'A ghoul?' Clarke's face was blank. 'Why would—?' Then it started to sink in. He staggered. I might not have been aware of what ghouls did for sustenance but Clarke knew. 'No. You're not telling me that he – that Julian – that my boy was—'

Uh-oh. 'Mr Clarke, let's go back to the station and talk about this. Give me the gun and we can resolve this peacefully.'

His horrified eyes went from me to the werewolves, and then to the gun in his hand. Something inside him broke. 'You fuckers! You supernatural slimy fuckers! You – you – you—'

'Oh calm down, you silly man,' Lady Carr snapped.

That was all it took. Clarke straightened up, swung the gun round and loosed off a shot. It went wide and slammed into the building behind us. One of the werewolves lunged straight at him, transforming in mid-air.

I threw myself forward and tried to drag the wolf away. 'Get off!' I yelled. If he heard me, he didn't react. His jaws snapped as he tried to pin Clarke's writhing body to the ground.

'Bryan,' Lady Carr commanded, her voice barely audible over the sudden clamour. 'Fall back.' The wolf should have retreated immediately, but he was too enraged by the threat to his alpha to hear her command.

Clarke's arms were flailing everywhere. He continued to clutch the gun, huffing and groaning. The wolf snarled, more than prepared to go in for the kill. I could hear the sirens as a posse of armed police approached, but they would be too late. Whatever was happening here would be finished in the next five seconds.

Out of the corner of my eye, I spotted Fred reaching

for the gun. 'Stand down!'

Clarke shifted to the side and the werewolf took the opportunity of his altered stance to lunge for his exposed neck. I gritted my teeth, grabbed a hank of the wolf's fur and hauled him back. 'Leave it!' I hissed at him. 'Listen to your alpha!'

He growled at me – and then there was a loud bang. Something slammed into me. Pain and hot wetness spread through my chest. I looked up and saw Clarke staring at me in horror, his finger still on the gun's trigger.

'No,' he said. 'Oh no. I didn't mean that. I didn't want to do that.'

The gun dropped with a clatter. I was barely aware of Fred's pale face as he snatched the weapon and moved it out of the way for safety. My vision started to go blurry at the edges and the world slipped sideways.

Goddamnit. Not again.

Chapter Six

'Welcome back!' Dr Laura Hawes' face came into focus, her brilliant wattage smile wreathing her face.

I managed a grunt. The smell of sulphur, which always seemed to accompany my resurrections, was stronger than ever. I wrinkled my nose and forced myself up to a sitting position. 'How long?'

'Twelve hours,' she said cheerfully. 'Just like the other times.' Then, in a bid to be helpful, she added, 'You were shot.'

Tell me something I don't know, I thought ruefully. I touched the spot on my chest where the bullet had entered. There was nothing there but smooth, unblemished skin. I had to hand it to myself – whatever the reasons behind my repeated risings, my body had the recovery process down to a fine art.

'How are you feeling?' Laura asked.

I considered her question. The truth was that I felt fantastic. Energised. Full of vim and vigour. 'Fine,' I said. 'More than fine.'

Laura nodded, like she'd expected nothing else. 'Good.' She raised her eyebrows. 'There's quite a collection of people here because of you.'

My brow furrowed. 'What? Why would there be—?' Oh. My shoulders sagged. I'd died in front of a whole bunch of witnesses. Until now, I'd been able to keep my strange ability to evade death a secret. After dropping dead in front of thirty werewolves, including Lady Carr and Fred, there was no doubt that my secret was well and truly out of the bag.

'If it bothers you,' Laura said, 'I can sneak you out of the back entrance. You can get out of the morgue without seeing any of them.' She looked rather excited at the prospect of some sneaky skulduggery. But that would only delay the inevitable. I might as well face the music.

'No. I appreciate the thought but I'll have to speak to them sooner or later. Who's out there?'

Laura reached for a clipboard. 'Four werewolves, including the head of the Carr clan.' I cursed inwardly. 'PC Frederick Hackert and Special Constable Liza May. A Mrs Vivienne Clarke.' My eyes widened. 'And DSI Barnes.'

'That's it?'

'Yep.' She sent me a wry look. 'No sexy vampire Lords this time around.'

'I wasn't… I didn't…' I grimaced. There was no point lying. 'Alright, I was hoping he'd be here too.' Lukas didn't owe me anything but I'd kind of expected that he'd rush here when he heard about my third death. His absence shouldn't have rankled, but it did.

Amusement danced in her eyes. 'I don't blame you.'

I pushed the vampire Lord out of my mind and stretched, checking my limbs and patting absently at a few tiny flames that were still flickering on my forearms. 'Was anyone else hurt?' I asked. 'After I died, did anyone else get shot?'

'From what I've heard,' Laura said, 'once you dropped, the atmosphere changed considerably. Your assailant was taken into custody and everyone else left the scene.'

I breathed out. That was something.

Laura handed me a small pile of neatly folded clothes. 'I took the liberty of finding things in your size. They look like the sort of clothes you'd wear.'

I smiled gratefully. 'Thank you.'

'Any time, Emma.' She wagged her finger at me. 'This is becoming a bad habit of yours.'

Yeah. I couldn't argue with that.

She left me in peace to get changed. I pulled on the functional underwear, tight-fitting jeans and professional-looking blouse, and ran a hand through my hair to tease out the knots.

Laura had helpfully left a small hand mirror too. I held it up and examined my face. It was still there. I was still me, at least on the surface. I couldn't help wondering if something had altered inside me. Realistically, how many times could I die and come back to life again while remaining the same?

I prodded myself doubtfully and thought about what Reverend Knight had said about the importance of souls over bodies. Was there a darkness seeping into my soul because of my multiple deaths? I shivered. Could I even tell if there was?

My chilling musings were interrupted by a knock on the door. I knew from the brisk rap who it was. I sighed and called out, 'You can come in, DSI Barnes.'

The door opened and she marched in, her arms swinging. 'Twelve hours. I could set my watch by you, DC Bellamy,' she remarked. She glanced round. 'This is the second time in as many months that I've visited a morgue on your account. I haven't spent so much time in the vicinity of the dead since I was a new detective.' She pursed her lips. 'I miss it. There's a peaceful serenity about a morgue. It's where problems get solved and life is wrapped up.' Her gaze drifted to me and hardened. 'Apart from where you're concerned, of course.'

'It's not exactly something I have control over,' I said, irritated by her implied censure.

She sniffed. 'I suppose not. But it would have been

far easier if you could have died without an audience.'

'I'll be sure to remember that next time.'

DSI Barnes folded her arms. 'There's no need for sarcasm.' She tapped her foot. 'By my count, thirty-three people, most of them werewolves, witnessed your death. We have a man in custody who's been charged with your murder. At least last time you took care of your murderer for us – this time I have no idea what to suggest to the Crown Prosecution Service. Clarke killed you, and yet here you are alive.'

She tutted. I wondered if dealing with Clarke was a genuine dilemma or if she was just concerned about the paperwork. Then she gave me a long look. 'Are you alright, Emma?' she asked. 'This can't be easy. I could speak to our counsellors and see if there's someone who can talk you through your experiences.'

I knew it was a genuine offer and I relaxed slightly. For all her gruff demeanour and business-like approach, not to mention her single-minded dedication to the Metropolitan Police Force, Barnes was kind and thoughtful at heart. 'Thank you. I'm fine though, honestly.'

She gazed at me a while longer, then nodded. 'Very well. All that remains is to arrange your reassignment.'

I blinked. 'Pardon?'

'I can arrange for you to be transferred to another force outside London. Newcastle is looking for new detectives. It's a lovely city.'

I was sure it was a great place but that didn't mean I wanted to move there. 'I don't understand,' I said. 'Why can't I stay where I am? You might think I've screwed up the Clarke case, but I've been making great inroads with the supe community. I don't think this is the time to transfer me out.'

'If you stroll into Lisson Grove after dying in such a

showy fashion in the middle of the street, everyone will know what you are.'

My muscles tightened. 'Except *I* don't know what I am. Neither do you.'

Barnes waved a dismissive hand. 'You know what I mean. You can't seriously think that you can wander around the streets now that everyone knows what you're capable of.'

Her voice softened. 'Much as I wanted you to be with Supe Squad, I am unwilling to put you at genuine risk. I've read your reports. I know that you've been repeatedly targeted by supes who want to make their mark because they're aware there's something different about you. That's not something I was expecting. Now that you've risen from the dead, those attacks will probably happen more often. You've made yourself the biggest target in London.'

'With all due respect, DSI Barnes, that's where you are completely wrong.'

Both Barnes and I jumped. Standing in the doorway and looking entirely unperturbed was Lady Carr.

'This is a private conversation,' Barnes snapped.

The diminutive werewolf alpha strode forward until she was nose to nose with Barnes. Despite the grimness of the situation, I was fascinated. This had all the potential of a prize-winning fight.

'I wouldn't have believed it if I hadn't seen it with my own eyes,' Lady Carr said, looking at me with a flicker of awe. 'I've never heard of such a thing before and, believe me, I've seen many weird and wonderful things in my time. There is no denying the truth, however.'

To give her credit, Barnes stood her ground. 'What truth is that?'

Lady Carr smiled. 'DC Bellamy is one of us. She is a

supe.'

'You don't know that.'

'How often do humans die and rise again?'

'How often do supes?' Barnes shot back.

'There are many different types of supernatural beings,' Carr said calmly. 'I was concerned that DC Bellamy was too enamoured of the vampires, and that her allegiance to them would be to our detriment. But, as a supe in her own right, her allegiance will be to herself. We can work with that. In fact, now that we know of DC Bellamy's make up, she will be afforded far more respect. In the space of twelve hours, she's gone from a mere irritant to someone with incredible power and authority.'

As much as I disliked being called a 'mere irritant', given the work I'd put in over the last few weeks, I had bigger concerns. DSI Barnes' ultimate goal was for the police to have greater control over the supes, not just now but in the future. If that control was only temporary, and contingent on my presence, it wouldn't please her in the slightest. It certainly wouldn't persuade her to leave me in Supe Squad.

It was ironic; six weeks ago I'd been utterly dismayed to be sent to Supernatural Squad by DSI Barnes, and now I was devastated at the thought of being forced to leave by the same person.

I cleared my throat. 'I am a police officer first and foremost,' I declared, slightly too loudly. 'The fact that I come back to life after dying might only be temporary. It might never happen again. I might drop dead in a couple of hours and that will be that. We don't know. Neither do we know how the supes on the ground will react to it. They might like the idea or they might hate it. So let's not jump the gun. I believe I've dealt very effectively with the minor attacks. I see no reason for that to change.'

Lady Carr was almost gleeful. 'We agreed to allow Supe Squad greater power after what happened to her predecessor, Tony Brown,' she said to DSI Barnes. 'Now it's your turn to make concessions. We will revoke that agreement if DC Bellamy leaves.'

'You can't threaten me like that,' Barnes said, her mouth twisting.

'It's not a threat.' Carr's tone was mild. 'This is good for both of us. Yes, word will get out among the supes about DC Bellamy's ability. Even I can't prevent that from happening. But *you* sent her to us in the first place. That means you'll be afforded respect too, simply through association. She lays the ground for your future plans. And she's the sort of detective we can truly accept. Our werewolves will not attack her – quite the opposite.'

'You can't speak for the vampires. Or the Others.'

'Lord Horvath has already discussed it with me. He contacted me immediately after DC Bellamy's death twelve hours ago.'

I started. So Lukas knew I'd died again, he just hadn't come to check that I'd also resurrected. That was fine. It was his prerogative. I had no reason to be hurt. Honest.

'With the vampires and werewolves in DC Bellamy's corner, the Others will follow suit. They will have no choice.' Lady Carr glanced at me. 'That is a good thing.'

DSI Barnes exhaled. 'I have a responsibility towards my detectives in the same way that you have a responsibility towards your wolves. It's not merely supes we have to worry about.'

She was talking about humans. How many humans out there would be desperate to do what I did? How many would want to cheat death, either for themselves or for a loved one? How many would want me locked up and experimented upon?

'That,' Lady Carr said, 'is on you. The supernatural community will keep DC Bellamy's secret to themselves.'

I had no real reason to disbelieve her and neither did DSI Barnes. My boss looked at me. 'I know you might feel invincible, Emma,' she said softly, 'but that doesn't mean you are. Your … ability puts you in danger as much it protects you.'

I met her eyes. 'I've died three times. Believe me, I don't think I'm invincible. But I want to stay with Supe Squad. It's where I belong.'

DSI Barnes sighed. 'Happy as I was that you chose to remain, I also told you that you would end up regretting it. Now I fear it's only me who will regret it. But this has to be your call.'

I was surprised at how relieved I was to hear that. 'Thank you.' I lifted my chin. 'I will stay.'

The morgue room door burst open again and Fred and Liza fell through it. Clearly, they'd been eavesdropping.

DSI Barnes glared at them. 'Is nothing private in this place?' she snapped.

Neither of them could stop themselves from grinning. Fred bounded over and gave me a tight hug. 'I'm so happy you're not dead!' He squeezed me harder. 'It's amazing!'

'I'm happy, too,' I said into his shoulder.

'You should have told us that you can't die,' Liza said. 'You can trust us. We won't tell anyone.'

'You'd better not,' DSI Barnes muttered darkly.

I shuffled my feet. 'Fred?'

'Yes?'

'I can't breathe.'

'Oh!' He released me and stepped back. 'Sorry.'

I smiled at him. 'It's fine.' And it really was. A

weight had been lifted off my shoulders. I decided that I wasn't a fan of big secrets. The truth might be more complicated – but that didn't mean it wasn't easier to deal with.

'It's nuts.' Liza poked me with her finger to check that I was real. 'When Fred told me you were dead, I...' She shook her head and choked up. 'I'm glad you're still here.'

'Hale and hearty.'

'Can you do anything else?' Fred asked eagerly.

'Anything else?' Like cheating death wasn't enough?

'Zap lasers from your eyes? Click your fingers and teleport across the world?'

I thought about my crossbow training with Kennedy and the ease with which I could now hold a heavy weapon. I also thought about the way I'd avoided being run over by that car. Okay. Maybe I'd still keep a few secrets of my own after all. 'Nope. Nothing like that.'

'Well,' DSI Barnes said, 'I suppose that's settled for now. There's only one final matter left.' She looked at me. 'What we do about the Clarkes.'

I grimaced. 'Mrs Clarke is here?'

'She showed up about half an hour ago and refused to leave,' Fred said. 'We tried to make her go home but...' He gestured helplessly. 'I don't think she knew what to do with herself.'

'I'll go and talk to her.'

DSI Barnes' eyes narrowed.

'Don't worry,' I said. 'I'll be careful what I say. She wants to believe that I'm alive. The last thing she needs is for her husband to be locked up for murder for the rest of his life.'

'Whether you're still breathing or not,' Lady Carr said, 'that pathetic excuse for a man shot you.'

'He didn't mean to. I'm not denying that the Clarkes

have their faults, and I'm not suggesting that they are grieving angels whose actions should be excused. But they do have their reasons. They want their son back.'

'We all know that's not going to happen,' DSI Barnes snorted.

'They know it too,' I said sadly. 'They always did. And that's the problem.'

***

Mrs Clarke was sitting in the small waiting room near the front desk, surrounded by framed pictures of soothing landscapes and pretty flowers. A leaflet for bereavement counselling was clutched in her right hand; it was crumpled and twisted beyond repair.

When she looked up and saw me, her face whitened. 'You … you're alive,' she gasped.

'Yes. The force of the bullet knocked me out, but I was wearing a bulletproof vest under my shirt so no real harm was done.' And then, because the devil was in the details, I added another lie. 'It helped that your husband used a silver bullet. If it had been a lead one, I might not have been so fortunate.'

'They told me you were dead. And,' she looked round, 'we're in the *morgue.*'

Mmm. Yes, that was more difficult to explain away.

Mrs Clarke exhaled. 'You wanted to teach us a lesson, didn't you? You wanted to show us that Julian's death doesn't give us carte blanche to threaten others. Or to hurt others.'

Good grief. I couldn't imagine a more callous 'lesson'.

'Being here in the morgue is a mistake,' I said. 'Nothing else. Somebody somewhere messed up.' I was using an old defence we'd been taught about in the

Academy. Suspects would claim that it was another guy who screwed up and committed a crime, so it was nothing to do with them. Honest, guv.

'Whoever they are,' she said, her head hanging low, 'they've not screwed up as badly as we have. Julian would have been horrified that things had come to this.'

'What your husband did was wrong. What happened to Julian isn't the werewolves' fault. They aren't to blame for his death. Nobody is.'

All the rage had been sucked out of her. This was a different woman to the one I'd met earlier. I suspected that anger and the desire for revenge was all that had been keeping Mrs Clarke and her husband going.

'He shouldn't have gone there,' she whispered. 'He certainly shouldn't have taken that gun.'

'No,' I agreed.

'What's going to happen to him? Will he be charged?'

'That's not up to me,' I told her. 'I don't know what will happen next.'

She wrung her hands. 'Can't you … can't you put in a good word for us?'

Our legal system didn't allow for that; it was designed to prevent victims from being coerced into withdrawing any allegations. But as I was neither dead nor injured, I suspected that it would be possible for Mr Clarke to be charged on the more minor offences of possession of an illegal firearm and discharging a weapon with the intent to harm, rather than attempted murder.

'It's out of my hands,' I told her. 'Although it would be a lot worse if he'd actually killed anyone.' Patrick Clarke didn't know how lucky he was.

'I don't think it can get any worse.' Mrs Clarke seemed to collapse into herself. 'What will happen now? What am I supposed to do?'

'I can call someone for you…'

'No.' She straightened her spine and sniffed, and I caught a brief glimpse of the iron will she'd shown me during our first encounter. 'I'll talk to our solicitor and find out what's happening to Patrick. He's not a bad man, I swear he's not. What happened with Julian affected us both. But you're right. I know it's not the wolves' fault that my son died. It was a Ford Escort.' Her voice dropped. 'A fucking Ford Escort killed him. Every time I see one now, I feel like kicking it.'

I didn't blame her for that.

She looked at me. 'They told me my son's body was taken by ghouls.'

'That's what we think.' I nibbled my bottom lip. 'Why there?' I asked. 'Why bury your son in St Erbin's? It's not the nearest graveyard to your home and, given its proximity to the supernatural community, it seems a strange choice.' I paused. 'Did the Sullivan clan demand that he was buried there?'

Mrs Clarke looked surprised at the question. 'No,' she said. 'They returned his body to us. It was about the only decent thing they did.' Her eyes flashed with fury but it didn't last long. Her desolation was a far more overpowering emotion.

'The old vicar there was helpful. He gave us a lot of guidance and support after Julian was forced to join the wolves, and again when Julian died. He was a good man. So is his replacement. I don't blame either of them for what happened to my son's body. This isn't their fault.'

With trembling hands, Mrs Clarke reached into her designer handbag and pulled out a photo. The face of a young man who looked a lot like her grinned out at me.

'This is Julian?'

She choked back a sob. 'Yes.'

I gazed at his photo and the youthful optimism

shining from his eyes. I knew without asking that the picture had been taken before he was changed into a werewolf because of the shark's tooth necklace hanging round his neck. Wolves didn't wear jewellery. It didn't tend to last long when you repeatedly shifted from one body form to another.

'I know it's a lot to ask,' Mrs Clarke said shakily, 'and I know I have no right to ask it but—'

I interrupted her. 'I'll do it. I'll find the ghouls and see if there's anything of Julian for you to bury.'

'Thank you,' she said simply. 'It would mean a lot. And I'm sorry about what happened to you.'

My answer was quiet. 'I know. I'm sorry for what's happened to you, too.'

Chapter Seven

All the way back to Supe Squad, I felt like I was being watched. For the most part, I was sure that wasn't remotely true and that I was being ridiculously paranoid. It was still the middle of the night, and all the people we saw on the streets had their own cares and worries.

A few vamps and werewolves goggled at us once Fred turned into the Soho streets. Word had already gone around: Emma Bellamy was back from the dead. I resisted the urge to wave at the few onlookers like I was the Queen, and kept my head down.

'I can take you straight home, you know,' Fred said. 'You just died. I'm sure you can take the day off.'

I smiled. It was difficult to explain that the desire to be active and do something was fizzing through my veins. Dying didn't make me want to curl up and sleep – it had quite the opposite effect. 'No, I'd rather get to work and keep busy. But I appreciate the lift. *You* can certainly take the day off. You've been up all night hanging around the morgue while I've been dead to the world. Literally.'

'I'll go and get a shower,' he said bravely. 'But then I'll be right by your side again.'

This certainly was a different Fred to the one I'd met when I first walked into Supe Squad. That one had spent most of his time slumped in front of the television. I appreciated the effort he was making, even if it wasn't necessary. 'I need you to be rested,' I said. 'Not half dead through lack of sleep. Take the day off. Liza is going to do the same.'

'Half dead?' he grinned. 'That's an odd turn of phrase given I'm not the one who's been lying on a slab for the last twelve hours.'

I shrugged. 'The English language is full of idioms to do with death.'

He pulled up right outside the front door. 'You're dead right.'

I gave him a long look. 'This could get very tiring very quickly.' I unclipped my seatbelt. 'Go home, Fred.'

He yawned. 'Okay. I left the list of ghouls and their whereabouts on your desk,' he said. 'From what I know about them, they only stay awake during the night so you've got a few hours left to track them down.'

'Perfect.' I stepped out of his car and closed the passenger door.

'Knock 'em dead, boss,' he smirked. Then he drove off before I had the chance to scowl.

I tutted, ignored the dark glower Max's night-time replacement gave me, and headed inside. That guy still despised me and I continued to be baffled that he'd chosen a job in customer service in this area. Neither his position nor his location appeared to suit him very well. But, as long as he remained on the right side of the law, it wasn't my place to judge his life choices.

I flicked on the kettle, grabbed Fred's list of ghouls and scanned it. He was right – there weren't many of them: I counted only a dozen names at three separate addresses. Not that the addresses would be particularly easy to find. What was the postcode for somewhere that was 'the third drain on the right-hand side of Cleveland Street, twelve paces along and five spans down'?

I gazed down doubtfully at the clothes Laura had given to me. It didn't look as if they would stay clean for very long. I was starting to wish that I'd spent more time recently swotting up about the Others rather than focusing my attention on the vamps and werewolves.

Every time I thought I was getting a handle on all this supernatural stuff, something else came along to remind that me that I was a virtual babe in the woods, no matter how many times I died and came back to life. I didn't have another experienced detective to work alongside, nor did I have a knowledgeable mentor to whom I could go for advice. Unless I counted Lukas as a mentor but, considering his lack of interest in my latest venture into death, that probably wasn't wise. Besides, regardless of how helpful he'd been in the past, he was still a vampire. The Lord of all vampires, in fact.

I shrugged off my uncomfortable thoughts regarding black-eyed Lord Horvath and stuffed the list into my back pocket. Then I picked up the thin file Liza had put together on the ghouls. Any insights, no matter how small, would be helpful.

According to Liza, a ghoul's lifespan was around five hundred years. That in itself was problematic; it was far harder for evolution to do any work when individuals lived for that long. Without new blood in their family trees, and a range of inherited immunities as a result, they'd also be far more susceptible to new diseases. Judging from the sketch she'd acquired from somewhere, ghouls weren't particularly pretty, either. They rarely exceeded three feet in height, their facial features were exaggerated to the point of deformity and their skin tended towards the grey and leathery end of the spectrum. They didn't appear to possess any special powers, other than the ability to scrabble through the earth, which explained their long claw-like hands. And, of course, they survived on a sole diet of human corpses. Yum yum.

The only positive was that apparently ghouls tended to be peaceful beings. It was just as well. Given

Kennedy's suggestion that I leave the crossbow at home until I could use it confidently, I had little more than a baton with which to defend myself.

I sighed. I owed the Clarkes nothing, but I'd promised Mrs Clarke I would help. It was my job, exactly the sort of thing I'd signed up for when I'd agreed to become Supe Squad's only detective.

I checked my watch. There were only two hours left until dawn. If I was going to find the ghouls in question, I'd have to get my arse into gear.

***

Twenty minutes later, I was standing on Cleveland Street. I noted two pubs that were still open, their windows fogged up and faint strains of music drifting from their doors. I ignored them both and walked up the litter-strewn road in search of the third drain.

Taking the most northerly part of Cleveland Street as my starting point, I gazed at the ground. One drain hole. Two drain holes. I kept moving. There – the third drain hole.

I skipped over and gave its cylindrical iron cover a doubtful glance. I understood that ghouls were creatures that dwelled in darkness, whose activities made my skin crawl – but did they really live in sewers?

I scratched my head and knelt down. I didn't have much choice: if I wanted to find the ghouls, I had to go down there. I grimaced and scrabbled at the cover with my fingertips. This was certainly one of the weirder things I'd done lately – and that was saying something.

I'd barely managed to raise the cover enough to peer inside the inky blackness below when I heard a voice from above my head. 'Are you quite alright there?'

Dropping the drain cover back into place with a loud

clang, I straightened up and came face to face with a man who looked to be in his early sixties. For someone wandering around the streets at five o'clock in the morning, he was very well dressed – if you thought people like geography teachers dressed well. He was wearing tweed, a *lot* of tweed. He was even wearing a jaunty flat cap made of the stuff.

I peered at him, expecting to see a flash of vampiric fangs. His teeth looked too sharp to be human, but they certainly didn't belong to a vampire. I was too obvious in staring at his mouth; he knew what I was up to straight away.

'I'm not a blood sucker, DC Bellamy,' he said with a bland expression. His clipped English accent perfectly matched his clothes.

'You know who I am.'

He smiled and bowed from the waist. 'I am a supernatural being. It is part of my very existence to know who you are.'

I had the distinct impression he was playing a well-mannered game with me. 'And,' I enquired, 'who are you?'

He reached into his top pocket, drew out a monocle and screwed it in his left eye socket. 'My name is Albert Finnegan.' He bowed again. 'It's a pleasure to make your acquaintance.'

I very much doubted that was his real name. All the same, I inclined my head in acknowledgment. 'Is there anything I can help you with, Mr Finnegan?' I asked, hoping he'd say no. I had plans for the last couple of hours of darkness.

'You are the one who looks like they need help,' he remarked mildly. 'What on earth are you doing?'

'I'm on important police business,' I told him. 'There's no need for you to be concerned.'

From the faint quirk at the corners of his mouth, the last thing Albert Finnegan was feeling was concern. 'I shall try to hold my anxiety at bay.'

'I'm glad to hear it. Move along, sir.' I crouched down and renewed my attempt to flip open the drain hole. This clearly wasn't a very well-used entrance. The cover appeared to be almost totally rusted.

'You know,' Finnegan said, 'if you're looking for the ghouls, there are easier ways to reach them.'

I froze, then I stood up slowly once more. 'What do you know about the ghouls?'

He smiled more broadly this time. 'Plenty. Because I am one. It's a pleasure to make your acquaintance.'

I looked him over. By my reckoning, he was a smidgeon under six foot. His skin was a smooth nut-brown, which suggested that he spent a considerable amount of time and money on moisturising products. My gaze drifted to his hands. They were not remotely claw-like.

'I take it that I'm not what you expected,' he said drily.

'Assuming,' I said, taking care not to give offence even if I wasn't quite ready to believe him, 'that you are what you say you are, then no. You are not what I was led to believe a ghoul looks like.'

He bowed. 'I will take that as a compliment.' He half turned and swept his arm in the direction of a smart red door several feet away from the drain hole. 'If you'd like to come inside, perhaps I can explain further.'

I looked from the door to Finnegan and back again. I still had DSI Barnes' warnings ringing in my ears. Going inside a house at the behest of a man I didn't know was a rather foolhardy move.

I slid out my phone and tapped out a text to Fred, informing him of my location. Finnegan waited patiently.

'Thank you,' I said, once the text had been sent. 'That would be very helpful.'

'You don't have to worry, DC Bellamy,' he said. 'I wouldn't harm you. For one thing, we ghouls are peaceful creatures. And for another, it wouldn't be wise to do anything untoward to a police officer.' He raised his eyebrows meaningfully. 'Especially a police officer who is currently enjoying the protection of both the clans and Lord Horvath.' He paused. 'Regardless of silly drunken pranks that occur along the way.'

Ghoul or otherwise, Albert Finnegan was very well informed. I filed that away mentally and followed him.

The inside of the house was unremarkable; it could have belonged to anyone with deep pockets. A rich, red wallpaper covered the walls. The well-maintained period features, from the decadent tiled fireplace in the front room to the elaborate coving and original ceiling rose, would have had an estate agent's toes curling with excitement.

I glanced at the large windows that faced onto the street. There was a clear view of the outside but I spotted heavy unrolled blinds above them.

Finnegan tracked my gaze. 'Modern advances have altered our lives considerably. It is certainly true that once upon a time we lived underground – even the slightest hint of sunshine can cause untold damage to ghoul bodies. The blackout blinds have all but eliminated those worries. They allow us to live above ground.'

'And have these modern advances also allowed you to grow to twice your natural height and develop new skin?' I enquired baldly.

Finnegan threw back his head and laughed. 'I see the old stereotypes are still alive and kicking.'

I didn't smile. 'I would appreciate an explanation.'

His eyes twinkled; he certainly was enjoying himself.

'Humans are delicate creatures with strange sensibilities. They are comfortable when they can pigeonhole both their own kind and other species. Our ancestors discovered very early on that it was far easier to appear as grotesque monsters than in our normal forms. Humans could accept that corpse-eating creatures existed when those creatures looked like something from their worst nightmares. When those creatures look just like they do,' he gestured to himself, 'humans find it far harder to accept. And it is wise to be wary of humans and their … fears.'

'So you learned how to shapeshift to keep yourselves safe?' I asked, still feeling very dubious. 'Like werewolves do?'

Finnegan chuckled. 'The truth is far simpler.' He walked over to a large ornate cabinet and opened its doors. He drew out a rubber mask, of the sort you could obtain in any fancy-dress store, and a pair of gloves styled into claws.

He looked at them fondly. 'This mask is practically an antique now. We don't use costumes like this any more – we've found that we don't need to. The old stories persist quite enough for our needs.'

I stared. 'You dressed up? For hundreds of years, you dressed up to make everyone think you look like monsters?'

'Pretty much.'

'What about the height thing? Ghouls are supposed to be three feet high.'

Finnegan smirked and doubled over, folding his body in half before angling his head up towards me. 'Short monsters are far less scary to humans than ones their own size.'

I shook my head. 'Unbelievable.'

'Yes,' he agreed. 'What we do is very strange.'

'Why has this never come to light before?'

'Other supes are well aware of us and our true selves. It's only humans who haven't bothered to pay attention. There are a mere eleven ghouls living in London. Numbers in other cities and other countries are similar. We are not numerous enough to warrant much interest.'

'You steal dead bodies from graves and eat them while wearing fancy dress,' I said. 'I should think that warrants considerable interest.'

Finnegan tutted. 'Oh, DC Bellamy. From what I've heard of you so far, I expected far better.'

I folded my arms. 'What's that supposed to mean?'

He checked his watch. 'Any minute now, you're going to find out.'

'What does that—?' I was interrupted by the loud ring of the doorbell. I jumped. 'You have many visitors at this time of night?'

'As I've already mentioned,' Finnegan told me, 'the one part of our legend that is true is that we are strictly nocturnal. For ghouls this is rush hour.' He smiled at me. 'Come on.'

I followed him out to the hallway. A woman, who was as well dressed as Finnegan, had already answered the door and was in conversation with the dark-suited man standing on the doorstep.

'We'll deliver him round to the rear,' the man said. 'This will be the last one for a while. I hope that won't be a problem.'

'Oh no,' the woman said. 'We're well-stocked right now.'

A chill ran down my spine. 'Wait,' I said. 'Is this …?'

Finnegan nodded. 'A delivery.'

'A corpse?' I whispered.

'Signed, sealed and delivered, DC Bellamy. I can

assure you that we haven't stolen bodies from graves for a very long time.'

'1828,' the woman chirped. 'That was the year when the Burke and Hare murders came to light. They were more than enough to put a stop to further attempts at those sorts of activities. Grave robbing wasn't the same after that.'

'Burke and Hare were a couple of Scottish murderers,' Finnegan explained. 'They supplied corpses to a doctor for dissection purposes. Unfortunately, they murdered the occupants of those bodies first. As you can imagine, their actions caused a considerable stir. The laws around corpse donation changed quite dramatically, so we had to change too. Ghouls, like most supernatural creatures, are skilled at adapting.'

I wetted my lips. 'I still don't...'

'Some humans donate their bodies to medical science. Some humans donate their bodies to us. Not a lot,' Finnegan continued, as the man on the doorstep nodded, 'but enough.'

'We treat them with respect,' the woman said earnestly. 'Donors understand that they will die but also that they can sustain life with their death. If we could survive on broccoli alone we would, but the simple truth is that we can't. Think of us as a version of a Tower of Silence.'

I wrinkled my nose. 'A what?'

'Zoroastrians use a Tower of Silence for their dead. Bodies are placed high up within a built-up circular structure and left open to the sky and scavenging birds. It's nature at its most sensible.'

'I'm a vegetarian,' I told them both. 'I understand the logic of what those donors do but—'

'You couldn't imagine doing it yourself.' Finnegan's tone was kind. 'You're not alone. Our actions are considered monstrous by many. That's why most humans who know of our kind prefer us to look like monsters. Please understand, we don't go looking for donors or pressgang any poor souls into donating their bodies. They come to us.'

The man on the doorstep nodded vigorously. 'I can attest to that. My funeral parlour offers this service, together with cremation and burial.' His chest puffed up with pride. 'We are the only funeral parlour in the country that does. When someone wants to give their body to the ghouls, they come to us. There are more people who want to do it than you'd think. I can show you all the paperwork, if you like.'

I'd take him up on that. I'd also be scouring the law books to double check that all this was above board. It continued to amaze me what sort of things went on that I had no idea about, not just in the supe world but the human world too.

'You said there are eleven ghouls in London?' I asked.

Finnegan nodded. 'And they all use this service. I can guarantee that no ghoul has robbed a grave for almost two hundred years. We don't need to. Neither do we want to.' He gave me a long look. 'I heard about what happened with the young werewolf. I've been expecting your visit and I was keeping an eye out for your arrival. Whatever happened to that boy had nothing to do with us. For a start, we gain no nourishment from the bodies of werewolves. Something in their blood doesn't agree with us so we would have no reason to take any human from their grave. And even less reason to take a wolf. I promise you that.' His eyes narrowed. 'Regardless of public perception about our kind, I'm upset at the idea that we are being blamed for such a thing.'

I thought about what Knight had told me. He'd said

there were two occasions since he'd started at St Erbin's when he believed that graves had been disturbed. 'It's not the first time,' I said quietly. 'Julian Clarke was not the first.'

Finnegan's mouth thinned. 'Then I doubt he will be the last either. Something very sinister is going on here.'

I met his eyes. I certainly agreed with that. And I would find out exactly what.

Chapter Eight

Tallulah spluttered all the way to Supe Squad. When we finally made it, I turned off the engine and leaned forward. 'Okay,' I said. 'I get it. You don't enjoy being forced to work in the dark. You have to remember, Tallulah, that this is the way things are. You're a Supe Squad car and I'm a Supe Squad detective. We do our best work at night. You've had things easy for the last few decades because humans have been pushed out of supe business, but that's changing now. It's a change for the best. We're less likely to end up at the knacker's yard as a result.' I gestured to the sky outside. 'And look. Dawn is here already.'

Then I saw the tall figure leaning against the Supe Squad wall watching me. 'And,' I added quietly, 'so is he.'

I climbed out of the car. Lukas eyed me, his expression hooded. 'Tony often spoke to Tallulah, too,' he said. 'Does she ever talk back?'

'She's not the chatty type.' I tilted my head and gazed at the vampire Lord. 'Dropping by for a wee visit and a chat of your own?'

He pushed himself off the wall and moved towards me with his long-legged stride, coming to a halt a few inches from me. His black eyes searched my face then he nodded to himself as if satisfied. 'I wanted to make sure that you were okay. And that there are no ill side-effects after your most recent encounter with death.'

I stretched out my arms. 'As you can see, I'm fine.' I

glanced to my right, noting the cantankerous bellman eavesdropping on our conversation. 'Let's go inside. We can talk better in the office.'

Lukas didn't disagree. He waited while I unlocked the door, then followed me down the narrow corridor and into the main office space at the back.

'Would you like a drink?' I asked. 'We don't have anything alcoholic or any blood, but the coffee is passable.'

'No,' he said. He sat down on the sofa usually occupied by Fred. Despite its squashy appeal, he didn't look comfortable in the slightest. 'You need to take more care,' he said suddenly, his voice surprisingly rough. 'You have to train harder with the crossbow so you can defend yourself.'

'It was a human who killed me this time around,' I replied, with more lightness than I felt. 'A crossbow wouldn't have done me any good. I'm only permitted to use them against supes.'

Lukas's expression tightened. 'Not if your life is in danger, as it so often appears to be.'

I waved away his concerns. 'I told you, I'm fine.' I peered at him. In fact, I was feeling a darned sight better than Lukas looked. His clothes were as immaculate as ever, his tailored suit moulded to his body and his white shirt crisp against his neck. But there was a shadow around his jawline, indicating the beginnings of stubble, and a weariness around his eyes that I'd not seen before.

'Something's wrong with you,' I said softly. 'What's happened?'

He ran a hand through his ink-dark hair. 'There was an incident with one of my vampires. I've been dealing with it.' His eyes met mine with silent apology. 'It's the reason why I wasn't at the hospital when you woke up.'

'It's not your job to look after me, Lukas,' I told him.

'I'm not a vampire and plenty of other people have my back.'

He didn't answer. He simply dropped his hands into his pockets and looked away.

I walked over and sat next to him, then I reached out and touched his arm. His gaze snapped to mine. 'What happened? Is your vampire alright?'

A brief spasm of anguish crossed his face. 'No. She's not alright. She died.'

I sucked in a breath. 'I'm sorry.'

'She was attacked.' Venomous rage rippled through his voice. 'Some fucking bastard did this to her deliberately. We believe it was a human.'

I rocked back on my heels. I'd never heard of a human daring to attack a vampire. There might be plenty of people out there who disliked the vamps but, as a rule, they were sensible enough to avoid them. A million questions sprang into my head but, rather than press Lukas for answers, I waited and gave him the time he needed.

His jaw tightened. 'She was in Knightsbridge,' he said. 'Shopping.' He rolled his eyes, not at the fact that she was shopping but at the thought that she was killed while performing such a mundane activity. 'She had coffee with an old friend, bought herself a scarf and some make-up from Harrods, and was mugged on her way home.'

'Mugged?' I blinked. 'In broad daylight?'

'Her purchases were taken.' He shook his head. 'The theory is that it was a spontaneous attack. She fought back because she was a vampire and that's what we do, and she was killed while defending herself.'

It wasn't easy to kill a vampire; in fact, unless you deliberately set out to do so and were properly equipped, I'd have said it was nigh on impossible. 'How?'

'She fell,' he said starkly. 'And landed badly. There was a stack of broken wooden pallets next to where she was attacked. Moira fell, and one of the pieces of wood pierced her heart.' He took his hand out of his pocket and held it out, uncurling his fingers to reveal a memory stick. 'I have the CCTV footage here.' His mouth flattened. 'In all its bloody glory,' he added.

I glanced at the memory stick then at him. 'Do you want me to have it?' I asked carefully.

'Yes.' His tone was clipped. 'Take it and find the fucker who did this to her. He looks human, and that means my hands are tied.' Lukas stared at me. 'I don't have the means to find him, but you do. You can track him down and tell me where he is.'

'Lukas,' I said, 'five weeks ago I found the werewolf who was responsible for Tony's death. I wanted her brought to justice.'

'Cassidy was taken care of,' he growled. 'She *was* brought to justice.'

'Werewolf justice. Not my justice. You and Lady Sullivan were very clear about that. And you were right. This is exactly the same situation, but in reverse. I can and will do everything in my power to find the man who attacked your vampire, but any punishment will belong to the human legal system.'

His fingers curled round the memory stick and his grip tightened. Then he released it. 'I understand.'

I knew he understood; it was whether he accepted it that concerned me. It had been a bitter pill for me to swallow when I'd been forced to walk away from Cassidy – and I'd barely known Tony. There wasn't much I could do about my worries right now; I'd have to take Lukas's words at face value.

'Very well.' I reached over and took the memory stick and our hands touched. I was surprised again by the jolt I received at that touch, not to mention the heat of Lukas's bare skin. Until I'd come to work at Supe Squad, I'd assumed that vampires were cold to the touch. Lukas's face betrayed nothing apart from his pain at the loss of his vampire.

'Her name was Moira,' he said. 'She was fifty-seven years old. She was turned when she was twenty-five. I've known her for a long time. Find the man who hurt her, Emma. Her death might have been an accident, but her attack was not.'

'I'll do my best.' It was all I could promise for now.

Lukas nodded. 'I know you will. Thank you.' He stood up. 'I should go. Typically, services for vampires are held twenty-four hours after their passing. I have to oversee the preparations.'

'Will she be buried?' I asked, still mindful of my investigation into the mysterious disappearance of Julian Clarke's body and my conversation with Albert Finnegan.

'No. We consider that fire is cleansing. Her body will be cremated, as per vampire tradition.' He paused. 'Why do you ask?'

I chose my words carefully. 'The reason I was only just returning to the office is that I was meeting with the ghouls.'

A ghost of a smile crossed Lukas's mouth. 'Their proclivities are … interesting. Vampire bodies don't offer sustenance to ghouls, so at least we're spared that particular problem.' He gave me a long look. 'I imagine that you have many questions about what you've learned from the ghouls. I heard about the young werewolf – Julian, was it?'

'Yes. It was his father who shot me.'

His expression hardened, but he didn't comment. 'I can fill in any gaps in your knowledge. I know the ghouls reasonably well, better than most supes do. And we should discuss a few other matters, too. I can tell you more about Moira. I've also been speaking to Kennedy. He had some observations about you that would merit closer inspection.'

Like the fact that I was far stronger now than I was prior to my first death. 'Okay,' I said. 'Let me know when is good for you.'

'Tonight would work. We can talk over dinner. Moira's funeral will be finished by then, and I could do with the distraction. I'll pick you up in front of your flat at seven o'clock.' He hesitated. 'If that suits you.'

I pushed Liza's earlier comments firmly out of my mind. He was grieving. He definitely had no ulterior motives. 'Perfect,' I said. 'I'll see you then.'

***

After Lukas left, I made a coffee and wrote out a list, prioritising what needed to be done, then plugged the memory stick into my computer. As I opened the video file, I steeled myself for what I was about to see. Police detective or not, I wasn't immune to pain and suffering – and for that I was glad. The day I became inured to such things was the day I should resign.

The United Kingdom has more CCTV activity than any other European country. In London alone, there is one CCTV camera for every fourteen citizens. There are tough privacy laws that prevent the cameras' footage being used for nefarious purposes, but the vast majority of cameras are still operated not by the government but by private businesses and people. As soon as the video started, I knew that was what I was looking at. Lukas had no doubt tracked down the owner of the camera and persuaded them to hand over the footage. With his almost magical vampiric skills of manipulation, that would have been easy.

I sipped my coffee and leaned in to watch.

I didn't recognise the street but it looked like the camera was positioned at the rear of a restaurant. It wasn't long before Lukas's vampire came into sight, swinging her shopping bag with its famous Harrods' logo. Her face had the fixed, blank expression of someone lost in thought; there wasn't so much as a flicker of wariness when the man in a hooded top came up behind her. Feeling the tremor in my own hands at the reminder of the attack when I'd died for the first time, I put down my coffee mug and tried to remember to breathe. I was past the worst of that trauma but the memory could still attack me when I was least expecting it.

The hooded man was walking quickly, his pace far faster than Moira's. He caught up to her and, to begin with, it looked like he was merely attempting to pass her. At the very last moment, though, he swung towards her with his arm raised.

Moira was a vampire and therefore had lightning-fast reflexes, even when she was taken by surprise. She raised her hands and blocked his first lunge, while her face transformed into a silent snarl.

I paused the video and examined his hands. He was holding some sort of weapon. I squinted. A knife – and a lethal-looking one at that. I took a screenshot and started the video again.

The attacker lunged for Moira. She did what I suspected any self-respecting vamp would do and lunged right back, her jaws open and her fangs fully extended. She wasn't planning on taking any prisoners; she went straight for his jugular.

It was difficult to see what happened next. The

attacker lifted his arms, although whether it was to block her attack or to swipe at her with the knife was impossible to tell. Either way, it didn't matter; Moira's teeth were already at his neck. His hood fell down, revealing the back of his shaved head. Then she staggered backwards and stumbled. She lost her footing and fell, straight onto the pile of broken pallets. That was when I realised that whatever shard of wood pierced her heart had done so by entering through her spine. She'd barely had time to blink. My heart wrenched. It was over in a matter of seconds.

I rewound the video and watched her fall again, this time focusing on her attacker. At the very moment she stumbled, he reached for her. He wasn't fast enough to grab her and stop her falling, but it was an instant reaction on his part.

I chewed on my lip. Even after it must have been clear that she was dead, he didn't leave the scene. With his back to the camera, he knelt down beside her. From what I could tell, he seemed to be trying to hoist her up again. There was a panicked jerkiness about his actions. He hadn't wanted her to die. He probably hadn't realised she was a vampire until it was too late.

The attacker stepped back and stared down at her body. Then his head snapped to the left, and my eyes narrowed. What was that about? Was someone else there, just out of shot? A moment later, the mugger swooped down on Moira's body and grabbed something – presumably her jewellery – before scooping up her fallen shopping bag and sprinting away.

I scratched my neck and continued watching, hoping that whoever had caught the attacker's attention would wander into view. Unfortunately, no-one appeared until Moira was discovered by some poor soul who came out of the rear of the restaurant with a cigarette in hand.

I rewound the video yet again. For almost the entire attack, the man's face was turned away from the camera. When he panicked and started to run away, however, there was a fleeting moment where his features were visible. I crossed my fingers and focused my gaze. There. It might have only been a split second in real time, but it was more than enough for the camera.

It isn't always possible to tell who is supernatural by their appearance. Sometimes it's a small thing that gives them away, such as Albert Finnegan's unnaturally smooth and unblemished skin. Sometimes the differences are far more stark. For example, naturally born werewolves' bodies are often heavier and more squat, and they tend to have more hair when they're in human form, and vampires' physical attributes are enhanced after they are turned. Sometimes there are no obvious supernatural characteristics, as with werewolves who are made rather than born into the clans, or with some of the Others.

Moira's attacker looked and acted human. Like Lukas, I strongly suspected that was the case, but I would reserve judgement until I had proof. The good thing was that if he were indeed a run-of-the-mill mugger, he probably had form – and that meant that the police at the Met would already have his face on file.

I copied his image and enlarged it. He looked to be around thirty years old, with heavy dark eyebrows and a shaved head. I couldn't see any earrings or piercings, but there something under his chin that made me think he might have a tattoo. Unfortunately, the angle wasn't clear enough to be certain no matter how hard I squinted.

Potential tattoo aside, he would have been a perfectly ordinary looking man if it hadn't been for his eyes. They were a cold, glacial blue which both drew my attention and made me want to look away. I shivered, committing his face to memory, then I logged into the facial recognition programme and uploaded the photo.

The software immediately started to do its work running his features through all known criminals. While that happened, I ran a quick search for similar crimes in the area. Knightsbridge was a rich tourist hotspot, so it was a prime location for would-be muggers. Unfortunately, that meant I ended up with a long list of similar attacks. Even if I enlisted Fred and Liza's help, it would take too long to go through them all. That was where it helped to have contacts.

I tapped through my phone until I found Molly's number. We'd gone through a lot of our detective training together but, while I'd ended up in Supe Squad, she'd eventually been sent to CID after a brief stint with Special Branch. Molly might have been disappointed that she was no longer dealing with matters of national security and having to focus on assaults, murders and burglaries, but at that particular moment I was delighted.

She picked up after several rings. 'Detective Constable Emma Bellamy,' she drawled. 'What a pleasant surprise.'

'Detective Constable Molly March,' I replied. 'The pleasure is all mine.' The greeting, and the mutual use of our full names and titles, had become a ritual between us. It was a way of acknowledging that we both still felt the thrill of becoming detectives. I hoped it would never go away. In the human world names – as well as titles – had power too, even if that power wasn't quite similar to what the supes experienced.

'Alas,' I continued, 'I'm calling you about work rather than pleasure.'

I heard her yawn. 'I expected as much. You do realise that it's barely seven o'clock? We're not all like the night owls of Supe Squad. I've only just rolled out of bed.'

I jerked guiltily. I'd become so wrapped up that I'd forgotten about the time. 'Sorry. I can call back later.'

'Don't be ridiculous. I'm already too curious. What's up, Emma?'

I outlined what I'd learned from both Lukas and the CCTV footage before adding, 'I have a list in front of me with all the usual suspects who've been nabbed for muggings and burglaries of that sort around Knightsbridge. But it's a long list and I was hoping you could help me narrow it down.'

'Piece of cake,' Molly told me. 'I don't need to check any records. You're looking for the Flock.'

'The what?'

'It's a gang that runs out of Knightsbridge. They don't live there, obviously. If they could afford a house in that district, the last thing they'd be doing is petty thievery. They're all over the area, and they frown on competition. Chances are your vamp attacker is one of them.'

It was exactly the sort of intel I was looking for. 'Does this Flock have a leader?'

'A man who goes by the name of The Shepherd.'

'How very imaginative. Let me guess,' I said drily, 'their mugging targets are sheep.'

'I expect so,' Molly said with a faint snort. 'The Shepherd's real name is Devereau Webb. We've been trying to pin something on him for years, but he's a slippery bastard and the members of his Flock are loyal to a fault. It doesn't help that he has friends in high places. Word is that several members of the current government are in his pocket.'

Hmmm. 'Any ideas where I can find him?'

'He's got a flat somewhere across the river. I don't know the address but I can look it up when I get into work and let you know.'

'That'd be great. Thanks, Moll.' I paused. 'Aren't you going to warn me off approaching such a dangerous character?'

'I've not had my porridge yet. My warnings are at a minimum. Not to mention that I know nothing I say would do any good.'

I grinned. Nope. By the sounds of things, The Shepherd was the one person who could lead me straight to Moira's assailant. He would get a visit from Supe Squad's finest detective, whether he wanted one or not.

The computer dinged, indicating the facial recognition programme had completed its search and found no match for the bald attacker. Right now, The Shepherd was my best and only lead.

Chapter Nine

Given that he'd barely had any sleep, Fred looked remarkably well rested. His knee jiggled when I told him what I'd learned from the ghouls. He was as discomfited by the thought of corpse-stealing as I was. 'Can we trust this Finnegan fellow?'

'He certainly came across as truthful,' I said. 'But that doesn't mean one of the other ghouls hasn't turned rogue and decided that they'd rather hunt down their own food instead of getting it delivered on a plate.' I paused. 'So to speak.'

Fred grimaced. 'You want me to check out the other ghouls?'

'It's daylight. You won't be able to get hold of them until night falls again. What concerns me is that Reverend Knight and the church authorities are convinced that ghouls are responsible for the disturbances at the graves at St Erbin's. Knight said quite clearly that there have been two occasions since he started there when there was evidence of ghoul activity. Speak to him and see if you can get the exact dates. That way we can link them to any recent burials.'

'How about prior to Knight's arrival?'

I nodded. 'See what you can find out on that front, too. How long has this been going on for? How many graves might have been affected? Is there any actual evidence that points to the ghouls, or is it all supposition?'

Fred scratched out a few notes on his pad. 'I'll get on it right away.' He raised his eyes to mine. 'Is there any other reason why someone would steal bodies out of their graves?'

I thought about what Finnegan had told me about Burke and Hare's chilling activities. We weren't living in those times any more.

I shook my head. 'Honestly, Fred, I can't think of a thing.'

***

Molly was on the ball. The first thing she must have done when she got to her desk was to look up The Shepherd's details. I still had a few hours before Kennedy showed up again for our next crossbow session so, as soon as I received her text with an address, I grabbed my coat and headed out of the door.

Surprisingly, Tallulah's engine started first time. Maybe our little 'chat' last night had done some good. We whizzed through the busy London streets at almost record speeds, arriving in front of the tower block where The Shepherd lived before half the city had digested their breakfast. Tallulah deserved an oil change for that sort of performance.

After murmuring my thanks to the car without a trace of self-consciousness, I clambered out and angled my head upwards to examine the building. The tower block had a shabby quality, despite being relatively new. Maybe crime didn't pay after all, I thought wryly. I went towards the main door and steeled myself for the smell of stale urine that was usually present in such buildings.

I was pleasantly surprised. Instead of the graffiti-laden entrance and litter-strewn floor I'd expected, I was confronted by some healthy-looking pot plants, the fresh scent of lemon cleaning products and what appeared to be a working lift.

I paused long enough to read the community notice board. Details of bingo, Pilates, and even a neighbourhood committee bid to get council funds for a tennis court had been posted on it. I chastised myself for my prejudices. I managed to keep an open mind about supes; I should be able to do the same about humans. The exterior of The Shepherd's tower block didn't reflect its interior. There was a lesson in there for all of us.

The address was for the thirteenth floor. Rather than take the lift, I opted for the stairs. I'd not managed my morning jog because of my new caseload – and the unfortunate matter of my third death; the least I could do was to get some cardio while on the job.

Running up steps was hard work, and I fully expected that by the time I got halfway I'd be out of breath. That wasn't the case. I sprinted, taking the stairs two, and then three, at a time. I'd never had it so easy. I didn't pause until I reached the tenth floor; even then, it wasn't fatigue that stopped me but rather the lack of it.

I considered my body with awe. I'd always been reasonably fit but this was something new. I flexed my muscles and stretched my legs, marvelling that it wouldn't matter to me if The Shepherd lived on the hundredth floor. It was getting harder and harder to deny the evidence: the more times I died, the more powerful I became. I wasn't sure if I should be pleased or terrified.

I was about to bound up the next set of stairs when I heard the sound of raised voices below me. I hesitated, cocked my head and listened to the argument. With the fire door leading to the stairwell closed, I could only make out a few words but I was sure that one of them was Devereau. It wasn't exactly a common name in these parts. Whatever the people on the ninth floor were yelling about, it was something to do with The Shepherd. I tiptoed to the door and pressed my ear against it.

'I don't care what you think you need,' a gruff female voice said. 'It's too early to disturb him.'

'We both know he's up. I won't take a lot of Devereau's time. I only want to find out why I've been taken off the Harvey Nichols' crew.'

'I already told you. We're putting our efforts into other areas.'

'Can't I go out today?' The voice of the man arguing his case had a whining quality. 'You know Thursdays are the best.'

'Nobody is going out today. Devereau's orders.'

My eyes narrowed. Interesting.

'Let me through. I want to see him.'

The woman's response was tired. 'Fuck off, Gaz. I've already told you.'

I pulled back and considered. My little bout of eavesdropping had been fortuitous. From what I'd overheard, it was obvious that The Shepherd's claws were all over this entire building. It wouldn't surprise me if all his crew lived here. And although the address Molly had given me was for the thirteenth floor, it sounded like Devereau was here on the ninth. It made sense. He probably owned several of the flats and moved between them so that when the police came knocking – as no doubt they did regularly – he could either delay them or escape them. Surrounded by his Flock, The Shepherd was a canny criminal. No wonder he'd managed to carve out his own little empire.

Before I could debate my next move, I heard the sound of another fire exit door opening not far below me, and footsteps pounding up the stairs. A second later, the young freckled face of a girl appeared. Beneath her freckles her skin was very pale, suggesting she spent more time in front of a screen instead of outside playing. It wasn't my place to judge.

She came to a halt as soon as she saw me, her pigtails quivering as she stared, open-mouthed.

I smiled in return. 'Hello,' I said. I could do kids. Kids were easy. 'I'm—'

She threw back her head and screamed with all her might, 'Pigs! Pigs are here!'

For a split second nothing happened, then the door next to me was flung open. The girl vanished, hurtling down the way she'd come and I was confronted by two snarling faces – one woman and one man. No doubt these were the two who'd been arguing.

The woman looked exactly like I'd pictured her, with a weathered face, platinum blonde hair and suspicious eyes. She glared at me. 'Gaz,' she muttered.

He jabbed a number into his phone and held it up to his ear. Then he shook his head. 'She's alone.'

'It doesn't explain why the fuck they didn't tell us earlier,' the woman snapped. 'They're supposed to be keeping an eye out for visitors. Those idiots need to get their act together.'

'She ain't a copper,' Gaz said, with one ear still glued to the phone. 'She came in a Mini. An old one. No police officer drives a car like that.'

I decided this wasn't a good time to disabuse him. The woman circled round me before eventually coming to a halt in front of my face. 'Who are you?'

'My name is Emma,' I started.

'I didn't ask for your name. I asked who you were.'

I met her eyes, stare for stare. I knew if I told her that I really was with the police, I wouldn't get close to Devereau, so I'd save that piece of information until I was face to face with the man himself. 'I will tell The Shepherd who I am,' I said calmly. 'He's the man I'm here to see.'

She leaned in, her stale, tobacco-tinged breath

90

clouding in my face. 'No-one sees him without my say-so.'

I went in hard. I reckoned it was the only way to get the woman's respect. 'Listen up,' I said. 'I don't know who you are and I don't care. I'm here to see The Shepherd and I won't take no for an answer.'

Unfortunately, my approach was a mistake. I knew it as soon as she smirked. 'We'll see about that.'

'Window?' Gaz asked, his earlier antagonism with the woman forgotten. He pocketed his phone.

'Yeah.' She smiled nastily. 'Window it is.'

Uh-oh. That sounded ominous. I had a dilemma: if I told them I was a detective, it would be a million times harder to get to Devereau Webb. They would simply toss me out on my ear unless I could produce a warrant. But if I didn't tell them I was a police detective, they'd have no qualms about using violence.

As it was, I didn't have any time to say anything at all. Gaz lunged at me with surprising speed for a man of his size.

I leapt to the side to avoid him. In theory that was all very well, but the stairwell was narrow and there wasn't much room to manoeuvre. It didn't help that the freckled kid who'd raised the alarm had drawn more of the Flock. Others were coming up the stairs behind me. I was trapped between the two in front and the several behind.

Gaz lunged again, this time managing to grab hold of my right wrist. His large fingers curled round it and his dirty fingernails dug into my flesh. He yanked me forward. 'Come here, bitch,' he snarled.

The woman jabbed him in the ribs. 'Don't use that word! I've told you before and I won't fucking tell you again.' She was a politically correct henchwoman, then. That was good to know.

I took advantage of the situation and wrenched

myself free. Get to Devereau, I decided. It was the only way out of this.

I spun and started to launch myself up the stairs. Gaz, the woman, and the others followed. I pelted up eight steps, then turned a 180 degrees and threw myself over their heads, aiming my body behind the furious group. My landing was undignified, but it worked. While the members of the Flock cursed and tried to re-group, turning round to get hold of me again, I threw myself through the fire door and into the ninth-floor corridor.

I slammed the door shut behind me. Now all I needed was to find something that would jam it and keep it closed. I pulled on it hard, doing what I could to prevent Gaz or whoever from yanking it open from the other side, while my eyes scanned round for anything I could use. I was out of luck.

I heard a grunt, followed by a wheeze and several mutters. I had the strength to hold the door against two or three of them, but I'd never manage once several of them tried to force it open. A second later that's exactly what they did. The fire door burst open, despite my best efforts to keep it closed. I twisted and pelted down the hallway – and the Flock threw themselves after me.

There were at least a dozen doors leading into flats and there was no way of telling which one led to The Shepherd. I gritted my teeth. This was a very bad mistake. I should have told them who I was at the beginning. In front of me was a dead end, behind me were several angry gang members, and I had no clue where their leader could possibly be. Unless…

I gazed down at the carpeted floor as I passed door after door. No. No. No. There was a roar from behind me. The Flock were still coming.

No.

Yes.

I whirled right, jerked on the door handle and fell into the flat beyond. In the middle of the room, stood a well-dressed man in his early thirties with blond hair so carefully styled that it looked like it belonged on a Ken doll. Despite his immaculate appearance and the cup of tea in his hand, there was a hardness behind his eyes that belied his mild facade. This was Devereau Webb. It had to be.

I gasped and straightened. Gaz and others barrelled in behind me. I felt one of them reach for me but Devereau held up his hand and they instantly moved back. 'She's with the police,' he said, without a trace of rancour.

'I told you!' exclaimed a furious voice.

I glanced round, noting the young girl who'd raised the alarm. She was standing in the corridor, barely visible behind the dozen or so others who'd come after me. She looked mightily pleased with herself. She was the only one who did.

'Detective Constable Bellamy,' I said. 'It's nice to meet you, Mr Webb.'

He strode forward, still with the cup in his hand, and examined me in a detached, curious fashion. 'So much for our early warning system,' he murmured. 'This sort of thing isn't supposed to happen.'

I couldn't see the expressions on Gaz, the woman or the others' faces but I suspected they were all wincing.

'Tell me,' Webb said, 'how did you know I was inside this particular flat?'

I had nothing to gain by not telling him. 'The carpet,' I said with a shrug. 'It was more worn outside this door than the others. I expect you receive more traffic than your innocent neighbours.'

Devereau took a sip of his tea. 'Bravo, DC Bellamy. That was very observant of you. Although I'm not sure anyone is truly innocent.'

I chose to ignore that remark. 'How did you know that I'm with the police?'

'Your car,' he said without preamble. 'Its reputation precedes you. You, DC Bellamy, are with Supe Squad.'

I tried not to look too surprised. While every supe in London would recognise Tallulah, most humans didn't have a clue. Devereau Webb was very well informed. The assembled Flock gazed at me with renewed interest.

'Do you know why I'm here?' I asked.

'I believe I do.' He placed his cup down on a nearby table. 'Leave us,' he said, without raising either his voice or his eyes.

Not one of the Flock hesitated, not even Gaz who'd been so desperate to gain a minute of his boss's time. They all trooped out of the flat, leaving me alone with Devereau.

'Close the door!' he called. 'This isn't a barn!'

The girl who'd raised the alarm bounced back. With a cheeky grin in my direction, she pulled the door shut.

'Please take a seat,' Devereau said, waving at an incongruously flowered sofa.

I remained standing. 'Thank you,' I said, 'but I'm fine.'

He appeared more amused than offended. 'Suit yourself.' He sat down and leaned against the cushions. 'You know, you should have said who you were from the beginning. It would have made things far easier.'

'I didn't think you'd talk to me.'

Devereau raised an eyebrow. 'I have no reason to hide from the police.'

Yeah, right. 'I heard the word "window" mentioned.'

'Ah.' He smirked. 'Allegedly, when intruders appear we hold them out of the nearest window by their ankles to show them the error of their ways.'

'Allegedly?'

'Of course. Nobody who works for me would ever do such a thing. That would be against the law.'

Deverau Webb was a scary, scary man. It wasn't his words that sent a chill through me, it was the mild-mannered way he said them. I tried not to think too hard about whether I'd rise from the dead after I'd been splattered on the ground from nine storeys and got to the point. 'There was an incident in Knightsbridge yesterday.'

'The dead vampire.'

'Indeed.'

He didn't miss a beat. 'And you think I had something to do with her death.'

'It's been suggested that your Flock operate out of that area.'

'I can't begin to imagine what you're talking about, DC Bellamy.'

I had the feeling this was a dance we could do for a very long time. 'Look,' I said, 'I'm not here for you. I'm here because there's a vampire who was attacked and who subsequently died from her injuries. We have CCTV footage of the incident. We know her death was an accident but her mugging was not.' I gave him a meaningful look. 'I don't believe, Mr Webb, that you wish to make an enemy out of the vampires. Lord Horvath is not someone to be trifled with.'

There was a glint of anger in Devereau's eyes. Ah-ha. Finally, I was penetrating his mask and getting to the man underneath. 'Neither am I, DC Bellamy.' He linked his fingers together. 'The incident you're referring to had nothing to do with either me or my Flock.'

He was denying it. What. A. Shock. 'Mr Webb,' I started.

He rose to his feet, stalling me. 'However, despite our lack of involvement, it might surprise you to hear that

I am willing to help you with your enquiries.' He paused. 'In return for a small favour.'

This time I kept my mouth shut and waited.

'I have information that will help you find your mugger. I guarantee it. I will give you this information freely if you can arrange an audience for me with the clan alphas.'

The werewolves? I blinked at him. 'I have no influence over the clans.'

'That's not true. Besides,' he smiled, 'I'm only requesting a meeting. Nothing more, nothing less.'

'That's not how this works, Mr Webb. I ask the questions and you answer them. End of. I don't grant favours.'

He raised his shoulders in an elegant shrug. 'Ask as many questions as you like, DC Bellamy. Until I get that meeting, I won't answer a single one of them. And you can tell that to your Lord Horvath as well. Vampire or not, he doesn't intimidate me. You might say,' he added with a glint of humour, 'that I am a wolf in sheep's clothing.'

I looked into Devereau Webb's eyes and I knew without a shadow of a doubt that he was telling the truth. The Shepherd, and by extension his Flock, wasn't going to open his mouth unless I arranged that meeting.

'The werewolves aren't quite as fond of the night as the vampires are, but I won't be able to contact any of them until after midday,' I warned. Before noon, all meetings were strictly wolf only.

Webb's expression didn't alter a jot. 'I can be patient, DC Bellamy.' He paused. 'The question is, can you?'

Chapter Ten

Nobody stopped me when I left Devereau Webb's tower block. In fact, I didn't glimpse so much as a shadow of a person, although I knew I was being watched every step of the way back to Tallulah.

Molly had told me that the Flock were solidly loyal, but I was only just beginning to grasp what that meant. I thought about the expressions on their faces when they realised they'd failed their boss by letting me get close to him. Except it wasn't fear that drove the likes of Gaz, it was a genuine desire to please. They were more worried that they'd disappointed Devereau Webb than that he would punish them.

There was no doubt that The Shepherd was a career criminal. But that didn't necessarily mean he was evil too. That was something I was still pondering when Kennedy and I walked into the weapons room for our next bout of crossbow training.

'Stop it,' he said, when I reached for the weapon.

I stared at him. 'Stop what?'

'Thinking.'

I must have frowned, because Kennedy sighed dramatically. 'Thinking is dangerous. It doesn't mix at all well with lethal weapons. Do you meditate?'

Uh…

He rolled his eyes. 'Of course you don't.' He pointed at me. 'You should start. You need to be able to empty your mind when you pick up a crossbow. The moment you start thinking, whether it's about the bow or about whether you left the iron switched on, you're too distracted to hit your target effectively.'

I bristled. 'I'm not thinking about whether I left my damn iron on. I'm thinking about the nature of evil.'

Kennedy gave me a long look. 'Don't. Over-thinking is an anaesthetic for the soul. It should be conducted over a good whisky, or in a hot bath, or not at all. It shouldn't be something you do when you hold the power of life and death in your hands.'

'Surely that's exactly when you should be thinking the most,' I argued.

'No.' He tapped his temple. 'If you're in that moment and you take a shot, you do it because you *know* that's what you have to do. There's no need to stop and think about it. Become distracted by your own thoughts and you'll miss your target – and quite possibly end up dead.' Kennedy paused. 'And that might be fine for you, but you don't know what will happen to those around you who can only die once and who are counting on your protection.'

My eyes flew to his. 'You know? About my … deaths?'

'By now every supe knows,' he said grimly. 'Don't make the mistake of believing what you have is a gift, Emma. It could very well end up being a curse.'

'You know that I'm going to be thinking about that statement now?'

'Don't.' He wagged his finger. 'Don't think.'

Easier said than done, but I understood what he was getting at. Thinking was a distraction; I had to be in the moment and I had to focus.

I grabbed the crossbow, cocked the string, loaded it with a bolt and fired at the practice dummy. The bolt flew out, skimming the top of the dummy's head. 'Hey!' I exclaimed, delight skipping through me. 'I almost hit it!'

'That's because you were still thinking,' Kennedy muttered. 'Almost is not good enough.' He glared at me. 'Again.'

I set my jaw. Okay, then, again it was. I'd show him. I would become the best markswoman this side of the Thames. Kennedy would grovel at my feet when he saw how good I could become. He would...

Kennedy roared. 'Emma!'

I glanced at him. 'Yes?'

'Stop bloody thinking!'

Oh, yeah.

***

By the time we were done, I had blisters on the bases of my thumbs and my fingers were starting to resemble raw mincemeat. On several occasions I'd let frustration get the better of me. Frankly, if it hadn't been for Kennedy's exhortations, I'd have given up. Using a crossbow wasn't hard, but using a crossbow to hit a target accurately –that was something else.

I waved goodbye to him, even managing to thank him for his time, and checked my watch. It was still a bit early for either Lady Carr or Lord Fairfax, and Lord McGuigan would ignore my calls until he felt he had no other choice. Lady Sullivan might respond, however.

I slid out my phone and jabbed in her number. It rang several times before anyone picked up. Caller display wasn't always a useful tool – not when you had the likes of Lady Sullivan's beta, Robert, to deal with. He did enjoy his little games of one-upmanship.

'DC Bellamy,' he said, when he finally answered. 'To what does Clan Sullivan owe this honour?'

'I need to speak to Lady Sullivan,' I said. 'Sooner rather than later.'

'Well,' he replied, 'that is very fortuitous. She would

like to speak to you, too.'

Unfortunately, I knew exactly what she wanted to speak to me about. And it wasn't something I wanted to get into.

'Why don't you come round in the next hour?' Robert suggested. 'We'll make you feel very welcome.'

That's what I was afraid of. 'I would very much appreciate it,' I said, trying to be as polite as possible, 'if you could put her on the phone right now.'

'*Put* her on the phone? What kind of relationship do you think we have?'

I counted to ten in my head. 'You know what I mean. I need to speak to her now.'

'Come and see us, DC Bellamy. One hour.' He hung up.

I gritted my teeth. Then I rang again.

'Good afternoon,' Robert purred. 'You have reached Clan Sullivan. How may we help you?'

'It's DC Bellamy,' I said. 'As you well know. Let me speak to your boss.'

'DC Bellamy! Didn't we just make arrangements? Are you calling to cancel them already?'

I drummed my fingers on the table. 'Tell you what, Robert,' I said, 'either put Lady Sullivan on the phone now, or I'll refuse to answer any of her questions about what I am and what I can do. I will, however, provide a precise explanation to Lord Fairfax, Lord McGuigan and Lady Carr.'

There was a beat of silence. I knew I had him. The clan alphas continually jostled for position and superiority. Any of the alphas who gained knowledge that the others didn't possess had an advantage. That was why Lady Sullivan wanted to talk to me – and why she wouldn't want me to talk to the other alphas without her.

'Wait a minute.' The amused pleasure in his tone had

been replaced with irritation. That was fine by me.

'Emma.' Lady Sullivan's cut-glass voice filled the line. 'I understand you wish to talk to me.'

'Actually, Lady Sullivan,' I said, 'it's Detective Constable Bellamy.'

'If you insist, dear.'

She had the ability to patronise down to a fine art. 'Lady Sullivan, I need to see you and the other clan alphas this afternoon. It's regarding an important police matter, and I was hoping I could count on you to help me arrange it.'

'Hmm. It's Thursday.'

I frowned. 'So?'

'Fairfax is busy on Thursdays. Back, sack and crack.'

'He gets waxed?' I said, without thinking. The confidential informant I'd enlisted from the Fairfax clan liked to pass on gossip, but he'd never mentioned anything like beauty treatments. 'But he's a werewolf.'

'Yes.' She sighed dramatically. 'The mind boggles. Meet with me, and I will pass on whatever you have to say to the others.'

'I'm afraid that won't work, Lady Sullivan. It has to be all four of you. In person. At the same time.'

'You do demand rather a lot, DC Bellamy.'

I didn't want to bring this up, but I would. While it would be an easy matter to ask Lukas to help me meet the werewolf alphas, especially as I was doing all this on his behalf, I wasn't going to interrupt him today. Moira was probably being cremated at this very moment. 'Well,' I demurred, 'the agreement we came to after one of your wolves murdered my predecessor does state that...'

'Fine,' Lady Sullivan snapped. 'I'll make the arrangements. But I expect something in return from you.'

Everyone did these days. 'Go on, then.'

She didn't miss a beat. 'A DNA sample. A simple cotton swab whisked round your mouth. It won't hurt and it won't take long. I always knew there was something about you, DC Bellamy, and your antics outside Lady Carr's house prove it. With a DNA test, I can get to the truth of what you are, and I don't have to worry about any of your lies or misdirection during the process.'

Given I had no idea what I was, or how I repeatedly managed to cheat death, I had no lies or misdirection to offer. And I certainly wouldn't call being shot to death 'antics'. But Lady Sullivan's demands might play into my own hands. If she could find out what manner of supernatural being I was, it would save me the trouble. Now that everyone knew what I was capable of, I didn't have to keep it secret.

I didn't want to agree too rapidly, however. A show of reluctance would go a long way. 'You're asking too much,' I said. 'To give you that sort of information freely would be foolish.'

'You've seen our medical facilities. They are state of the art, and all our doctors adhere to strict data protection policies. I will not share what the lab discovers about you with anyone else.'

'My private life shouldn't be open to your scrutiny simply because I'm trying to do my job.'

'Emma.' Lady Sullivan clicked her tongue. 'If you want my help in getting the alphas together at such short notice, this is what I require in return. You can trust me.'

I most definitely could *not* trust her, but right now our desires converged. I huffed loudly and then agreed. 'If there's no other way…'

'There isn't.'

'Alright, then. Meeting first, however. I'll give you what you need afterwards.'

'Done. Robert will contact you with the time and

place.'

I smiled to myself. 'I'll see you soon.'

As soon as I hung up, Fred popped his head round the door and waved a sheet of paper at me. There was a manic jerkiness about his movements; he'd been gulping down far too much Red Bull. 'You're going to want to see this, ma'am,' he told me.

I stared at him. 'You just ma'amed me.'

He grinned. 'You're the Supe Squad boss.'

'You've never ma'amed me before.'

'That's a mistake I aim to make up for,' Fred said airily.

My mouth flattened. Nope. I didn't like it. 'Please, Fred,' I said, 'call me Emma when it's just us in the office.'

'You know, you're a lot like Tony. He hated us calling him sir. The two of you would have worked well together.'

I felt a tug at my heart. 'Yeah,' I said quietly. 'I reckon we would have.' I shook myself. 'What have you got there?'

Fred beamed proudly. 'They say that dead men tell no tales.' He waved the paper again. 'But they're wrong. These guys have got plenty to say. I've spoken to Reverend Knight and I've been cross-referencing what he believes are ghoul incursions with burial dates.'

I steeled my stomach. 'Go on.'

'The one thing the church is good at is keeping records. St Erbin's was established towards the end of the sixteenth century and, according to the parish records, graves were disturbed on a regular basis for almost two hundred years.'

I suppressed a shudder. Fred was too absorbed in revealing his discoveries to notice.

'The ghouls were always blamed for the

disturbances, but there are different patterns to the grave robbing. Sometimes it appeared that they were dug out from the surface and sometimes they seemed to be disturbed from underground. It was believed that the surface robbers were human and the underground ones were ghouls.'

That made sense. I nodded. 'Okay.'

'By the 1830s, almost all of that stopped. The government had cracked down on corpse donations to medical science. For nearly seventy years, the graveyard at St Erbin's was left in peace.'

My eyes narrowed. 'And after that?'

'The ground started being disturbed again. Frequently.'

My suspicions about Albert Finnegan and his fellow ghouls stirred again. Had they merely decamped to other cemeteries and graveyards for their dietary requirements, and then returned to St Erbin in the twentieth century when they thought they could get away with their grim burglaries again?

'In 1901,' Fred continued, 'St Erbin's started to record more grave robbing. There were twenty instances in that year.'

I blinked. 'Twenty?'

'Yep.' He beamed at me. 'Even more the year after that. Records of ground disturbances from St Erbin's increased year on year. On every occasion, ghouls were blamed. The church didn't advertise any of it. After all, who'd want their loved ones laid to rest in such a place?'

'Who indeed?' I curled up my fists. Bloody Finnegan. So he'd been lying. I'd been too desperate to believe his protestations of innocence. Some hotshot police detective I was.

'But,' Fred told me, blithely unaware of my scowls, 'there were a few years when all seemed quiet.' He grinned proudly. 'And you know what else happened in those years?'

'No, Fred,' I said. 'I don't.'

'I found the old receipts. It all matches up.' He jigged from side to side. 'I can't believe nobody spotted it before.'

I was beginning to wish he'd get to the point. 'Spotted what?'

'During the years when St Erbin reported decreased ghoul activity,' he crowed, 'they also paid local workers to undergo routine pest control.'

My brow creased. 'What do you mean?'

'Moles.' Fred's grin was so wide it all but split his face from ear to ear. 'Whenever St Erbin's paid for mole control, ghoul activity disappeared. Whenever they didn't do anything about moles, the ghouls returned. So either ghouls have a mortal fear of small subterranean mammals or…'

'It was the moles all along.' I exhaled. 'Moles disturbed the ground, and the church automatically thought it was deformed creatures breaking into coffins and nabbing corpses. Partly because of their history, and partly because of their location. But the ghouls really did stop stealing from graves back in the 1800s.' Praise be. Finnegan was in the clear. 'Well done. This is great work.'

Fred swept a bow. 'The evidence might be circumstantial but all the dates match up. The church authorities were too wrapped up in their fear of the supernatural to realise what was going on literally in their own backyard. And nobody else thought to question it. Even Liza believed that ghouls still rob graves.'

Some of the tension in my shoulders eased, but not all of it. 'Moles don't explain Julian Clarke,' I said.

Fred held up a finger. 'Indeed. But there are two

important points to consider. In the past four years, there've been five occasions when St Erbin's has reported grave disturbances. On each occasion, there's been photographic evidence taken by both Reverend Knight and his predecessor, a Reverend Reginald Baxter. All five times, the ground was noticeably disturbed. In theory that could still mean moles, but the patterns of loose earth from the photos suggest otherwise. I checked the weather reports. Before any disturbances were noted, there was bad weather – storms, mist, driving rain, that sort of thing. The sort of weather that would help hide anyone who was digging for a few hours in a graveyard in the middle of the city. Plus, all five times someone had just been laid to rest in the graveyard in the previous ten days.'

'A rogue ghoul? Someone not on Albert Finnegan's radar?'

Fred shook his head. 'No. It can't be.'

'Why not?'

'Because the people buried on all those five occasions weren't human.' His eyes met mine. 'They were all werewolves and, as we now know—'

'Ghouls don't eat werewolves,' I finished for him.

Chapter Eleven

It wasn't long after I'd finally persuaded Fred to go home and take the rest of the day off that the Supe Squad buzzer sounded. I opened the door to a young werewolf with a yellow tag on her arm indicating her zeta status. Whoever she was, she was a ranked wolf, albeit one still on the bottom rung.

She gazed at me, her eyes wide as saucers. There was only a faint yellow tinge to her irises, but her shoulders were wide and her stance was squat. I also noted the thin golden down on her arms. Every physical attribute indicated that she'd been born into the clans as a baby wolf instead of being recruited at a later age.

I gave myself a mental pat on the back. Not only was I growing more observant, I was now more knowledgeable about supes in general too. Perhaps there was hope for me yet.

'What's that smell?' she asked, obviously fascinated.

'Verbena blended with wolfsbane,' I told her. I'd refreshed the herbs that morning. Both were completely harmless, even to werewolves, but they were a foolproof method of separating the supes from the humans. If you couldn't smell the herbs you weren't a supe, no matter what beliefs you held to the contrary.

'Cool,' she breathed. She continued to stare at me. 'Is it true that you can't die?'

'Uh…' I grimaced. 'I can die. It's just that when I do, I … uh…' I gave up. 'It's complicated.'

'Cool.' She blinked at me. 'Can I touch you?'

I frowned. 'No.'

'Okay.' The werewolf nodded. 'Cool.'

'Is there something I can help you with?' I asked. 'Would you like to report a crime? Do you need assistance?'

She stared for a moment longer then she shook herself. 'No.' She hesitated. 'I have a message for you. You're to meet the alphas at Lord Fairfax's club in twenty minutes. I can escort you, if you wish.' She held her breath, obviously hopeful that I did indeed require her help to travel less than mile from here in broad daylight. Of course I didn't need any such thing – but one of my missions was to cultivate as many supe relationships as I could.

'That would be very helpful.'

The werewolf blushed. 'Cool.'

'Let me grab my jacket.'

She nodded and I nipped to the office, grabbing my phone and firing off a quick text to Devereau Webb as I did so. When I returned to the doorway, the wolf was examining her perfectly manicured fingernails with considerable interest.

'Thanks for waiting,' I said. 'What's your name?' I cleared my throat. 'I mean, what name would you like me to know you by?'

'It's Pa—' She stopped. 'Actually, it's Buffy.'

I gave her a long look. 'Buffy?'

'Yeah.' She leaned in and whispered in my ear. 'But don't tell the vampires.'

Alriiiight. I was beginning to see what was going on here. Lady Sullivan still seemed to be under the impression that she could play me for a gullible fool. Yes, I was often gullible, and yes, I was often foolish – but I wasn't quite at that level.

'Buffy' was acting the role of naïve ingénue with

fluff for brains when I suspected the opposite was true. I'd play along with her for now. If the werewolves were going to continue to underestimate me, I'd continue to let them. It could only be to my advantage in the long run.

Buffy gave me a pretty smile. 'Lord Fairfax's club is this way,' she said.

'Great,' I exclaimed brightly. 'Lead the way.'

We turned right, and away from Supe Squad. Halfway down the road, the werewolf took out a pocket mirror from her bag and started to examine her reflection. She puckered up her lips, pouted and tossed her hair ostentatiously. I also saw her watching me in the reflection. It was only for a split second, but it was more than enough to confirm my suspicions.

'How long have you been a zeta, Buffy?' I asked.

'Almost three years.' Her eyes shone with a fervency I often saw in the wolves. It was the one part of Buffy that I believed in.

'So you're looking to move up to epsilon soon?' I asked, referring to the rank above zetas.

Buffy giggled. 'Oh, goodness. I'd love to make epsilon but it'll be a while before I get that far. I have to prove myself first.'

Uh-huh. One way to prove herself would be to ingratiate herself with me and pass anything she learned back to her clan. I wasn't the only person in this part of London who was building a network of informers; apparently Lady Sullivan was at it too – and she'd sent me someone who was adept at playing the fool to lull me into a false sense of security. I suspected that Buffy was planning to attach herself to my side like glue, hoping that her ditzy façade would make me more inclined to trust her.

'Can I ask you a question?'

'Of course, you can,' I said. 'Fire away.'

'What's happened to your fingers? They look sore.'

I glanced down at my bruised hands. 'Crossbow training,' I said. 'As a Supe Squad officer, I'm permitted to carry a crossbow to use against supes if I need to.' I grimaced. 'But it's a lot harder to use it properly than I thought. I should invest in a pair of gloves.'

Buffy bit her lip. 'That's amazing. I could never learn how to use a crossbow.'

'I'm not sure I can either.'

'I bet you're really good. Can you load one up?'

'That much I can do.'

'And can you shoot it?'

I nodded. 'I can hit a target with about fifty percent accuracy. Go me.'

'Wow.' She shook her head in amazement. 'That's brilliant.' She looked me up and down. 'I don't see a crossbow on you, though.'

'No. Until my accuracy is over ninety percent, my teacher won't let me take it out with me.'

'I bet you'll be armed and ready in no time.' Buffy's voice was far too fawning. Did Lady Sullivan think I'd fall for this guff?

'We'll see,' I said with a smile.

'Maybe one day you can show me how to use one.'

'Mmm,' I agreed non-committally. 'Maybe.'

We crossed the street and went past the row of open shops towards the main crossroads. Buffy stopped in front of a small dress shop and pointed at the mannequin in the window. 'Look at that skirt! I'd love to be able to wear something like that. I don't have the legs for it. I've got too much natural wolf in me to pull it off.'

'If you like it, you should get it,' I told her. 'And you should wear it as often as possible.'

She giggled. 'I wish.' She pointed at a side street. 'There's another shop down this way that sells similar clothes. It's a short cut to Fairfax's club. We can have a look in the window as we pass – if that's alright with you,' she added hastily.

I smiled easily. 'Sure.'

Buffy's answering grin was dazzling. 'Thank you!'

I sighed. She was pulling out all the stops. It was almost a shame that her efforts were going end up thwarted.

We turned into the side street. I'd been down this way a few times before and I knew that it was very narrow and very quiet. I was vaguely aware of the shop Buffy was talking about; its contents were a bit too dressy for my liking, but I could see why she would like them.

I checked my watch again. I hoped the detour wouldn't make us too late. And then I felt an odd prickle at the back of my neck and an unpleasant thought struck me. Perhaps this wasn't about Lady Sullivan attempting to get insider information. Perhaps matters were far more sinister.

Buffy started to stride ahead, pulling away from me. I glanced back. Two silhouetted figures appeared at the far end of the narrow street, effectively blocking any exit route. Anger flashed through me. I didn't have time for this shit. No wonder she'd been asking me so many questions about my crossbow.

'Buffy,' I said, 'if you're thinking about doing anything right now, I strongly suggest you alter your course of action.'

She spun round so she was facing me. Much of her face had already transformed, and whiskers and fur were sprouting all over her skin. 'What on earth do you mean?' she enquired. Her mouth transformed in front of my eyes, developing into an unmistakable muzzle, and there was a cracking sound as her bones shifted.

I hissed under my breath. 'No,' I said, throwing as

much power into my voice as I could. 'Stand down.' I felt the thrum of compulsion reverberate through my words.

Sometimes it worked, but Buffy was no weakling and I didn't have her true name. Mere zeta wolf or not, my attempts to sway her fell flat. Clearly she'd been chosen for this task for more reasons than her acting ability and, without her real name to use, my attempts to control her floundered. Her yellow eyes glinted with cold amusement. I had seconds at best.

I looked round quickly for something to defend myself with. A dustbin lid would be good – even some discarded litter that I could throw at her could help. Alas, there was nothing to hand. I was stuck on a narrow road with high walls on either side, a werewolf in front and two behind. There was the strong likelihood that I was screwed.

The anger I'd felt was sliding into panic, old traumas re-surfacing. No, I told myself. There was no time for that. I gritted my teeth and steeled my stomach, lowering my centre of gravity to prepare for what was about to come.

A split second later, Buffy lunged.

Her wolf form crashed into me. Her objective was clearly to knock me to the ground so I'd be a completely defenceless target. What Buffy didn't know was that I was stronger than I looked. I held my upright position and, when she bounced off me, I managed a sharp kick in her direction. She let out a brief whine. That should have given me a glimmer of satisfaction but unfortunately I could already hear pounding feet from behind.

I didn't bother to turn around and look. I knew who was coming and why. Instead, I pulled my head down and ran forward. The best I could do now was to get past Buffy because I doubted I'd ever outrun a wolf, regardless of how many times I died or how much faster and more powerful I became. But if I could put a small distance between me and the wolves, I might get to the main road and its relative safety. They wouldn't attack me when there was a chance others would notice.

I hurtled past her. For a moment I thought I'd done it, until I heard ripping fabric and felt her teeth scrape against my lower calf. I yanked my leg out of the way before she could pierce the flesh. Out of the corner of my eye, I caught a glimpse of my other two pursuers. Both had transformed – and both were fixed on me with the focus of determined predators.

Kennedy's admonitions sprang into my thoughts. I gulped in air and allowed my mind to go blank. It worked. My body took over, flight taking precedence over fight.

I sprang to my left, using my momentum to spring off the wall on one side and reach for the top of the wall on the other side with one twisting movement. My fingers curled round the rough surface while my toes dug into the bricks for purchase. The muscles in my biceps bunched and strained. I hauled myself up, kicking back the wolf that was snapping at my heels.

The wall was several inches thick and easy enough to balance on. I started to run, speeding along it like a gymnast on a balance beam. I had no idea how I'd manage the dismount, but I trusted my instincts to see me through. Right now, they were all I had.

All three wolves beneath me snarled, running alongside the wall on the ground and matching my every step. As soon as they decided to come at me together, I'd be toast. I picked up the pace, the wind whipping at my hair as I ran.

I couldn't keep going like this for long because a tall building lay ahead, effectively cutting off the wall. It was too high and its surface was too smooth to do me any good. I clenched my jaw tightly, wondering if I could leap to the opposite wall. Then I spotted the house under reconstruction to my right. It was practically a shell, with neither doors nor windows barring my entrance. That'd do.

I jumped off the wall away from the werewolves, before landing badly in the debris-filled garden. Agonising pain spasmed through my ankle. One of the wolves howled from the other side of the wall. I pushed past the pain, clambered to my feet and barrelled into the house.

There was no sign of any builders. That was unfortunate – but not devastating. All I had to do was run through to the front door and out into the street beyond and I'd be safe. Unfortunately, as I ran into the corridor, I realised that the way to the front door was barred; two heavy piles of wood were blocking my exit.

I cursed. The only way out now was the way I'd come in – and the wolves would be there by now. With no choice, I leapt for the stairs instead and ran up them with even greater speed than I'd achieved at Devereau Webb's tower block. On the first landing, empty rooms stared at me; the bare floors and chalky clumps of plaster flaking away from the old walls seemed to be mocking my attempts to escape. I ran up the next set of stairs. Same again. This building was only three storeys tall. If I didn't find something or someone useful soon, I was finished.

I wheeled round onto the final landing. To one side was an old bathroom but its door was hanging off its hinges and would provide no protection. I darted into the largest room, which overlooked the busy street below. The windows were covered by a single sheet of plastic. I ripped through it and went onto the slim Juliet balcony. I could already hear the wolves' paws thundering up the stairs behind me.

It was a long way down and I didn't rate my chances of jumping and landing on the pavement below without seriously injuring myself. It would be easier to land on my head and die another death. However, I had plans for today and they didn't involve yet another trip to the morgue.

I looked up. The roof wasn't far above me.

I climbed onto the narrow iron balcony rail. If I stretched up, I could just grab the guttering. It looked rusted and loose, and I doubted it would hold my weight, but I was out of options. I held my breath and sprang up.

As I'd suspected, the moss-filled gutter gave way almost instantly, dropping a foot down and taking me with it. I scrambled for purchase, my legs swinging loosely in the air below. There was a loud crack. I glanced to the side at the last guttering joint; the old nails holding it in place were straining free from the bricks. With one final spurt of energy, I released my grip and swung upwards towards the sky.

At first, I didn't think it had worked. I was half expecting to see the ground rushing towards me before everything went black. Instead, I found myself balanced precariously on the slick tiles of the roof. I wasn't sure how I'd managed it – but somehow I had.

I pushed myself up unsteadily, bracing one hand against the sloping roof with the other extended outwards for balance, then I started to shuffle along. I didn't look back. The growls and snarls of the foiled wolves were enough for me.

I kept going until I reached the end of the row of terraced houses. The last building was a guesthouse – and that meant it had a fire escape. I slid down three metres until my feet hit solid metal, then I jogged down to the ground and joined the people on the main street below.

I'd done it. But I was very, very pissed off.

Chapter Twelve

Ten minutes later, I strolled up to the entrance of Lord Fairfax's club, hoping that my appearance was carefree and my attitude seemed chilled.

The solitary doorman stared at me with a less nonchalant expression. 'Detective Constable Bellamy,' he said carefully, his eyes drifting to my cheek and back again. 'What can I do for you today?'

'You're not expecting me?'

He licked his lips. 'Uh, no. But I can check inside…'

I held up my hand. 'There's no need.' Clearly Lady Sullivan hadn't expected me to make it this far, so she hadn't set up the meeting I'd requested. 'Is Lord Fairfax in?'

'He is.'

'I need to see him.' My tone was hard and allowed no room for manoeuvre. For once it worked.

'Go straight in,' the doorman told me. He pressed his earpiece and muttered, 'Supe Squad Short Arse is here for the boss.'

I'd been called far worse. I sniffed and nodded, striding through to the main room of the club. I'd been here once before with Lukas at my side. Then the club had been a bustling hive of activity but at this hour it was virtually empty, save for a few cleaners mopping the dance floor and some staff setting up the tables. They glanced curiously in my direction. When I spotted the furrowed brows, my hand went up to my cheek. It came away sticky and wet. I gazed at the oil on my fingertips.

If a few dirty smears were the worst I had to show for what had just happened then I'd done well.

The door at the far end of the large room opened and Lord Fairfax walked through, flanked by several wolves I now recognised as his trusted betas. His face was plastered with a smile but I had a definite sense of underlying tension. 'DC Bellamy. To what do we owe this pleasure?'

'I need to see you, Lady Carr and Lord McGuigan,' I said. 'All at the same time. Right now.'

He peered at me. 'Can I ask why?'

'I'll explain when they get here. It's important police business, Lord Fairfax, and I'm expecting your compliance.'

'I wouldn't dream of not complying,' he said, 'but I can't speak for the others. We're all busy people and, despite recent changes in our relationship with Supe Squad, I don't expect the other alphas will be as amenable as me.'

I was no longer willing to play Miss Nice Guy, or to follow the unwritten rules. 'You can tell them that if they don't present themselves here within the next twenty minutes, I'll make it my sole goal to disrupt their lives from here on in, whether the law allows it or otherwise.'

Fairfax appeared more intrigued than upset by my empty threat. He rubbed his chin. 'In which case, shall I contact the others for you?'

'That would be great.' I pulled out a chair and sat down.

Fairfax turned to his nearest beta. 'Call the other alphas, will you? Tell them to get here as soon as they can.'

I raised my chin. 'Not Lady Sullivan. Don't bother with her.' Devereau Webb would have to manage without her. If he had a problem with that, so be it. I had my limits.

Lord Fairfax flicked me a look. 'Very well. Do as the detective constable says.'

The beta wolf bowed and took off. I leaned back. Hopefully this wouldn't take very long. Fairfax sat down opposite me and watched me for several moments, obviously trying to decipher what was going on. When he couldn't, he asked, 'Would you like a drink, detective?'

'Water.' I paused. 'Please.'

Within seconds a tall glass was placed in front of me. Condensation was already forming on its sides. I drained it in three seconds and wiped my mouth with the back of my hand.

Fairfax motioned for another one and continued to watch me. 'You're the talk of the town, you know,' he said.

'Mmm-hmm.'

'I've never heard so much as a whisper about anyone else with your skills.'

I met his eyes. 'The word "skills" suggests something that I've worked at and have control over. Rising from the dead isn't a skill, it's a strange quirk of fate.'

'Fate, and not luck?'

Buffy's face, as it twisted into a wolf's, flashed into my head. 'I'm not feeling very lucky right now,' I muttered. I glowered at Fairfax, indicating that I no longer wished to talk about it. He got the message and fell silent.

I was on my third glass of water when Lady Carr and Lord McGuigan walked in. Neither of them looked happy.

'We are not at your beck and call, Ms Bellamy,' McGuigan frowned, without so much as a hello.

'Good afternoon, Lord McGuigan,' I said pointedly. 'And it's DC Bellamy.' I glared at him to emphasise my point. After the hour I'd just had, I wasn't taking any prisoners.

Lady Carr's mouth pursed. 'Is Lady Sullivan joining us?'

'No,' I said, at the exact time the lady wolf herself walked in.

'Good day.' She strode up and sat down next to me, not looking in my direction.

I turned towards her. 'Your presence is no longer required.'

The three other alphas looked at me with interest. I folded my arms.

'You cannot exclude me,' Lady Sullivan said. Her voice was quiet, but there was no denying the steel underlying her soft tone.

'I can and I will.' I lifted my head and looked at the others. 'I should apologise for my dishevelled appearance,' I said. 'The reason I look this way is because I narrowly escaped an attempt on my life on the way here.' I pointed at Lady Sullivan. 'Orchestrated by her.'

I was gratified to notice that all three of the other clan heads looked shocked.

'Ridiculous,' Lady Sullivan dismissed. 'For one thing, we now all know that you can't die. So an attempt on your life would never occur – and I would certainly never agree to such a thing.'

I didn't deign to answer that but Lady Carr was more persuadable. 'Sullivan makes a good point,' she said. 'If you truly can't die, there can't be an attempt on your life.'

I schooled my expression into a mask. 'As I'm sure you all know, I *can* die. It just so happens that twelve hours after my death, I reawaken. Someone who wants to know why that happens might kill me, take possession of my body and then observe what happens next. And perhaps perform some experiments on my temporary corpse in the meantime.'

I leaned forward. 'One Supe Squad detective has already been killed this year as a result of werewolf activity. The Met Police bigwigs decided that it was in everyone's best interests to keep the circumstances of his death quiet – there's already enough anti-supe sentiment without adding fuel to the fire. Let me be clear, however. If there are any more attacks on me, I'll broadcast what happened to Tony Brown to the world. I will also seek retribution for any hurt caused to my person. No matter what you may think of me – and Supe Squad in general – I *am* a police officer.'

I turned my head and met Lady Sullivan's eyes. 'Try anything like that again and you'll live to regret it, I promise you.'

From the fleeting emotion that showed on Lady Sullivan's face, I half expected her to deny her culpability again. Instead, she dropped her gaze. For a werewolf alpha to show submission like that was extraordinary.

'Very well,' she muttered. Then, 'I apologise.'

Lord Fairfax's nose wrinkled with disapproval. 'I'm very unhappy about this. Although I am wholly innocent of Sullivan's actions, and I would have prevented them had I known about them, please accept my apology, DC Bellamy.'

Lady Carr rolled her eyes. 'Brown nose.'

Lord McGuigan nudged her in the ribs and mouthed a word at her. I couldn't be sure, but it looked like 'Horvath'.

'Clan McGuigan,' McGuigan said aloud, 'also extends its shock and apology, DC Bellamy. In fact, we would like to offer you some protection. I have several well-trained werewolves who are more than capable of ensuring that such a thing doesn't happen again.'

Lady Carr jumped on the bandwagon. 'Clan Carr's wolves are more suited to that. I will send you my own personal protection. They will see to your safety.'

My spine was ramrod straight. 'I neither want, nor need, any protection. What I want is to walk the streets without fear of attack from your damned werewolves. You might consider things are bad now, and that you preferred how things were run before I came along, but think about it. If I go, what comes next will be everything you never wanted. My boss, DSI Barnes, will see to that.' I gazed at each of them in turn. 'Don't bite the hand that feeds you.'

I received four grudging nods of agreement. Lady Carr rose to her feet and prepared to leave.

'Sit down,' I snapped. The werewolf alpha immediately sank into her chair. She looked surprised; it was probably a long time since anyone had told her what to do. Tough. I wasn't in the mood for playing around.

'I wanted this meeting for a reason other than my well-being.' I checked the time. 'There is a human, who I imagine is already waiting outside, who wishes to speak to you. I told him I'd try and arrange a meeting for him. In return, he will provide information that will hopefully lead to the capture of the person who attacked a vampire yesterday. Last month Lord Horvath helped with your problems. Now it's your turn to help him with his.'

Fairfax shrugged. 'Fine by me.'

'That is perfectly acceptable,' Lady Sullivan agreed. The other two alphas nodded.

I almost laughed. I had no doubt that if Lady Sullivan hadn't tried to have me killed, they'd all have put up far more of a fight, regardless of my deliberate mention of Lukas. They'd have agreed in the end, but they'd each have wanted to make a show of denial first. The wolves enjoyed asserting their power in a way I'd not seen from Lukas or any of the vamps. Maybe it was a good thing I'd nearly died again.

Lord Fairfax addressed one of his betas, who was standing guard at the exit. 'Go and see if there is a human waiting outside. His name is—'

'Devereau Webb,' I supplied.

'If he's out there, escort him in,' Fairfax ordered.

We waited in silence – and it wasn't a friendly silence. It was one of the silences where everyone felt awkward, the sort that grew and grew, creating chasms of twitchiness and discomfort. We avoided each other's eyes, Lady Sullivan in particular.

When Fairfax's beta reappeared with Devereau Webb in tow, we breathed a collective sigh of relief. I was thankful that Webb had taken me at my word and hotfooted it here from his home. Whatever he wanted to discuss with the alphas, it was clearly important and I was intrigued.

If Webb was aware of the tension, he didn't show it. He swaggered into the room behind the beta wolf, his shoulders back and his hands in his pockets. With a confident smile, he strode up to us, grabbed an empty chair and sat down, spreading his legs so wide that his knees brushed against Lord McGuigan's.

Rather than appearing unhappy about the contact, McGuigan looked charmed. That made one of us, then.

'Thank you, DC Bellamy,' Webb said. 'I'll take things from here.'

It was an obvious dismissal but I ignored it. I crossed my legs. 'The floor is yours, Mr Webb.'

I was certain he would demand I left the meeting but he seemed to think better of it. He offered a lazy shrug and an amiable smile. 'Very well, detective.' He looked round the small gathering. 'First of all, let me thank you all for coming. I know that you are important people and your time is precious.'

Lady Carr clicked her tongue. 'Yes, yes. Get to the point, young man.' I imagined it was a very long time since anyone had called Devereau Webb that.

'I am here seeking a boon. I understand that your recruitment policies are stringent and there are numerous rules about who can be turned into a wolf. I also know, however, that you often look for new blood to keep your clan lines as healthy as possible – and that you only recruit the very best.'

I blinked. Devereau Webb wanted to become a werewolf? Was that what this was about?

'And you believe you are the very best?' Lord McGuigan drawled, shooting a derisive look in my direction, presumably for bringing Webb here with such a routine and mundane request.

'I'm not here on my own behalf,' Devereau replied easily.

Interesting.

'We're waiting with bated breath,' Lady Sullivan said, sounding quite the opposite. 'On whose behalf are you here?'

'I'll get to that.' Webb leaned forward, his expression growing more serious. 'I'm not sure what DC Bellamy has told you about me. I might not be a supernatural being like your good selves, but I have considerable power and many connections.'

'We all have those.' McGuigan folded his arms and looked away. I reckoned he was about twenty seconds away from standing up and walking out of the door. Webb had better get to his point quickly.

'Let's just say,' Devereau said, 'without naming any names, I possess some damning information concerning several highly placed politicians. I'm in a position to negotiate with them – in fact, I've already done so. I know that you have the run of St James's Park during the full moon. I also know that it's far too small to meet all your needs. I have an agreement whereby exclusive use of Regent's Park will be granted to one clan and one clan only. Certain areas will be off limits.'

He smiled faintly. 'The zoo, for one. The sports pitches at the Hub, for another. But the area of available land is still considerable. This is the sort of gift that money can't buy.'

I didn't need to check the alphas' expressions to know what a coup this was. It was no secret that St James's Park was small and crowded when all four clans had to use it on the night of the full moon and every wolf in the city was compelled to transform. To have exclusive use of even part of Regent's Park was a game changer.

'And in return for this gift?' Lord Fairfax enquired, his tone so deliberately bored that I knew he was practically salivating at the thought of having such a vast space at his clan's disposal. 'What do you want?'

'You permit one person, who I name specifically, to be bitten enough to turn into a werewolf. That is all. I don't expect this person to receive special benefits. What they do once they are turned, and whether they end up as a ranked wolf or otherwise, will be up to them. I'm confident that the person in question has extraordinary potential and they'll prove an incredible asset to whichever clan takes them on.'

'If they are so extraordinary,' Lady Carr said, taking the words right out of my mouth, 'then why go to such lengths? Why not simply take the usual route and petition us to be turned? If they're as wonderful as you seem to believe, they're sure to be selected.'

Webb's left eyebrow twitched. Ah-ha. Now we were getting to the crux of the matter. I watched him, fascinated to hear what he was about to say next.

'Let's say that time is a factor and the normal routes are not open to this person.'

'You mean they're sick,' Lady Sullivan said flatly. 'And you think that becoming a werewolf will cure whatever ailment they suffer from.'

I gazed at Webb, checking his reaction. His eyebrow twitched again. Lady Sullivan was right.

'Leukaemia,' he admitted.

All four alphas exchanged glances. 'We don't tend to advertise the fact that werewolf transformation curbs cancer,' Fairfax said. 'After all, there are strict limits on our numbers,' he nodded towards me, 'which are set by the government and which we have no control over. We can't trigger the change in someone merely because they are sick, and there are only so many sob stories one can listen to. We can't even permit "accidental" transformations to occur.' He drew air quotations around the word. 'Our procedures to guard against them are strict.'

Webb inclined his head. 'I am aware of all that. I've done my research.' He smiled faintly. 'The Carlyle Library, in particular, has proved very helpful. I know that approaching the vampires is out of the question. Turning into a bloodsucker doesn't remove illness. In fact, in some cases it can accelerate the symptoms and make matters worse. But I also know that the reverse is true with werewolves. If this person is turned, they will also be cured.'

'It is unorthodox, but Clan Sullivan is prepared to recruit your person.' Lady Sullivan smiled at him. 'We are very welcoming to newcomers.'

'Hold on a minute,' McGuigan blustered. 'Clan McGuigan would like the opportunity to speak up. *We* will take this person. And,' he gave Lady Sullivan a glare, 'we are considerably more effective with new werewolves than other clans. We haven't had any murderers in our ranks. Unlike some others,' he added pointedly.

Lady Carr cleared her throat. 'The Carr Clan has spaces available. We can move on this within the week.'

Fairfax stood up. 'Mr Webb,' he intoned. 'This club belongs to my clan. Why don't the two of us go somewhere more private and discuss your proposal further? I have a room beyond that door where we will be undisturbed.'

'Just because we chose to meet here doesn't give you an advantage!' McGuigan snapped. 'I have a far grander property less than a stone's throw from here, Mr Webb. We can go there immediately.'

'We all have grander properties, you idiot,' Lady Carr muttered.

I blocked out their bickering and focused on Devereau Webb. He wasn't displeased by the sudden jostling for his attention, but he wasn't thrilled by it either. There was more to this than he was telling us.

'I thank you all for your interest,' he said. 'I'll allow you all time to think over my proposal.' He reached into his jacket, drew out four identical envelopes and passed one to each alpha. 'Inside those envelopes, you'll find draft legal agreements for the future use of Regent's Park, including any and all restrictions. You can examine the land yourselves and I will grant you enough time to consider all the advantages. Then, in twenty-four hours, I will bring the recruit here to be turned. If more than one of you want to go ahead, the recruit will choose which clan to join.' He gazed round them all. 'Does that sound suitable?'

There was a beat of silence, then all four alphas nodded agreement. I breathed out. Devereau Webb did have a way with people. He was effective at compromise and at deflecting disagreements. But there was still something he was holding back. I'd lay money on it.

'Good.' He got to his feet. 'In twenty-four hours, then.' He turned and started to walk towards the door.

I sprang up. 'All four of you stay here,' I instructed. I caught up to Webb. 'Wait a minute.'

He glanced at me. 'Ah, yes. DC Bellamy. I'd almost forgotten about you.'

As if.

Webb reached into his jacket pocket and drew out another envelope, far slimmer than the previous ones. I didn't take it. I was waiting to hear what he had to say first.

'It is known throughout the city that the Knightsbridge area is for my people only,' he said.

My voice was flat. 'You're referring to pickpocketing, burglary and mugging.'

'Oh no.' His expression was one of mock shock. 'I mean proselytizing. My people use Knightsbridge to spread the word of God. Other people are free to evangelise in other areas, but it is an unspoken rule that they will not venture into Knightsbridge.'

I just managed to avoid rolling my eyes. Evangelising, my arse.

'Therefore,' he continued, 'when we see someone else … preaching, we suggest that they find other areas to work in.'

'Whatever happened to love thy neighbour?' I enquired.

Webb gave me a long look. 'Do you want to hear this or not?'

I gestured towards him. 'Go ahead.'

'On the day in question, one of my team happened to notice another missionary in the area. He appeared to be following a vampire and seeking to … convert them.'

I stiffened. 'It was obvious that she was a vampire?'

He shrugged. 'It was to my team member. They followed the missionary and saw him approach the vamp. They witnessed the brief attack and subsequent death from the other end of the street.'

I thought about the CCTV footage I'd seen. No doubt that had been when Moira's shaven-headed attacker had looked up.

Webb continued. 'My team member was concerned about what they'd witnessed so, to ensure no further trouble arose, they followed the attacker.' He held up the envelope. 'Straight to the address you'll find in here.'

I sucked in a breath. This information, if it were real, was pure gold. 'Your … missionary didn't approach?'

'No. They called it in and were advised to pull back.'

'Why? If the attacker was encroaching on your turf, why give him a free pass?'

'He killed a vampire.' Webb smiled at me. 'It seemed wiser to keep out of the way and let the likes of Lord Horvath deal with him. Of course, I didn't realise that the vampire Lord had the police in his pocket.'

My eyes flashed but I didn't rise to the bait. 'And Regent's Park?' I demanded.

'What about it?'

'You're blackmailing senior politicians for access to it at full moon? I shouldn't have to tell you that blackmail is a crime.'

Webb tutted. 'It's not blackmail, it's merely an agreement between civilised parties.'

'Who are these politicians? What have you got on them?'

'Honestly, DC Bellamy, you don't want to know. Suffice to say that they haven't broken any laws. They have embarrassed themselves and are seeking to conceal their embarrassment from the public. Further investigation on your part is not necessary.' He jerked his head at the four alpha werewolves. 'Neither, I suspect, is it desired.' He waved the envelope. 'Do you want this address or don't you?'

I gritted my teeth and took it from him. 'Who is the potential recruit? Who do you want transformed?'

I caught a surprising flicker of sadness in his eyes. 'No-one to interest you.' He tipped his head. 'Thank you for your help, DC Bellamy. It is appreciated more than you know. Until next time.' And with that, he strode away.

I stared down at the envelope. I had the distinct feeling that I'd made a very bad deal with a very bad devil. I sighed and stuffed it into my back pocket then turned to the alphas. They were all preparing to leave. That was unfortunate because I wasn't done yet. 'Stay where you are,' I called. I marched over to them.

Lady Carr sighed. 'What now, Detective?'

'I need to run some names past you.' I took out the sheet of paper Fred had given me. 'Patrick McGuigan.'

Lord McGuigan's face darkened. 'What about him?'

'He died two years ago, right?'

'Of natural causes,' he replied stiffly. 'Not all diseases are cured by wolf transformations.'

'Why did Patrick die?'

McGuigan glared at me. 'Lupus.'

I made a note. 'Jane Sullivan.'

Lady Sullivan jerked. 'She's dead too.'

'How?'

'She fell. She slipped, lost her footing and fell off a cliff while on holiday.'

I checked the next name. Like the Clarkes' son, not all werewolves changed their surnames to match their clans. 'Thomas Kennilworth?'

'He was in my clan.' Fairfax gazed at me. 'Also dead. It was a car accident. Last year.'

'Uh-huh. How about Margaret Hoy?'

Lady Carr stared at me. 'She was mine. She died from sepsis from a wound incurred during a full moon. What exactly are you getting at? Is this related to Julian Clarke?'

'It is,' I said grimly. 'Those four werewolves were all buried at St Erbin's Church too.'

'So?'

'We need to exhume their graves.'

All the werewolves looked alarmed.

'Julian's body was missing,' Lady Carr said. 'Do you think…?' Her voice trailed away.

'I do,' I said. 'But I need official permission from each wolf's next of kin to check.'

'Because of his parents' insistence, Julian was an anomaly,' Lady Carr said. 'It is typical for each alpha to be next of kin for all their wolves. I can give you permission for Margaret.'

The other three nodded, indicating that they were doing the same for their respective wolves.

McGuigan's brow creased. 'This isn't ghouls?'

'No,' I said. 'I don't believe so. They don't gain anything from the bodies of werewolves. These days they get their, uh, needs satisfied by home delivery.'

He blinked. 'Really?' If even werewolf alphas like him believed the old stories, then the ghouls had no hope.

'As far as I can tell,' I said.

'But if that's the case, why would those graves be empty?'

'I have no idea. However, if they *are* empty, I will find out what's going on.' I glanced at Lady Sullivan. 'I do have my uses, beyond my physical attributes.'

'I'm beginning to see that, Detective.'

Only beginning? I told myself to remain professional. Moving away from the others, I motioned to her to join me. 'Did you bring it?' I asked.

'Bring what?'

My answer was terse. 'The DNA testing kit.'

'I…' she blinked. 'Yes, but…'

'Hand it over.'

She reached into her bag and withdrew a small plastic vial and a cotton swab. I ran the swab round the inside of my mouth and dropped it into the vial before returning to her. She seemed nonplussed. 'I don't understand,' she said.

'I made a deal with you. I gave you my word.' I injected as much conviction into my voice as I could. 'And although you didn't keep your end of the bargain, I got what I wanted. I have enough honour to see my promise through to its end.'

Lady Sullivan's eyes turned ice cold. 'You're trying to shame me, DC Bellamy.'

'I don't need to shame you,' I told her. 'You've already shamed yourself.' I pointed at the vial in her hand. 'I want a copy of any answers you find. If you leave anything out, I'll find out about it sooner or later and…'

'I won't leave anything out.' She paused. 'For the future of Clan Sullivan, I give you my word.'

I actually believed her. I nodded. 'Good.' I turned to go.

'One more thing, DC Bellamy,' she said. 'If I may?'

'Go on.'

'It would be in all our interests if you did not tell Lord Horvath about what happened between us. He has a great deal to contend with since his vampire was killed, and I wouldn't wish to add to his woes.'

She was more scared of Lukas than I'd realised – and

more concerned about his intentions towards me than she should be. 'I won't lie to him,' I told her. 'But I won't volunteer the information.'

'Thank you. I appreciate that.' She hesitated. 'And I am genuinely sorry about what happened. It was an error on my part.'

I nodded to acknowledge that I'd heard her. Then I walked out.

Chapter Thirteen

I could feel the beginnings of a headache pushing at my skull so I swallowed a couple of ibuprofen tablets as soon as I hopped out of the shower. Then I opened my wardrobe. What did one wear to dinner with a vampire Lord? Given what kind of day Lukas had endured, I knew he wouldn't give a rat's arse what I was wearing but I wanted to appear respectful. It was effectively a business meeting, so I certainly shouldn't look too dressy. In the end I chose a pair of dark trousers that would allow me freedom of movement and a slightly more formal blouse.

I examined my face in the mirror and thought about all the female vampires I'd met over the last few weeks. I was the least glamorous person Lukas knew. With that thought in mind, I carefully applied a layer of foundation, a dusting of blusher and a slick of mascara. It made me appear less tired – but I was still the same Emma.

I resisted the temptation to wipe it all off again and grabbed my coat just as the doorbell buzzed. I nipped over to the window and glanced down. Lukas, wearing a smart coat and a grim expression, tilted his head up at me. I waved and headed down to the ground floor.

As I reached the foot of the stairs, the front door opened and my neighbour Will stomped in. He caught sight of me and glowered. I'd inherited the third-floor flat as part of my position within Supe Squad; before that, Tony had lived there. After Tony had gone missing, I'd pretended to be Tony's niece to get information from Will. He still hadn't forgiven me for it. Neither did it help that I'd taken Tony's job as well as his home; Will was not a fan of supes – even when those supes included Lord Horvath.

'This building is my home as well as yours,' he sniped, jabbing his finger at me. 'Don't invite that vampire in. The last thing we need is to give a bloodsucker free access to all our blood.'

'You know that whole invitation thing is a myth, right? If a vampire wants to come in, they'll come in.'

'And I have no interest in your blood,' Lukas called from the doorstep.

Will shuddered.

'You have nothing to worry about,' I said, trying to soothe his anxiety

He clumped past me. 'Tell that to Anthony Brown!' he threw over his shoulder.

I sighed and watched him climb the stairs, then I headed out to join Lukas. 'Sorry,' I said.

'Your neighbours are not your fault.' He gazed at me. 'You look tired.'

So much for the make-up. 'It's been a long day.' I bit my lip. 'You look tired too.'

He laughed humourlessly. 'We'll make quite a pair when we both fall asleep in our soup.'

I managed a smile. I drew closer and angled my head to look up at him. 'How did it go today?'

Lukas ran a hand through his hair. There was a frustrated pain about the movement that made my heart go out to him. 'It was tough,' he said. 'Very tough. There aren't a lot of us and, with our longer lifespans, I don't have to deal with this sort of traumatic occasion very often. That's a good thing, of course, but it means that it hurts more when it does happen.' He let out a harsh laugh. 'Sorry. You know about the power of grief. You lost your parents, and then when your boyfriend...' He shook his head.

I bit back the old impulse, born out of years of practice, to tell him that I hadn't lost my parents. They'd been viciously killed by a man called Samuel Beswick who'd slaughtered them in a senseless rage and who had been locked up for his crimes ever since. Instead I touched his arm gently, feeling the warmth of his skin through the material of his coat. 'Grief is neither exclusive to one person, nor the same for everyone. Allow yourself the time you need, Lukas. It's not a weakness, it's a strength.' I hesitated. 'Let's cancel dinner.'

'No. I need this.' He gazed at me. 'And I'm hoping you have some information for me.'

I bit my lip. 'I do.'

Grim satisfaction lit his expression. 'I knew I could count on you, D'Artagnan.'

***

I'd learned since I started this job that vampires ate solid food like the rest of us. They had to supplement their diet with fresh blood in order to survive, but they didn't drink O neg as often as I'd assumed. Not that human blood was in short supply; people literally lined up to be given the 'honour' of having their veins opened by a vamp.

Rather than stay in the area and have other supes to deal with, Lukas suggested that we head away from both Soho and Lisson Grove and aim for a small pizzeria a couple of miles away. Given the circumstances and the day that all the vampires had just endured, I persuaded him to send his driver home. Lukas folded himself into Tallulah and I drove.

Lukas held the pizzeria door open for me. The maître d' either didn't recognise him or was too well trained to show it, and we were led to a small table towards the back without any fuss. I glanced round. The interior was cosy and intimate – certainly not the sort of place I'd have imagined finding the Lord of all vampires. Perhaps that was the point.

'We can go somewhere else if you like,' Lukas said, noting my expression.

I smiled. 'This is great.'

'I'm glad to hear it.' His black eyes held mine. 'People always seem to think that I only want to hang out in fine-dining establishments. Don't get me wrong,' he added, 'they can be excellent. But sometimes all you want is simple food cooked well. I'm not in the mood for any fuss.'

'I don't blame you,' I told him quietly.

He acknowledged my words with a tilt of his head. 'And you? How are you doing?' He paused, as if he were choosing his words carefully. 'Is your job at Supe Squad going well?'

Buffy's clever eyes and ditzy manner flashed into my mind but I pushed the image away. Today had been an anomaly and, if I thought about it, I was proud of how I'd dealt with the situation. 'Yes,' I said. 'I actually feel like I'm getting a stronger grip on things. And while I still have a long way to go, I've already learnt a great deal about supes.'

'What did you think of the ghouls?' Lukas asked.

'They weren't quite what I was expecting,' I admitted. I told him that the werewolves also seemed to believe that ghouls still robbed graves and a small smile crossed his mouth.

'Old stories and beliefs persist,' he said, as the waiter poured us glasses of water. 'I doubt that the clans have given the ghouls much thought up 'til now. They live peacefully and under the radar,' he shrugged, 'so there's little reason to seek them out and find out more about their kind.'

'You obviously have.'

He smiled. 'You have Kennedy to thank for that. He spent a lot of time telling me that I should learn from *all* supes, not just those who are so numerous that they demand attention. I expect part of that comes from him being a satyr. There aren't many of them around either, and they have their own reputations to contend with.'

I grinned. I'd done my research and I knew exactly what Lukas was referring to. 'They're supposed to be sex-obsessed, randy buggers, you mean.'

'Indeed.' Lukas took a sip of his water. 'Speaking of Kennedy, how is the crossbow training going?'

I held my hands up, displaying my red-raw fingers. 'I have a few war wounds,' I said cheerfully. 'But I'm making progress.'

Lukas reached across and took my hands in his. His touch was surprisingly gentle. 'I can help you with these,' he said.

I knew what he meant. His saliva held healing properties; a few delicate licks and my skin would return to normal.

I shook my head. 'These are hard won,' I said. 'They'll heal on their own and I might gain a few helpful calluses that will help in my future attempts with the bow.'

A flash of something akin to respect lit Lukas's eyes. 'Very well.'

We exchanged a smile, then I drew in a breath and reached for the envelope which Devereau Webb had given me. 'I think I've found Moira's attacker. He doesn't know we're onto him but I have his address.'

Lukas's eyes dropped and he stared at the envelope, though he made no move to take it. 'How did you find him?' he asked quietly.

I outlined what had happened with Webb. Lukas scratched his chin. 'I haven't heard of this Shepherd.'

'Neither had I until today. He's the king of a small empire that focuses on petty crime and intimidation. He's well known to the police in CID, but he's not stupid enough to expand his enterprise to the point where he loses his control and the police get enough evidence to charge him with his crimes. I wouldn't say he's particularly dangerous physically, but I do think he's very clever.'

'Can he be trusted?' He nodded towards the envelope. 'Can this information be trusted?'

I'd spent the last few hours pondering this very question. 'I believe so. I get the impression that Devereau Webb lives his life by a distinct code.' I paused. 'And that right now he needs supes more than supes need him.'

Lukas held himself stiffly. 'You were right before. About Moira's killer, I mean. Don't get me wrong. I want to rip his throat out, but you need to deal with him as the law sees fit.'

I exhaled. I hadn't realised I'd been holding my breath. 'Thank you,' I said quietly. 'For what it's worth, I don't believe he meant for her to die. I know that's cold comfort but—' I gestured helplessly.

Lukas nodded. He understood what I was getting at. 'I'd like to be there when you question him.'

I'd expected nothing less. 'I can make that happen.' I checked my watch. 'I thought I might take him unawares and pay him a visit after we've finished here.'

'Good.' Lukas's expression altered. 'Now let's order some food and talk about something else. I need to be reminded that there's more to this world than horror.'

'What would you like to talk about?'

He leaned forward, the intensity in his eyes

deepening. 'You.'

Damn it. I was fed up of being a curiosity to every supe in London. 'I still don't know what I am. I still don't know anything more about why I can do what I do.'

He shook his head. 'That's not what I mean. I want to know more about you as a person. What's your favourite colour?'

Uh... I blinked. 'Blue.'

'Music?'

I looked around, ostentatiously checking for eavesdroppers. 'I have a secret penchant for eighties pop. A-Ha. Duran Duran. Eurythmics.'

His brow furrowed. 'You're kidding me.'

'Nope.'

Lukas looked vaguely horrified. 'D'Artagnan. I thought more of you than that.'

I folded my arms. 'Oh, yeah? What kind of music do you like?' I raised an eyebrow. 'Jazz?'

He made a face. 'Good grief. No.'

I considered. 'Death metal with some decent thrash thrown in for good measure?'

'What are you talking about?'

I grinned.

'Remind me,' Lukas sniffed, 'to introduce you to some real music soon. Handel. Mozart. Debussy.'

I wrinkled my nose. 'Didn't he play for the Smiths?'

'No.' Lukas broke off a piece of bread, a glint of amusement in his face. 'But he was a remarkably charming man.'

'You can be quite charming yourself,' I said, the words falling out of my mouth before I had the chance to stop them.

Lukas watched me. 'Does that make you Cinderella?'

It took a second for his words to sink in. That was flirting. Right?

Lucas smiled slightly before winking as if to suggest he was merely speaking in jest. And then the waiter appeared to take our order.

Chapter Fourteen

The address Devereau Webb had given me was for a road on the edge of London's East End. While Lukas and I had kept the conversation light over dinner and I sensed he was relaxing after his terrible day, the mood changed dramatically after we paid the bill and left. Grim anticipation filled Tallulah's shabby interior and I noticed Lukas's fists clenching and unclenching.

Although there were cells at Supe Squad, they were in a state of disrepair and certainly not suitable for holding anyone. If the man who lived at this address was the same man I'd seen in the CCTV footage, then I'd arrest him and take him to the nearest police station for questioning – and charging. I'd already scoped out the station and called ahead. In the event that we got our man, they'd dispatch a couple of uniformed officers to meet us at the house. I wasn't sure how they'd react to Lukas's presence but that was a bridge I'd cross when I had to.

'It might not be him,' I cautioned, when I pulled up in the street.

Lukas stared ahead. 'I know.'

'And if it is him, we have to tread carefully. We're not in Soho, Lukas. There are a lot of laws to abide by. I'd get into serious trouble if anyone found out I'd brought you along. That means you need to do exactly what I say.'

'I understand.'

'You'll have to stay in the car.'

His head whipped round. 'That wasn't part of the deal.'

'If I don't follow procedure, he could get off on a technicality.'

Lukas muttered something under his breath.

'Lord Horvath…'

'Don't,' he said. 'Don't Lord Horvath me.' His black eyes met mine. 'Unless circumstances demand otherwise, I will do as you say. I will stay in the car.'

Circumstances? 'Lukas,' I started.

'If he tries to hurt you or runs,' he elaborated, 'you can't expect me to put my feet up and watch.'

'Okay,' I agreed. 'But I need you to keep your cool and stay where you are unless that happens.'

Lukas's expression didn't alter. 'I give you my word.'

Some of the tension eased from my shoulders. No matter what mask Lukas was displaying, I knew his emotions were running high – but he would keep his promise. He was that kind of man. I nodded and unclipped my seatbelt before getting out.

'Keep an eye on him, Tallulah,' I whispered. Then I straightened my shoulders and stalked to the door.

The house was a small, Victorian, terraced property. Judging from our location, and the identical red-brick houses along the street, it had probably once been a railway worker's home. Two up, two down and a small garden out the back; even when it was built, it would have been unremarkable. If you were a criminal without the network of someone like Devereau Webb and you wanted to hide in plain sight, you couldn't have chosen better than here.

I paused outside for a moment and looked at the house. The curtains were drawn and there was a glimmer of light somewhere inside. That was good, I decided. With luck, this could be over in seconds.

I glanced at Lukas, who had stayed true to his word and remained inside Tallulah. Then I leaned forward and rapped hard on the door. Alright, let's be having you.

The curtains in the front room twitched. I moved closer to the doorstep, angling my body so that whoever was inside couldn't see me. The last thing I wanted was for them to get spooked and run before I could make a positive identification. Rather than be reassured by the police, some members of the public had the opposite reaction and gave in to baser instincts to flee, whether they'd done something wrong or not. As we'd been told at the Academy, until you were in the position where the police knocked on your door late at night, you couldn't know how you'd react.

The curtains twitched again and there was a thud. A moment later, I heard footsteps clumping towards me. Excellent. I crossed my fingers.

There was the rattle of a key in the lock. I waited patiently until the door was opened a crack and a wary male voice called out, 'Yes? Who is it?'

I couldn't see the speaker's face. He was behind the door and the hallway lights were off. The best I could make out was his outline, and I needed more to be sure that this was our guy.

'Good evening, sir,' I said politely. 'I'm Detective Constable Emma Bellamy. I'd like to ask you a few questions, if I may.'

'Now? It's after nine o'clock at night!'

All the better to throw you off balance, I thought. 'It's important.'

There was a heavy sigh and the door opened further. At the same time, he flicked on a bright porch light. I blinked rapidly. It was shining directly in my eyes, making it hard to see anything.

'Sir,' I said, 'can you please turn off the light?'

'I want to see some identification.'

I delved into my pocket for my warrant card and held it up. 'If you turn the light off first then—'

'Are you alone?' he demanded. There was a beat of silence. 'Wait. That car...' The man sucked in a breath. 'Is that Lord Horvath in there? The vampire?'

'Sir,' I said, tense now, 'you need to turn off the light.'

I raised my arm to shield my eyes but it didn't help; I still couldn't see his features. But he'd recognised Lukas and that told me a great deal. Few people outside the supernatural community could put a face to his name.

The man's voice altered significantly. 'Well, well, well.' He sounded very satisfied. 'Isn't this a turn-up for the books?' A split second later, he slammed the door in my face.

I cursed. 'Sir!' I shouted through the closed door. 'Come back here!'

It was a wasted effort. Lukas was already out of Tallulah and running towards me. I gritted my teeth and jumped up, using my elbow to smash the light over the doorway and break the bulb. While my vision restored itself, I shoved my shoulder against the door to force it open.

Lukas burst past me with one leg raised. He kicked the door and it sprang back, the wood splitting. There was a crash from beyond and I hissed, 'He's running.'

I sprang into the house and glanced into the room on my left. The television was on but no-one was in there. There was no doubt in my mind that the man, whoever he really was, had scarpered through the back. There had to be a rear entrance.

I darted through the drab hallway into the small

kitchen, and spotted the glass-plated door immediately. It was locked. I had to marvel at the calm thought process of someone running from the police who'd taken the time to bar the way behind them. Few people were that careful when they were under pressure. It made me even more convinced that this was the man who'd attacked Moira and inadvertently caused her death.

'Out of the way,' Lukas said.

I did as he asked. With calm efficiency, he grabbed a heavy plant pot and threw it at the door. The glass shattered. I leapt forward, knocking the shards out of the way so we could get to the garden and the man's escape route.

'What's going on? Ted? Are you alright?' It was a neighbour from the next house.

'Police!' I shouted. 'Call 999!'

There was a muttered 'Fuck!' Then I heard nothing more. I hoped they were already on the phone but I didn't have time to look back and check; I was already sprinting after my target with Lukas by my side.

There was no easy route out of the garden, so the man must have vaulted over the fence. He had the advantage – he knew the area. He wasn't a vampire, however, and he didn't possess supernatural skills.

Lukas pulled away from me and sailed over the fence as if it barely existed. I was less than a metre behind, scrabbling up and over it. When I landed, I realised we were on a narrow path that snaked between the terraced houses. It was overgrown and strewn with weeds – and there was no sign of our target.

Lukas's head was raised upwards, his nostrils flaring. He didn't possess the perfect scenting abilities of a werewolf, but he was still better at sniffing out a trail than the average human. His eyes narrowed and he jerked his head to the left. 'That way,' he bit out.

We started running. Lukas pulled away from me, flying down the path. Regardless of my enhanced physical abilities, there was no chance I'd keep up with him. I did my best, though, my feet pounding the dirt and condemning several stringy dandelions in the process.

Within seconds, Lukas was at the far end of the path. His head jerked from right to left as he scanned the street for any sign of our prey. He spun back in my direction. Ted, if that's who he was, had leapt into someone's garden rather than head for the road. Now all we had to do was work out which one.

'His scent?' I called.

Lukas pounded his fists in frustration. 'I've lost it. There are too many conflicting smells.'

Damn it. I hissed and started peering into the gardens. Lukas tilted his head, listening for any suspicious sounds. I glanced at him briefly and then away again.

Wait a minute. There was something there.

I jogged a few metres until I was in front of a wooden fence. I bent down and peered more closely. That was a muddy handprint – and it was still damp. I jumped, bracing my hands on the top of the fence so I could look down into the garden below. There, planted in the earth next to a dormant rose bush, were two heavy footprints. Someone had jumped over the fence at this very spot. It could only have been one person.

As I heaved myself over, I beckoned to Lukas but also placed a finger to my lips. It would be easier to round up our target if he didn't realise we were right behind him. Silence rather than speed was the key. Lukas nodded his understanding as I landed in the garden with a soft thud, making footprints of my own. A second later he was by my side, his movements lithe and cat-like.

The garden belonged to another small, two-storey

house, although it had double patio doors rather than a single back exit and was semi-detached instead of terraced. The curtains were drawn but I could see light and hear muffled voices beyond them. If Ted knew his neighbours well, he could have knocked on their window and hidden in their house. But that would be strictly a short-term option, and it didn't sound as if the family inside had just encountered a surprise night guest.

Lukas and I swivelled round, searching the darkness for clues. We both spotted the side gate at the same time. I checked it. It was off the latch. He'd gone this way.

The snicket at the side of the house led out onto another paint-by-numbers residential street that curved away to the right at the far end. I squinted, then I drew in a sharp breath and ducked down, grabbing hold of Lukas's arm and bringing him with me. Up ahead, on the opposite side of the pavement, was the stumbling silhouette of a man who appeared to be limping. No-one else was visible.

We stayed low but kept moving in a bid to catch up. Our target disappeared momentarily as he rounded the bend. I crossed the street so I could keep a good distance behind him, while Lukas sped up in a bid to get closer. Without saying a word, we'd formed our own capture net.

When I finally pulled round the bend and saw what lay ahead, I knew that Teddy Boy didn't stand a chance. This street was a dead end; less than a hundred metres away a row of garages blocked the way out – and our limping man was darting into one of them. He probably thought he'd made a clean getaway.

There was a loud clang as the metal garage door closed behind him. I put on an extra spurt of speed and caught up to Lukas. He flicked me a sidelong look of triumph.

'Let's make sure there aren't any more back exits first,' I whispered as we drew closer to the garages.

Lukas shook his head. 'High wall to the rear blocking any way out from the rear. No side exit because he's not in the end garage. The roof is flat but there aren't any skylights. He's in there and he's trapped.'

I allowed myself a smile. 'Stay here,' I said, 'and I'll—' I hadn't finished my sentence when Lukas started striding ahead. 'Hey!' I hissed.

'He ran,' he said simply. 'I'm not letting that happen again.'

I cursed. As Lukas reached for the garage door, I started after him. Nothing had changed: I was still the police detective and, while Ted Whoever remained human, that meant he was mine to deal with. Not Lukas's.

Lukas pulled the string to raise up the canopy-style garage door.

'Police!' I called, re-asserting my authority. 'You have to stand down imm—'

And then, before I could finish my sentence, there was a blinding flash of light and a deafening bang and I tipped forward to the ground.

Chapter Fifteen

Panic descended. My throat felt as if it were closing up and I couldn't breathe, no matter how much I gasped. I scrabbled at the ground, cold seeping upwards from where I'd fallen. There was gritty dirt and something wet beneath my fingers. My vision had gone and the ringing in my ears was overwhelming. My stomach lurched and nausea threatened to overtake me. Then air rushed into my lungs and I blinked, and the world started to right itself. Sort of.

I choked and spluttered, raising my head to gaze blearily around me. Everything still seemed fuzzy around the edges and the tinnitus continued unabated. I yanked my leg out of the dirty puddle it was lying in.

Lukas. Where was Lukas?

I rubbed my head, and tried to stagger up to my feet. My knees gave up halfway and I sank down again, just as a figure marched towards me, arms swinging. Not Lukas. I squinted, then ice filled my veins when I realised it was Moira's attacker. His lips moved. He was saying something to me, but I couldn't hear a damned word. He had the sort of cheesy grin on his face that I'd normally associate with a gameshow host or a dodgy car dealer. His mouth moved again. He crouched down until we were face to face.

He reached out and I flinched, expecting pain. Instead, he brushed back a curl of hair. His fingers went to my mouth. I raised my hands to try and push him off or defend myself, but I was still too disorientated. My hands flailed and he gently knocked them away. With his thumb and index finger, he pulled my lips apart and examined my teeth.

Vampire, I thought dully. He's checking to see whether I'm a vampire.

He nodded to himself, seemingly satisfied. The shark's tooth necklace round his neck shivered. His hands moved towards my body and I squeaked, suddenly terrified. All he did, though, was remove my warrant card from my pocket and examine it. He pursed his lips.

At that moment, out of the corner of my eye, I saw Lukas lurch up from the ground less than ten metres away.

The man moved. Ted. *Was* he Ted? He was still grinning. He casually loped over in Lukas's direction. Now he'd find out what a mistake he'd made – Lukas would flatten him. I heaved myself upright once more, this time managing to stay on my feet. I started to stagger towards them, ready to provide what support I could.

Lukas's eyes met mine and I recognised relief – and something else. Then he turned his attention back to Ted.

Something was wrong. Lukas swayed unsteadily and his face spasmed, contorting into a snarl. I saw his fangs grow more prominent. Then Ted simply raised his hand. What was that? What was he—? I yelped as he pressed something into the side of Lukas's neck. Was that a fucking syringe?

Almost immediately, Lukas's eyes rolled into the back of his head and he collapsed. No. *NO*. Not on my watch, buster.

I gritted my teeth and staggered forward. Ted's head turned slowly. He seemed surprised to see me and, as he watched me, his brow creased. Then he shrugged and reached down. He grabbed Lukas under his arms and dragged him towards the open garage.

He wasn't taking Lukas. I wouldn't allow it.

Everything felt as if it were in slow motion. I forced myself to move as fast as I could but I was certain I was going to keel over or throw up – or both – at any moment. I shuffled and stumbled and forced my way forward. I tried to speak, to tell him to stop but my mouth didn't seem to be working properly.

Ted bundled Lukas's inert body into a dusty car inside the garage, then he reached into the glove box. A moment later, I was staring at the muzzle of a gun which was pointed right at my face.

Over the ringing in my ears, I heard something like a shot. Bastard. Had he shot me? Was that twice in one damned week that I was going to the morgue because of a gun? I opened my mouth and screamed in frustration, staring down at my body. Where had he hit me? Where did it hurt?

There was another sharp crack. I looked up and saw a sudden flinch of fear from Ted. He'd dropped the gun and was staring at something over his shoulder. He glanced at his car and I was sure I caught a glimpse of frustration. A second later there was yet another crack. This time, Ted took off.

As he ran past me I reached for him and tried to block his way, but he shoved me aside. He darted towards the first house on the left, shoved his way through the garden gate and disappeared into the darkness beyond.

My arms flailed. Come back. Come back, you bastard.

I dragged myself after him but I couldn't move fast enough. Bile hit the back of my throat as my stomach contents moved into my mouth. Then I couldn't hold it any longer. Vomit hurled out of me and I crashed down to my hands and knees again.

A shadow fell across the ground in front of me.

Hands reached for my arms, helping me up. I blinked and stared. Wh – what?

Gaz's mouth moved. He was saying something but I couldn't work out what. I shook my head, confused. He smiled, patted me on the shoulder, and directed me towards the back of the car that had just pulled up.

***

'It was some sort of stun grenade.'

I glanced at Devereau Webb. 'Pardon?'

'He used a stun grenade. It causes temporary blindness, deafness and disorientation.'

I grunted. 'Tell me something I don't know.' I still had a persistent ringing in my ears but I could hear better now, and I no longer felt so dizzy or sick. 'Like why Gaz was there.'

Webb smiled. 'Call it an insurance policy. I'd already asked a few of my guys to keep an eye on the address. That man had invaded my turf and I wanted to be sure that he'd be put out of the way for good. I wasn't going to forget about him until you made a move against him. When you did and it all went tits up, I told Gaz to intervene.'

'Why? We were even. You don't owe me anything.'

He shrugged. 'Maybe I'm a nice guy.'

I snorted. 'Yeah. And maybe you're looking for more favours.'

'It wasn't about that.' He gave me a long look. 'You helped me out, even though we are natural enemies. I don't forget that sort of thing.'

'I bet rescuing the Lord of all vampires will look good on your CV, too.'

'You wound me, DC Bellamy.' Webb winked. 'But you're right. Achieving such a momentous feat isn't a bad thing.'

I looked at Lukas. He was flat out on the floor of Webb's flat and hadn't stirred, but his breathing was steady and his colour was healthy. Whatever shit Ted had injected into his bloodstream, I was certain it wasn't fatal.

Despite my severe disorientation, I'd clocked the expression on Ted's face. He'd been delighted to have Lukas in his grasp, in the same way that he'd been disappointed when Moira had died. Ted wasn't looking to kill a vamp, he wanted to kidnap one. For what purpose, I had no idea.

'What now?' Webb asked. 'I can take you wherever you wish to go, or you can head to Soho once those other vamps arrive for Lord Horvath. They should be here soon.'

I scratched my head. I didn't think Lukas was in mortal danger but I wanted to be sure. I'd go back with him and wait until he regained consciousness. Then I'd make my next move.

'I'll go with the vamps,' I said. 'They're heading that way anyway. I'll come back and pick up Tallulah in the morning.' I was desperate to continue the investigation and go after Ted while the trail was still hot but I knew I was tired, and therefore prone to making mistakes. Such as not pausing to think why there'd been such an obviously muddy handprint on the fence or considering why Ted had run towards a dead end where he would be trapped.

Ted had outwitted me, plain and simple. I'd take my licks – I couldn't do otherwise – but I wouldn't let it happen again. That meant I needed to get some sleep before I did anything else. I might be immortal but I certainly wasn't invincible.

'I can leave a few of my guys to keep an eye on the house and the garage,' Webb said.

I shook my head. 'A few of the local police are already on it.' It didn't matter; I doubted Ted would return to his house. Not now. 'Thank you, though.'

Webb inclined his head.

'Who is it?' I asked suddenly. 'Who is it that you want to be turned in a wolf?'

'I like you, DC Bellamy,' he told me. 'But I can't answer that question.'

I persisted. 'Why not?'

There was a knock on the door. 'Vamps are here,' someone called.

Webb displayed his teeth in a grin. 'Saved by the bell,' he murmured. He looked down at Lukas. 'Time to get this sleeping prince to his bed.'

***

I had been expecting two, maybe three, vampires to show up; I hadn't expected dozens of them. I stared at the assembled cars at the foot of Webb's tower block and swallowed. Half the vamps in London must have shown up.

A female vampire, with scarlet-red lips, patent-leather stilettos and a wasp waist that wouldn't have looked out of place on Jessica Rabbit, marched up. She ignored me and focused on Lukas, who was lying prone on a makeshift stretcher. Her taloned fingernails gently stroked his cheek.

I felt a shiver of anger. What was she doing? What if she scratched him?

'Lord Horvath,' she said huskily.

My irritation grew. Didn't she know he couldn't hear her? Then I took a step back. Whoa. What was wrong with me?

The vamp smiled at him. 'You are safe now.' She

straightened up. 'This is most concerning.'

It took me a moment to realise she was addressing me. I shook off my irrational jealousy, aware that it was an emotion I had no right to. 'Very. He was ahead of me and took the main force of the stun grenade.'

She examined me coolly. I couldn't help wondering if she was blaming me for what had happened. And I also wondered if she was right. 'The man who did this managed to escape?'

I nodded.

She raised her head and looked at the crowd of vampires. 'We will find the fucker who hurt our Lord. And when we do, we will—'

I cleared my throat loudly, interrupting her in mid-flow. A trace of impatience crossed her face. 'What is it?'

'Your vampires need to stand down.'

'What?' she asked incredulously.

I straightened my shoulders. When all was said and done I was still Detective Constable Emma Bellamy, and I'd faced down worse things than this vampire. Much worse. 'First of all,' I said, 'the man who did this is human. That means he falls under human law, much as you might prefer it to be otherwise. If anything … untoward were to happen to him, regardless of his crimes, the fallout could have grave consequences.'

The vamp gave an imperious sniff. 'Are you suggesting that we are unable to control ourselves because we are vampires?'

I didn't flinch. 'I've been in a similar situation to the one you're in now, and I know how hard it was for me. That's all. In the heat of the moment, terrible things can happen.' I paused. 'There's also another reason to stay back. This man – the one who attacked Lord Horvath and who is responsible for the death of your friend, Moira – is deliberately targeting vampires. He *wants* you to go after him. He's smart, in possession of worryingly effective weaponry, and he's on some kind of mission. The best thing for you all is to stay put in Soho for the time being. I will track him down.' My voice hardened. 'And I will deal with him. This isn't something that's up for negotiation.'

She watched me. I had no idea what was going through her head. 'He speaks very highly of you, you know,' she said eventually.

I didn't need to ask who she was referring to. I met her eyes. 'I won't let his attacker get away with what he's done.'

'I believe you.' She held out her hand. 'You can call me Scarlett.' That figured. Her mouth twitched. 'It's not my real name. Your reputation precedes you, DC Bellamy.'

I decided to take that as a compliment. I reached out and shook her hand. She wasn't so bad.

Scarlett raised her voice again and addressed the other vampires. 'Change of plan. The police will take matters from here.' There was a rumbling of discontent and more than one dark glower sent in my direction.

'Thank you,' I murmured. Scarlett inclined her head. 'Could I get a lift from you?' I asked. 'I'd like to wait and see how Luk – how Lord Horvath is before I leave.'

There was a faint groan and I whirled round. Scarlett also focused her attention on Lukas. 'I'm fine,' he muttered, raising his head and struggling up to a sitting position. His black eyes darted round. 'Where the fuck is—' His gaze fell on me and his shoulders dropped. 'There you are.'

'Here I am.' I smiled. He was alright. I'd thought he would be, but it was a relief to have it confirmed.

Lukas exhaled a rush of air. 'Good.' He nodded to himself. 'Good.'

'Are you okay?' I asked. 'How do you feel?'

'Tired,' he grunted. 'Groggy. Sore. I'm fine, though.'

The rest of the watching vampires pressed forward, anxious to reassure themselves that he was conscious and alert. Lukas rubbed his head and lifted his hand to wave to them.

'You need to rest,' Scarlett chided. 'Enough talk for now.' She glanced at me, more relaxed now that Lukas's wellbeing was assured. 'We'll drop you at your door, DC Bellamy. Lord Horvath would not be pleased if it were otherwise.'

Hearing her words, Lukas muttered something. I couldn't make it out what it was, but Scarlett smiled at him.

I swallowed. She was right. Lukas needed peace and quiet and his own kind around him. He didn't need me. 'Okay.' I gazed at him. He stared back at me but his pupils were still unfocused. Conscious or not, whatever drug he'd been injected with was still in his system. 'Could someone call me if his condition changes?'

'I will make sure of it.'

I breathed out and relaxed slightly. My eyes dropped, and I noted the pretty chain round Scarlett's neck. Then I froze.

'What is it?' she enquired.

A chill ran down me. 'Nothing,' I said. 'That's a pretty necklace you're wearing.'

Scarlett's head dipped. 'Three quid from a charity shop near Covent Garden,' she confided.

I managed a laugh. Just.

Chapter Sixteen

Galling as it had been to have to give in to my physical limitations and sleep, I felt so refreshed the next morning that I knew the rest had been worth it. It helped that there was a voice mail message from Scarlett, stating that Lukas appeared to be fine and was back to his normal self. I hadn't expected otherwise, but I still felt remarkably relieved.

Freed from both fatigue and worry, my mind was clear – and grim resolution seeped from my every pore. When I stalked into the Supe Squad office, even Liza seemed taken aback.

'I wasn't expecting you this early.'

'There are important matters to take care of,' I told her. *Very* important.

'Are you … are you alright?'

'I'm fine. I still have some ringing in my ears but it's a lot better than it was. I expect it'll go completely by this afternoon.'

She blinked. 'Is that what happens when you die?' She leaned in, fascination getting the better of her. 'Does anything else happen?'

'What?' I stared at her. Then I remembered that she'd taken yesterday off and she had no idea what had happened during the last twenty-four hours. I'd almost forgotten about my third resurrection but, as far as Liza was concerned, it was still hot news.

'Oh. No, I wasn't talking about that.' I outlined what had happened the previous day. Fred joined us, his expression growing serious as I described the stun grenade and Ted's getaway.

'Fred and I need to get back to his house as soon as possible,' I said. 'Tallulah is still there, so you'll need to drive, Fred.'

He nodded. 'I can do that.'

'I've been in touch with the uniforms who are watching his street. There's been no sign of him, so it looks like he's gone to ground. He knows we're after him so he'll either try to disappear or he'll ramp up operations. Whichever route he chooses, we need to track him down and stop him. This man is dangerous.'

Liza looked disturbed. 'What shall I do?'

'Find out as much about him as you can. Every misdemeanour, every parking ticket, every scrap of available information needs to be sought out and collated.'

'Done.' She hesitated. 'There's something else, isn't there?'

Yeah. There was. I licked my lips. 'Julian Clarke,' I said.

Fred's face scrunched up. 'His investigation will need to go on the back burner. The other exhumations aren't scheduled until next week and nobody except the Clarkes thinks he's a priority. I know what happened to his grave is unsavoury, but real lives are at risk with this other wanker.'

'That's not what I meant.' They both gazed at me. 'Ted was wearing a necklace,' I said.

Liza was confused. 'So?'

'It was a shark's tooth pendant. I can't be a hundred percent certain but I think it's the same as the one I saw Julian Clarke wearing in an old photograph.' I hadn't even registered it until I'd seen the necklace hanging from Scarlett's neck. Now it was all I could think about.

'That has to be a coincidence,' Fred said slowly. 'Right?'

'I don't know.' I raised my eyebrows at Liza. 'Get on to Mrs Clarke. See if you can get a copy of the photo she showed me, and find out whether Julian was buried with the necklace or not. Ask her where he got it from.'

'On it.'

'And pull all the files we've got on Julian's death. I need to see everything.'

'Don't you think you're jumping to conclusions?' Fred asked.

'I hope so,' I said grimly. 'I really do.'

***

My phone rang as we were pulling into Ted's street. I glanced down at the caller ID then answered it immediately. 'Lukas,' I said. 'You're alright?'

Fred glanced towards me but didn't say anything.

'I'm fine,' Lukas growled. 'But what about you? You were there as well. You were hit too.'

'I was further from the grenade than you. You took the worst of it. I have some mild tinnitus but I'm good.' More than good – especially now. I stared at Ted's house, which looked innocuous in the morning sunlight. 'Do you know what he injected you with?'

'My blood has been tested,' he said. I wondered if Scarlett had tasted it herself to check. 'He used a sedative. Nothing more.' His voice grew rougher. 'Where are you?'

'Back at his house.'

'Any sign of him?'

'No.'

He drew in a breath. 'Stay there. I'll come and join you.'

'No. You need to keep away from this. It's a vampire he wants, not a human.'

'You're not human.'

'He doesn't know that,' I replied. 'And, frankly, neither do we.'

'Yes, we do.'

I didn't respond to that. 'He's not here and he's not going to return. Stay where you are and rest up. If I find anything, I'll let you know.'

'I won't let you put yourself in danger while I sit back!' Lukas snapped.

'I'm not in danger.' I stayed calm. 'This is my investigation, and I promise that I will find him.' I paused. 'Trust me.'

'This has got nothing to do with trust.'

'Don't leave Soho, Lukas.'

'Emma...'

'I prefer it when you call me D'Artagnan,' I said lightly. 'Stay at home. I'll call you in a few hours.'

'Wait.'

I ignored his clipped command and hung up.

Fred's expression was a comical mixture of horror and mirth. 'Did you just tell the Lord of all vampires what to do?'

'I did,' I said serenely. 'It's for his own good.'

My phone rang again. I glanced at Lukas's name on the screen and shut off the phone. 'Come on, PC Hackert,' I said. 'Let's catch ourselves a killer.' I got out of the car and started marching to the front door. A moment later, Fred followed.

At the doorstep, I pulled on a pair of gloves. One of the uniformed officers walked up and gave me a respectful nod. To my eyes, he looked terribly young with his short brown hair, dark, unblemished complexion and earnest expression. 'Ma'am,' he said, 'a forensics team will be here shortly.'

'Good to know,' I said. 'Have you spoken to the neighbours?'

'We've canvassed this street and the one behind it where the garage is. He's been described as a polite man who keeps himself to himself.'

I was unsurprised. I didn't know much about Ted, but everything indicated that he was a loner who was intelligent enough to keep up appearances and not draw any undue suspicion. 'Do we have a full name yet?'

'Edward Nappey. Next door reckons he's been at this address for almost ten years.' He consulted his notes. 'He purchased a leasehold on the garage two years ago. The seller is living in Thailand, but we've contacted him in case anything turns up.'

'Good work.' I smiled. 'I appreciate all your efforts. Supe Squad will take things from here. I'll speak to your superior about making sure there are eyes on both properties for the next few days in case Nappey comes back. For now, you can stand down.'

'Thank you, ma'am.' He didn't move.

'Was there something else?' I asked.

He shuffled his feet. 'I thought I'd take this opportunity to ask if there are any openings at Supe Squad.' He shot Fred a guilty look. 'If there are, I'd be interested in transferring.'

I blinked; I certainly hadn't expected that. 'I don't believe there are any vacancies at the moment. We're a small team.' Tiny, in fact. 'But email your details and I'll bear you in mind if anything turns up.'

The officer grinned, then he turned on his heel and returned to the waiting police car.

Fred nudged me. 'He ma'amed you.'

I grunted. 'I know.'

'And he wants to come and work for you.'

'He wants to work with *us*,' I corrected.

'Nobody's ever wanted to do that before,' Fred said. 'We're the pariahs of the Metropolitan Police Force.'

'We used to be.' I glanced again at Ted's house. 'Now I think we're the place where all the interesting stuff happens.'

Fred's smile dropped. 'Maybe that's not a good thing.'

'No,' I agreed. 'Maybe not.' I tossed him a pair of gloves. 'Come on. Let's see what we can find out about Ted Nappey. You take upstairs, I'll take downstairs.'

I pushed open the door and stepped inside. Untouched since last night, Ted's television was still on, tuned into BBC One. It was an ancient model, boxy and large, shoved into the corner of the living room. There was no sign of a satellite dish outside the house, and I suspected that Ted wasn't someone who was interested in streaming services. I'd lay money on him watching the news for mention of his own crimes and then abandoning the television entirely in favour of other pursuits.

The complex, half-finished jigsaw on the coffee table added weight to that theory. I squinted at it; it was an image of the elaborate wooden archway leading into Lisson Grove, where all the werewolves resided. Perhaps Ted was obsessed with all things supernatural.

I opened a small cupboard and gave the stack of books inside a cursory glance. They were all non-fiction and related to supe matters, although a layer of dust suggested that Ted hadn't looked at them any time recently. I snapped a quick photo anyway so I could send it to Liza; she could research the books' contents when she had time.

I went into the kitchen. Ted was a frugal sort of guy. All I could find in the cupboards were tins of spaghetti. There was one large dinner plate and one smaller side plate; in the cutlery drawer there was a single sharp kitchen knife, and a lonely fork, knife and spoon. I had a sudden image of the man sitting in front of his jigsaw eating cold spaghetti out of a tin. His was definitely not a party lifestyle.

The fridge was as bare as the cupboards. There was a pint of milk and a forlorn-looking pot of yoghurt. The fridge was clean, I'd give him that. I wandered around a little longer. Eventually, coming to the conclusion that there was nothing else to find, I headed upstairs to see what Fred had discovered.

I found him in the bathroom, frowning at the contents of the cabinet above the sink. 'What have you got?'

'Medication,' he said. 'Lots of it.' He pointed to a stack of similar-looking boxes. 'Nothing on prescription, but lots of herbal remedies and over-the-counter pills.' Fred gave me a meaningful look. 'By the looks of the pharmacy he's got here, Edward Nappey has long-term health issues.'

'Except he's clearly not been taking any of the remedies,' I mused. 'Maybe health problems are what he wants people to think he has.'

'Do you think he has that much control over himself?'

I thought about everything I'd learned of him so far. 'Yeah,' I said, 'I do.' I gazed again at the cabinet. The whole house, medicine cabinet included, felt staged though to what end I didn't yet know.

'Have you found anything else?'

Fred shook his head, his frustration apparent. 'Not a damned thing. His wardrobe consists of three identical hooded tracksuits. His bed is made with hospital corners and every single wall is whitewashed and bare.'

'Any religious paraphernalia?'

'Not a jot. No condoms or sex toys or magazines. No

colour.' Fred frowned, as if personally affronted by Ted Nappey's lifestyle. 'No joy.'

Hmm. I chewed on my bottom lip. 'Is there an attic space?' I asked. I was clutching at straws but I had to try something.

Fred opened his mouth to answer me, just as a nervous voice called up from downstairs. 'Hello? Ted? Are you there?'

I gestured frantically to Fred, indicating that he should follow my lead. He nodded, his expression wary. I walked out of the bathroom and looked down the stairs. 'Good morning! Please don't be alarmed. I'm Detective Constable Bellamy and this is my colleague, Police Constable Hackert.'

The lined face of a woman in her seventies peered up at me. 'What's wrong? Has something happened to Ted?'

'That's what we're trying to find out.' I offered her a reassuring smile and clumped down the stairs. Her eyes drifted to my gloved hands and she swallowed. 'We received a phone call from one of the neighbours who was concerned. When we arrived, we found his door open and no sign of him inside. In fact, there's very little in the house. We think he might have been burgled.'

Her hand went to her mouth. 'Oh my goodness.'

'How do you know Ted?' I asked, wanting to get my questions in while she was still off balance.

'He's my son.' She looked at me with wide, horrified eyes. 'Do you think something bad has happened to him?'

'We're looking into it,' I said non-committally. 'What's your name?'

'Agnes,' she said. 'Agnes Nappey.'

'Are you married?'

She shook her head. 'Divorced. A long time ago now. I still use my married name though, and I still use Mrs instead of Ms. Ted prefers it that way.'

He was controlling, then. And he was trying to keep his poor old mum from meeting anyone else romantically. He wanted her all to himself.

'Do you visit him here often?' I asked.

'Every week. Ted is vulnerable. He needs my help.'

Hmm. 'What help exactly do you provide?'

'I pick up his medicine for him. He depends on it, you see. I make sure he's looking after himself.' She wrung her hands. 'He struggles a lot.'

'Does he work?'

'No – but he wants to. He used to be in construction, and he was excellent at his job. Everybody loved him.' She spoke with the sort of conviction only a mother could have. 'But he had to give that up when he got ill. He started getting headaches, not sleeping at night, shooting pains in his legs, that sort of thing. Some days he can barely get out of bed. The doctors don't do anything. He's been to see them lots of times but they're useless.'

Or they realised he was faking his symptoms. Not that I would suggest that to Mrs Nappey. 'When did he first get ill?' I asked.

'About four years ago.'

That was round about the time bodies started disappearing from the graveyard at St Erbin's Church. It wasn't evidence of anything – not yet – but it was worth noting. Long term unemployment would provide Ted Nappey with a lot of time to spare, time to plan attacks against vampires amongst other things. Maybe I'd been wrong about the stacked medicine cabinet upstairs; maybe it was simply a way to keep his mother off his back and give him space to focus on other things.

'I don't mean to be intrusive, Mrs Nappey, but if your son is unemployed how can he afford to keep this house on?'

'His grandfather passed away. He left everything to Ted.' She sighed. 'That was right before Ted got sick. I often think that his grandfather's passing had a lot to do with his illnesses. They were very close, you see.'

I nodded. 'And the garage? Why did Ted acquire that?'

She stared at me. 'What garage? Ted doesn't have a car.' She certainly didn't know as much about her son as she thought she did.

'My mistake,' I said breezily. 'Ted doesn't own any other properties, does he?'

'No.' Mrs Nappey looked baffled. 'Why are you asking me all these questions? Why aren't you out there looking for my Ted?'

'We need to build up a picture of him. It will help us to locate him.' I paused. I wanted to catch her off guard with my next question so that I could gauge her reaction. 'Mrs Nappey, has Ted ever been violent towards you?'

She recoiled in horror. 'What? No! Ted would never...' She gazed at me aghast. 'Why would you even ask that? Has that Maggie woman suggested it?'

'Who is Maggie?'

Her lip curled in disgust. 'His ex-girlfriend. He was always too good for her.'

Ted had had a girlfriend? That didn't fit the profile I'd been building of him.

'Do you know her last name?' Fred asked.

'Tomkinson. Maggie Tomkinson. She's a nurse at Fitzwilliam Manor Hospital.' Mrs Nappey gave him a pointed look. 'She's not a very good one.'

Uh-huh. 'We'll speak to her,' I promised. 'Before we go, it would be helpful to have a description of Ted, particularly any identifying features and the clothes he might be wearing. It might make it easier for us to find him.'

'He enjoys sports when he's not ill. He always wears a dark tracksuit. It makes him feel comfortable.' She hesitated. 'And he has a necklace. He says it brings him luck. I don't like it myself, but he wears it all the time.'

'What sort of necklace?' I asked casually.

'A tooth on a silver chain. The tooth isn't real. My Ted says it's plastic. An old friend gave it to him. He's been wearing it for months.'

'Okay.' I smiled at her. 'I can assure you we're doing everything we can to find your son. We're very concerned about him. If he gets in touch, can you please let us know immediately?'

'Of course.'

Fred handed her a card. 'Here's our number.'

She took it from him. 'What – what should I do now?'

'Go home,' he said kindly. 'Let us do our job. When we find him, you'll be the first to know.'

She sank into herself, reminding me for one stark moment of Vivienne Clarke. Two mothers with very different reasons for missing their sons.

'Take care, Mrs Nappey,' I said softly.

She nodded to herself. 'Oh, Ted,' she sighed. 'My poor boy.'

Chapter Seventeen

'Do you feel guilty?' Fred asked, while we rummaged through Ted Nappey's garage. 'For not making it clear to Mrs Nappey that her son is a dangerous criminal?'

'No.' I frowned at the neat row of grenades laid out on the workbench. Ted had been preparing for some sort of showdown for a long time. At least bomb disposal were on their way to sort everything out safely. Grenades were far beyond my remit.

'Our priority is finding him as quickly as possible,' I said. 'She's the sort of person who'd warn him off if she knew what we did. It would be different if she were in any sort of danger from him, but it was obvious from her reaction that he's never harmed her physically. All the same, we should keep an eye and check in with her regularly. I don't think Ted will contact her, but you never know.'

Fred nodded. 'I'll check out Grandpa. There's always the chance that he offed him so he could get his grubby mitts on his inheritance.'

'Good idea. I'm going to jump into Tallulah and head to the hospital. I imagine Maggie Tomkinson has plenty she can tell us.'

A car appeared from the far end of the street, its engine roaring. It sped towards us, stopping scant metres away. I noted its sleek black exterior and the expensive make; no prizes for guessing who this belonged to. I muttered a curse under my breath as the driver's door opened and Lukas jumped out.

He strode up, his arms swinging.

'I thought I told you to stay in Soho,' I said mildly.

He glowered, his jet-black eyes searing into me. 'I don't do well with orders.'

'You might be a vampire Lord,' I started, 'but—'

Lukas held out his phone. 'Take it.'

'What?'

A tinny voice echoed from the speaker. 'DC Bellamy? Are you there?'

I gritted my teeth. It was unmistakably Detective Superintendent Lucinda Barnes. Lukas had gone behind my back and brought out the big guns. I glared at him and took the phone. 'This is DC Bellamy.'

'Ah, Emma,' DSI Barnes said. 'Good to speak to you. I trust you're not feeling any the worse for wear after your encounter yesterday with a stun grenade.'

'I'm fine,' I bit out.

'Excellent. How is the investigation coming along?'

'We have several leads to follow.'

'Even better. I've been speaking to Lord Horvath and I think it's best if he joins you for now. Given that the vampires are involved, it would be wise to keep him in the loop.'

I inhaled deeply. 'With all due respect, DSI Barnes, with the vampires involved as they are, it would make more sense for Lord Horvath to stay well away.'

'He's a powerful vampire. He's perfectly capable of looking after himself.'

'If he were perfectly capable of looking after himself, he wouldn't have been incapacitated last night.'

'And,' Barnes said, 'if you were perfectly capable of looking after *your*self, you wouldn't have been attacked by Clan Sullivan.'

I hissed through my teeth, my eyes flashing at Lukas. He folded his arms and watched me, his expression bland. 'I dealt with that,' I said into the phone.

'Regardless of which department you work for, you are still a Metropolitan Police detective. I will not permit that sort of ridiculous attack to occur. The very idea is reprehensible!'

I tried to remain calm. 'Dragging Lord Horvath into the mix won't help matters with the clans.'

'On the contrary,' she said, 'it will show the wolves that they'll be left out in the cold if they continue with this sort of behaviour. The last thing they want is for the vampires and the police to have a strong relationship that excludes them.'

I tugged at my hair in exasperation. For DSI Barnes, everything had to be about politics.

'This isn't up for negotiation, Emma,' she continued. 'Supe Squad is small, and I'm not yet in a position to argue for more detectives to be assigned to it. However, this might provide the necessary nudge to the powers-that-be.'

Yeah, yeah. I looked at Lukas. It wouldn't surprise me if he'd offered more to DSI Barnes that I didn't know about, but arguing further was pointless. I didn't like it – but I'd have to lump it.

I hung up and passed the phone back to him. 'You heard what happened with Clan Sullivan, then.'

He regarded me implacably. 'You're not the only one who's been developing sources and informers. I've been at this gig for a long time, D'Artagnan.'

'You hate the thought of Supe Squad growing and getting more powerful. This is playing right into DSI Barnes' hands.'

He shrugged. 'That's what she thinks. What I'm doing is proving that Supe Squad doesn't need more officers or detectives – not when the supe population is so helpful to your kind selves.' He nodded at Fred and me.

Then he pointed towards the car and Scarlett stepped out. 'She will help PC Hackert. I will help you. Dividing our resources like this makes sense.'

Maybe it did, but not if it meant they ended up in harm's way. 'You're both targets. This isn't a good idea.'

Lukas moved closer and dipped his head. His tongue darted out and he licked his lips. I wanted to step away but somehow I couldn't. 'If I didn't know better,' he said softly, 'I'd say you don't want to spend time alone with me.' His black eyes glittered. 'But I know that's not true, D'Artagnan. It's nice of you to be concerned for my safety but I'm perfectly well. And,' his voice hardened, 'I will not be caught out like I was last night. I guarantee it.'

I glanced at Fred. From his flushed cheeks, I got the impression he was very keen to spend the next few hours in Scarlett's company. I sighed. 'It's not like we have any choice.'

Lukas grinned suddenly. 'Indeed.' He tilted his head. 'You should have told me about Lady Sullivan.'

I sighed irritably. 'I can look after myself. You can look after yourself. We're all good at looking after ourselves.' It sounded like I was conjugating Latin verbs. 'Come on, then.' I jabbed a finger at his expensive car. 'That will have to stay here. We're taking Tallulah. She's been out here all night on her own.'

The corners of Lukas's mouth turned up. 'You genuinely care for that car, D'Artagnan.' He paused. 'And now I know you genuinely care for me too.' His lips brushed against my cheek unexpectedly, then he turned and walked to Tallulah.

For a good few seconds, all I did was stare after him.

***

I owed Dr Laura Hawes a great deal. Not only was she on

hand every time I woke from the dead, but she'd also managed to get hold of Maggie Tomkinson for me.

When Lukas and I reached the hospital, the nurse was already waiting in the lobby. She glanced at the vampire Lord, her eyes flickering as she registered what he was even if she didn't know who, but she didn't pass comment. Maggie had a no-nonsense approach to life; how she'd ended up with a boyfriend like Ted Nappey was bizarre.

'I can't say I'm surprised that the police are knocking on my door to ask about Ted,' she said. 'I always thought it would come to this.' She led us towards a small room. 'Come on. We can talk in here.'

Lukas and I exchanged glances then followed her. The room was set up with a table and chairs. We sat down and started.

'You dated Ted?' I questioned.

Maggie nodded. 'For my sins, yes. We were together for a couple of years. Before he started to turn weird.'

'How did you meet?' Lukas probed.

'Here. Ted had an accident at work. He fell off some scaffolding and broke his wrist. It wasn't serious, but it took a long time to heal. He was in and out as a patient a few times. Once he was fully discharged, he got in touch and—' Her mouth flattened with the sort of distaste only hindsight can bring. 'We went out.'

'You say he turned weird,' I said. 'What do you mean exactly?'

Maggie sighed. 'It was small things at first. He became obsessed with my work – he was convinced that I was constantly picking up all sorts of germs.' She nodded at Lukas. 'And he developed a strong hatred for supes. He was sure that you're keeping the secrets of your health and strength to yourselves, but if you'd let us test you and take samples from you for laboratories all over the world, it would be better for the human population at large. He wrote to his MP about it. Many times.' She smiled faintly. 'He never got a reply.'

Lukas crossed his legs. 'We have been tested. In fact, we often submit ourselves to all sorts of tests and studies. It's the easiest way to keep the government off our backs.'

'I told him that but he didn't want to know the truth. He'd already got his own version that he believed. Nothing could persuade him otherwise, no matter what facts I presented. He spent hours on the internet poring over conspiracy theory forums. He'd never write anything himself because he didn't trust the internet any more than he trusted anything else, but he read what others believed. And then he found the book.'

'The book?'

'Some ancient heavy piece of crap called *Infernal Enchantments*. He carried it everywhere with him. He must have read the damn thing from cover to cover a dozen times. It was his prized possession and no-one else could touch it – if I went near it, he'd yell at me.'

I sneaked a look at Lukas's face. If he'd heard of this book, his expression wasn't giving it away.

'We visited his house,' I told her. 'It was quite … sparse.'

Maggie looked unsurprised. 'Yeah. He started to get rid of all his stuff. He reckoned his possessions were controlling his life and that he'd have a clearer mind if he had a clearer home. He tried to make me do the same.' She wrinkled her nose. 'He could be quite manipulative. He wanted me to think the same way that he did, and when I didn't agree with him he'd argue. It's hard when you're involved with someone who becomes consumed by darkness.'

My body stiffened. Yeah. But at least Maggie had

been aware of her boyfriend's taste for darkness; with me and my boyfriend Jeremy, I'd been completely ignorant about his real character. It had cost me my life. Twice.

Lukas's foot nudged mine underneath the table. It was a small movement of reassurance but it was surprising how much it helped. 'Was he violent towards you?' he asked Maggie.

'No, quite the opposite. Violence frightened him. The whole world frightened him. He was strange and argumentative, but he wouldn't have hurt anyone.'

I thought about the array of weaponry in Nappey's garage, and his attacks on Moira and then on us. He might not have been violent once, but he certainly was now.

'And yet,' I said, keeping my expression bland, 'you're not surprised that we're here asking about him.'

Maggie took her time before answering. 'The longer I was with him, the worse he became. He would get really ... obsessive. Part of me thought he'd end up running away to join a cult – or that he'd start one himself. It didn't help that he took our break-up hard. It was a long time before he stopped contacting me out of the blue, although it's more than a year now since I last heard from him.'

She drew in a breath. 'Truthfully, I was expecting to hear that he'd got himself killed by approaching the wrong person and spouting off his usual nonsense. It was only a matter of time before he made a move towards the supernaturals,' she said quietly. 'Getting in a vamp's face and blasting off your conspiracy theories is asking for trouble.'

'We're not all bad,' Lukas said with a slight grin.

Maggie smiled wanly. 'Try telling that to Ted.'

Chapter Eighteen

'So he's not typically violent but he dislikes supes immensely,' I said.

Lukas put his hands in his pockets. 'It sounds less like dislike and more like jealousy. He doesn't have the power or the health or the prowess of a supe. He wants what we have.' He tapped his mouth. 'I'll get someone to look through our petition records. If he's ever made an application to be turned into a vampire, we'll have his details.'

'It's worth checking,' I agreed, 'but it doesn't sound like his style. He wants the skills of a supe, but I don't think he wants to *be* a supe. Not from what I'm hearing.' I chewed the inside of my cheek. 'There's something else I should tell you. There's a slim chance that Ted is the one who's been stealing werewolves' bodies from their graves.'

Lukas started. 'What?'

I told him about the shark's tooth.

'There's more than one shark's tooth necklace in the world.'

'I know. I don't like the coincidence, that's all.'

Lukas scratched his chin, musing. 'St Erbin's is in the middle of Soho. How on earth could anyone dig down to a grave without someone noticing? The place is teeming with humans and vampires at all hours of the night and day.'

'Bad weather,' I said. 'Every time there was a grave disturbance recorded at St Erbin's, there was bad weather.'

'Even in the worst weather it would still be risky.' He

grimaced. 'But then we already know Ted Nappey likes taking risks. We both have the bruises to show for it.'

I made a face. 'Yeah.' I paused. 'I have a confession to make.'

Interest flashed on Lukas's face. 'Oh yes?' he enquired silkily. 'What might that be?'

'I might have suggested to Reverend Knight that I'd encourage you to visit him. He's finding things ... hard. I thought you and he might have a chat.'

'Me? Have a chat with a vicar?' He shook his head. 'That's not what I was hoping your confession would be, D'Artagnan.'

I wondered what he'd been hoping for. I slid my gaze away. 'It might be worth paying the church another visit. When we do, if you could talk to Knight I'd appreciate the gesture.'

'How much?'

I blinked at him.

'How much will you appreciate it?' There was an edge of teasing to his tone. And perhaps something else too.

I swallowed. 'A lot.'

I felt Lukas watching me. 'Very well,' he said finally. 'It won't hurt. First, however, we should track down this book that Nappey was so enamoured of.' His mouth curved into a predatory smile, his fangs suddenly visible. 'And I know exactly where we can find a copy.'

I looked up. 'The Carlyle Library?'

Lukas's smile stretched. 'None other.'

***

Located close to King's Cross Station, the Carlyle Library is a mammoth building. It was created by an old philanthropist back in the eighteenth century. His idea had been to open an institution that would give the general public greater access to rare books and guarded knowledge. Sort of an old-fashioned version of the darker corners of the internet. Unlike its more modern counterpart, the British Library, the design and arrangements of the Carlyle Library are hopelessly disorganised. Unless you know what you are looking for, finding a title can be a gargantuan task. But when the book happens to be related to the supernatural, it is slightly easier. Far down in the bowels of the main building, there is an entire section dedicated wholly to supes. Contrary to Malcolm Carlyle's wishes, access to the Arcane Works room is restricted, even to most Carlyle Library staff; there is all manner of dangerous books in there, the contents of which have to be protected. When you were Lord of all vampires and the detective in charge at Supe Squad, however, gaining entrance was a piece of cake.

'You can't take any of the books out,' our grey-suited guide told us, as we followed him down to the room. 'But you're at liberty to peruse any of the books for as long as you like.'

'It's one book that we're interested in,' I said. 'It's called *Infernal Enchantments*. If you have records of anyone who's requested a copy, it would be most appreciated.' It wouldn't help us track Ted Nappey down, even if he'd come here, but it would help to confirm what Maggie Tomkinson had told us. We might not be any closer to finding Ted, but we were certainly building a strong picture of him.

'I'll look into it,' the librarian promised. 'It shouldn't take long.'

Good. 'How many people request access to the Arcane Works room?'

He frowned. 'Not many. Would you like a list of them? I'm sure I can print one out.'

'That would be great. Thank you,' I said.

He certainly was very eager to be help, though I wasn't convinced how much use such a list would be. Devereau Webb had suggested that he'd conducted his own research here before he'd approached the clans; any number of people could have visited. The information might still be useful, however.

The librarian nodded happily, then led us down a narrow spiral staircase. He pointed at an ornate door, barred by an elaborate iron gate designed with twisting curlicues and fleur-de-lis. He produced a large key from his pocket with a flourish and unlocked the gate. 'Arcane Works is all yours.'

I peered inside. The Arcane Works room was probably what people thought of when they imagined supes. Instead of laptops and Wi-Fi and shabby police headquarters, they had a picture of grand rooms with ancient fireplaces and flickering candles, and shelves upon shelves of old books,. I shivered. It might be reasonably warm and sunny outside but in here it was chilly.

'No electricity?' Lukas questioned.

'We considered it several years ago.' The librarian, who had remained on the threshold and seemed genuinely afraid of stepping into the Arcane Works room, chuckled slightly. 'But this collection is rarely visited. Besides, to bring it up to date would mean disturbing the old texts.' He gave us a meaningful look. 'Words have power. Books even more so.' He said the words with such a flourish that I almost expected a drum roll to follow.

When neither Lukas nor I commented, he bowed. 'I'll check the request records for the book in question and get back to you.'

'Thank you,' I murmured. I picked up a box of matches and walked from candle to candle, setting each one alight. Rather than exude a comforting glow, the flickering flames gave the room an even more eerie atmosphere.

Lukas opened the old-fashioned cabinet near the door and started to search through the antiquated filing system. I joined him. 'Anything?' I asked.

His brow creased as he pulled out a grubby index card. As he did so, a faint breeze arose seemingly from nowhere. The candle flames wavered and the shadows lengthened. 'Relax, D'Artagnan,' he said softly. 'It's just a draught.'

I swallowed and nodded. Of course it was. 'Is that it?' I asked, gesturing towards the card. 'Is that the book?'

'*Infernal Enchantments*,' he read. '*An Encyclopaedic Compilation of Magicks.*'

'Magic doesn't exist.'

'No,' he agreed. 'But this book does.' He squinted at the shelves. 'I think it should be over there. Come on.'

I tiptoed behind him to the section, not sure why I needed to keep my footfall silent. The surroundings seemed to demand it somehow. Give me a criminal gang over this creepy room any day.

The shelves were stacked high with leather-bound books, some of their spines worn and barely readable. Others looked like they'd never once been cracked open. Lukas looked up. 'I think it's there,' he said. He jumped, his fingertips snagging on one of the heavier books. It slid out easily. He landed silently and held it up so I could see.

I gazed at the faded red cover, its gilt letters still visible. 'That's the one,' I said grimly. I pointed to a desk near the exit. 'There's enough light over there.'

We sat down side by side. I reached for the book at the same time as Lukas and our fingers brushed against each other. I drew back as if stung.

Lukas allowed himself a faint smile. 'Let me.' He blew off a thin layer of dust and opened the book. I half expected fluttering moths to escape, or to hear an ominous crack of thunder, but nothing happened. I was letting my imagination run away with me.

'Breathe,' Lukas told me.

I hadn't realised I'd been holding my breath. I expelled the air in my lungs in a whoosh. It was only a book, I told myself. There was no reason to feel scared.

We leaned over and read the list of contents. The chapter headings weren't particularly helpful: *Distilled Concoctions. Blood Works. Forest Herbs.*

'Try the index at the back,' I suggested. 'Start with *Vampires.*'

Lukas flipped to it. There were dozens of cross-referenced entries for vamps. At this rate, we'd be here for hours. 'We have to narrow it down,' he muttered.

I chewed on the inside of my cheek. '*Corpses,*' I said. 'Try that.'

He glanced at me sideways then flicked the pages again. There were only four referenced notes relating to corpses. My fingers twisted in my lap as Lukas turned to the first entry.

'*A human corpse in the correct stage of decomposition,*' he read aloud, '*can be used for numerous purposes. The fingernails of a female who has been dead for fourteen days contain properties which…*'

I shuddered. 'Not that one.'

He nodded and turned the pages again. '*Ghouls gain nourishment from…*'

'No. Not that one.'

Lukas grunted in agreement and leafed through to the next section. '*The corpse of a werewolf is very useful indeed. The skull can be utilised as a vessel for mixing potions and, should you wish to divine the future, the clipped fur of a transformed wolf can be burnt with a selection of carefully chosen herbs.'* He paused and looked up. 'I'm beginning to think that this book is a pile of horseshit.'

I wasn't going to disagree. 'Keep going anyway.'

'The bones of a young werewolf,' he read, *'can be ground down to brew the Elixir of Fortitude.'*

A chill descended down my spine. 'That one,' I whispered. 'Cross-reference that one.'

Lukas did as I asked and located the right page for the elixir. We stared at what was written there.

'Finely ground bone dust from a werewolf newly dead. A cup of holy water, held in an oak bowl away from sunlight. A pinch of dandelion pollen harvested on Good Friday.' Lukas exhaled sharply. *'This Elixir will strengthen both body and mind, curing physical disease and solidifying psychological spirit. The successful recipient of this Elixir will possess the strength to match any being, living or otherwise.'* He pushed the book away in disgust. 'It's mumbo-jumbo claptrap.'

I leaned over and continued reading. *'If the desired effects are not achieved, the Elixir can be enhanced. Three cups of blood from a still-breathing vampire will—*
'

Lukas sucked in a breath and yanked the book back. He scanned the words. 'Fuckers,' he bit out. 'Surely this isn't what Edward Nappey is trying to do? Brew some crappy potion from an old joke book? He's crazier than I thought. This is a wild goose chase, D'Artagnan.'

'The book doesn't have to be true for Ted Nappey to believe in it,' I said. I rubbed my palms together in a vain bid to generate some heat. Instinct told me that this was what he'd been doing all along: Ted wanted to play witch and mix up a magic potion that would put him on an equal footing with any supe in the country. I was convinced that we'd found his motive. Unfortunately, that didn't help us find Ted.

'Cooeee!'

Lukas and I jumped.

'I've got the information you asked for,' the librarian called out. He waved a wad of paper. 'I printed out the list of everyone who's tried to access this room during the last ten years.'

I blinked. That looked like a lot of names.

Lukas pushed his chair back and got to his feet. I gazed at the open pages of *Infernal Enchantment* for another frozen moment, slid out my phone and snapped a photo. We had what we'd come for. I closed the book. Something occurred to me and I opened it again. There had been four entries for corpses. We'd only checked three of them.

I found the final corpse reference towards the back of the book.

As much as it may be wished otherwise, reanimation of corpses is not possible. Death cannot be cheated and, sooner or later, we all must meet our Maker. The only creature able to evade death temporarily is the elusive phoenix. Although this particular being lives a natural life span, it cannot be killed through unnatural means. Any attempts to destroy it will only result in the phoenix rebirthing in fire. While able to produce progeny, it should be noted that the magicks of a phoenix are unique. There can only ever be one phoenix in existence at any one time.

'Is everything alright?' Lukas enquired from over my shoulder.

I slammed the book shut. 'Yep.' I sprang up to my feet. 'Yep. Everything is fine.'

He shot me a curious look. 'Our librarian friend has dug up three names. In the past forty years, only three people have sought out this book.' His mouth flattened. 'None of them are Ted Nappey. According to the library records, Mr Nappey has never visited.' He paused. 'But there's something else. There used to be two copies of *Infernal Enchantments*. During the last Arcane Works audit a few years ago, it was discovered that one of the copies had gone missing.'

I shook off what I'd read and focused. 'From what Maggie Tomkinson said, Ted had his own copy. He could have picked it up anywhere – a second-hand bookshop or a charity shop. Maybe someone's attic.' I grimaced. 'Or he used false ID to sneak in here and steal the copy that's now missing.'

'It's certainly possible,' Lukas agreed. 'Although we can't prove anything.'

I chewed on my lip. 'I'd be curious to hear why those other three people were interested in it.'

'I've got their details.' Lukas held up a printout. 'At least it might be more useful than this list of wannabe supe scholars.' He waved the thick wad of paper at me. 'Do you still want this? There are a lot of names here.'

I stared at the copy of *Infernal Enchantments*.

'Emma?'

'Mm?' I realised Lukas was frowning at me. 'Oh. Yeah, I'll take the list. It might prove useful later.' I reached for the book, my fingers tingling when I touched its cover. 'I'll put this back on the shelves.'

Lukas watched me. He knew something was up but he didn't know what. 'What aren't you telling me, D'Artagnan?'

I raised my chin and met his intense gaze. 'That I can't wait to get out of here,' I said simply. And then I turned away to avoid looking at him any further.

Chapter Nineteen

A phoenix. Was that what I was?

'Spread your legs a little wider.'

Surely a phoenix was a bird. I didn't have wings. I couldn't fly.

'Focus on your breathing.'

Only one phoenix in existence at any one time? So was I unique? Literally unique?

'Aim.'

How on earth did that happen?

'Fire.'

There was a faint whistle as the silver-tipped bolt flew through the air. I dropped the crossbow, re-loaded it and raised it yet again. Then I glanced at Kennedy. His lips were pursed, though not in an expression of disapproval. Far from it.

'Well done.'

I looked at the stuffed dummy. Huh. I'd shot it right through the head. I squinted, adjusted my aim and released my second bolt. It thudded into the dummy, less than an inch away from the first one.

'I'm not often impressed,' Kennedy declared, 'but I reckon you've nailed this.'

'Shooting at a dummy is a bit different from shooting at a living being.'

'True.'

'It's not exactly a moving target.'

'True.'

'My life isn't currently in danger. Neither is anyone

else's.'

'True.'

'But yeah.' I flashed the satyr a grin. 'It turns out all I needed was some expert tuition to set me on the right track. Thanks, Kennedy.'

'You're welcome.' His long, fur-covered ears quivered. He was a lot more pleased with my progress than he was letting on. He strode over to the far wall. 'Don't ever forget that the crossbow is an extension of yourself. You're not detached from it. As a ranged weapon, it can be easy to shoot it then walk away. And the best motives can still result in the worst murders.'

He lifted one of the hanging daggers and inspected the blade before turning and walking towards me. Then he held the dagger up until its sharp tip was scratching the skin on my cheek. I didn't move.

'When you wield a blade,' Kennedy said softly, 'you have to get up close and personal. It's far harder to hurt someone when you're in their face and when you can feel their breath. A crossbow can be used at a distance – but killing never should be. If you're not prepared to kill someone from here,' he told me, his breath hot on my cheek, 'you're not prepared to kill someone from one hundred metres away.'

The crossbow didn't have that sort of power but I understood what Kennedy was saying. 'I've been on this side before,' I said. 'I've felt a knife sliding into my skin. I know what death feels like and I don't take it lightly.'

'In that case,' Kennedy whispered, 'what they say about you is true.'

'What do they say?'

He smiled enigmatically and didn't answer. He simply replaced the dagger in its spot, picked up his bag and prepared to leave.

After a moment or two, I shrugged. 'Thank you,' I

said again, 'for all your help.' I grabbed a jar of salve that Liza had procured for me and rubbed some into my raw fingertips.

'Take care out there.' Kennedy paused at the door. 'And take care of yourself with Lukas. As vampires go, he's one of the best. But he's also Lord Horvath and he didn't reach that position by being warm and cuddly. He's a dangerous man. You wouldn't be the first to fall for his charms. Know that it doesn't usually end well. His priorities will always be his vampires.'

My head jerked up. 'I've not fallen—' I started.

Kennedy had already gone.

I cursed under my breath. I wouldn't deny that my feelings about Lukas were growing more complex by the day, but I would never put myself in the position where a man – any man – could harm me again. I'd already learnt my lesson. And the last thing I would ever be was a vampire's plaything.

I pulled on my blouse, fastened the buttons and headed down to the main office. The interlude with Kennedy had been useful and diverting but it was time to get back to the real business of the day.

The room was busier than I'd ever seen it. Fred and Scarlett were in one corner, their heads close together. Lukas was standing by the window with three sombre-looking vampires around him. Liza was at her desk, finishing a phone call.

I took a moment to absorb the focused buzz. I enjoyed the freedom that my status as the sole detective at Supe Squad granted me, but there was a lot to be said for this sort of atmosphere. We were all working towards one goal and it felt good to be part of an energetic team.

My eyes drifted to Lukas. A lock of his dark hair had fallen across his forehead and his eyes were sharp with intensity. Kennedy's words echoed back at me.

I swallowed and cleared my throat. 'Team meeting,' I called. 'I need to hear where we're at, and what information we've got.'

The vamps looked to Lukas but he was already moving towards the centre of the room. They followed suit and gathered behind him. Fred perched on the back of his favourite sofa and Liza straightened her posture.

'I'll start,' she said. 'I've been through every database I can find but there's not much out there. In terms of criminal activity, Edward Nappey has either kept his nose clean or is very good at staying under the radar. He drove a car until last year, when it was sent to be scrapped. No outstanding parking tickets or speeding fines. He's never been named as part of any illegal activity. He is thirty-two years old, with one surviving parent. He's been unemployed for the last five years and has made repeated attempts to claim disability benefit. He has considerable savings, however, so each claim has been denied.'

'Those savings will be thanks to his grandfather,' Fred interjected. 'He ran a small chain of hardware shops until the early nineties when he retired. The shops were all closed down and sold off.'

'Did you find out anything about his death?' I asked.

'Heart attack,' Scarlett said. 'We've checked all the records and spoken to the hospital. There was nothing sinister about it.'

I wasn't surprised by that. While there was no doubt that Ted Nappey had benefited enormously from his grandfather's passing, I reckoned that he wouldn't harm a member of his own family. Or his girlfriend. In fact, it was possible that Nappey didn't want to kill anyone in his quest for the daft Elixir of Fortitude. Moira's death had been an accident, and Nappey had tried to capture Lukas rather than murder him.

Then an entirely different thought occurred to me and my blood chilled. 'His car,' I said to Liza, 'what make and model was it?'

She consulted her notes. 'A blue Ford Escort.'

I sucked in a breath. 'Where's the file on Julian Clarke's hit and run?'

'Wait,' Fred said, 'you don't think—?'

Liza waved a manila folder. 'Here it is.' She opened and scanned it. 'The car that hit Julian Clarke was never found. It was identified as a blue Ford. Possibly an Escort, but the eye witnesses couldn't be sure.'

The atmosphere in the room altered significantly. It wasn't proof that Nappey had mowed down Julian Clarke but that's what we were all thinking. According to Maggie, his ex-girlfriend, Ted Nappey had once detested violence in all forms, but we also knew he'd spent a lot of time surrounding himself with death and that he hated supes. And he'd developed his own protective arsenal. If he was obsessed enough with creating the elixir, there was no telling what depths he might have descended to in pursuit of it. People changed all the time.

'Okay.' I nodded. 'Okay.' I glanced at Liza. 'Did you manage to get in touch with Vivienne Clark? Julian's mother?'

'Yes.' Her expression was grim. 'Julian obtained the shark's tooth necklace during a family holiday to Australia when he was seventeen. I have a photo of him wearing it.' She held up the image. I stared at it; the necklace certainly looked similar to the one Ted Nappey had been wearing. 'Mrs Clarke said that he was buried with it.'

'A trophy,' Lukas muttered. His hands bunched into fists. 'He took Moira's jewellery as well. Edward Nappey has persuaded himself that he's on a mission to make that elixir. He's probably convinced himself that he's a force for good. But he's taken a trophy, and that suggests he enjoys what he's doing. He gets a thrill out of killing and he's kept the necklace to remind himself of that.'

I wished I could disagree with him but unfortunately I knew he was right. The only silver lining was that thrill seekers took risks, and risk takers made mistakes.

'What elixir?' Fred asked.

I explained what we'd found at the Carlyle Library. Everyone in the room looked sickened.

'Strengthen body and mind?' Scarlett snorted. 'If he wants to do that, he ought to become a supe.'

I didn't fail to notice the adoring look that Fred sent her.

'That's the problem,' I said. 'He wants the sort of power that supes possess but he despises the supes themselves.'

'Would it even work?' one of the other vamps asked dubiously. 'Could something like this elixir crap really cure disease?'

'It's highly unlikely,' Lukas said.

Liza raised an eyebrow. 'How do you know for sure?'

I answered for him. 'Because Ted Nappey has been trying to create the elixir for the last five years and he's not had any success. If he had, he wouldn't be trying to kidnap a vampire to use their blood to enhance what he already has.' I paused. 'We can assume that he has a makeshift laboratory somewhere. That's probably where he's holed up now. If we can find that laboratory, we can find him.'

'Easier said than done,' Fred grunted. 'The garage was the only other property registered in Nappey's name.'

'And,' Lukas bit out, 'he wanted us to find that.'

I was beginning to think that we were being played

like puppets. Until Ted Nappey chose to stick his head above the parapet again, we were floundering.

'He was in construction,' I said. 'He's been out of work for five years, but he may have worked on a lot of local building sites before that. He probably knows several places where he could hide away without anyone noticing.' I nodded at Fred. 'Speak to his old employers. See if you can get hold of a list of where he worked.'

Scarlett stepped forward. 'I'll help,' she said. 'Freddy and I can visit the sites together.'

Fred's cheeks reddened.

'Liza,' I said, 'see if you can use your computer wizardry to track where Nappey might have gone after he ran from the garage. CCTV. Bus routes. Reports from residents nearby that sound suspicious. Anything that might hint at the direction he went in.'

She bobbed her head. 'Will do.'

Lukas folded his arms. 'My people will look into the book, *Infernal Enchantments*, and track down those three people who requested it.' The stern trio of vampires behind him lifted their chins in unison.

'Take care,' I warned. 'And stick together. Remember that Nappey wants a vampire. He might be human, but he's got the weaponry to bring any number of vampires down.'

Lukas agreed. 'Don't get cocky.' He raised an eyebrow in my direction. 'How about it, D'Artagnan? Shall the two of us pay a visit to the church and have that chat with Reverend Knight?'

I checked my watch. It wouldn't be long before Devereau Webb showed up at Fairfax's club. 'Actually,' I said apologetically, 'can I meet you there later? I have somewhere else I need to be first.'

Lukas's eyes narrowed. 'Somewhere else?'

'It's a wolf thing.'

'I'll come along.'

I straightened my shoulders. 'It doesn't involve you.'

'Last time you had a wolf thing that didn't involve me, they tried to kill you.'

Liza's head jerked towards us, alarmed.

'I told you already,' I said, the very definition of calm placidity, 'I dealt with that. They won't try anything again.'

Lukas opened his mouth to continue arguing but I forestalled him. 'I don't need your protection. You can look after you, and I can look after me. Remember? The last thing we need is heightened tension between the vamps and the wolves. We have enough to deal with as it is.'

His mouth flattened. 'Fine. I'll see you at St Erbin's later?'

I nodded. 'Yep.'

One by one, everyone filed out until only Liza and I remained in the room. 'It sounds like you've a lot going on,' she said. 'And I'm not talking about the Nappey investigation.'

I sighed. 'You don't know the half of it.'

'Has he asked you out for that business dinner yet?'

My eyes slid away and Liza laughed.

'Fred seems rather taken with Scarlett,' I said, keen to shift her attention away from me and onto someone else.

'Smitten,' she agreed. 'I've seen it happen many times before. I'm only surprised that it's taken Fred this long to be roped in.'

At my questioning look, Liza smiled slightly. 'It's what they do,' she said. 'They're vampires – they tease and play and draw you in. Theirs is a dance of seduction, sometimes for sex, sometimes for blood, but always for power. It's very hard to deny a vampire when they're fixated on you.'

'That sounds like the voice of personal experience.'

'I've worked here for a long time,' she told me. 'Sooner or later, the vamps always try it on with Supe Squad. It's the ultimate notch on their bedpost. Or coffin.' She eyed me. 'Or whatever. Lord Horvath has never got involved in any of that but you're not like the detectives we've had here before. There's a first time for everything.'

Cold discomfort prickled through my veins. First Kennedy had warned me off, and now Liza was doing the same. Lukas's flirting had been gentle, but the notion that this was nothing but a game to him caused a heaviness to settle in the centre of my chest.

'I'd better go,' I said, changing the subject. 'I'll take a crossbow with me. If you don't hear from me by four o'clock, get hold of DSI Barnes and tell her I went to Lord Fairfax's place.'

'So the werewolves did try and kill you before?'

'Lady Sullivan did, but I don't think the others were aware of what she was up to.' My mouth turned down. 'Probably because they didn't think of it themselves first.'

'So you think they'll make another attempt, even though you told Horvath otherwise?'

I grimaced. 'Frankly, Liza, the way my week is going, just about anything is possible.'

Chapter Twenty

I knew I was being followed almost as soon as I left the Supe Squad building. The hairs on the back of my neck prickled and there was a frisson of tension running down my spine. Despite my words to Liza, I hadn't seriously expected the werewolves to come after me again but, as the sensation of being watched grew stronger, I wondered if I'd been wrong.

I debated sticking to the main streets and making sure that my tracker had no opportunity to try anything untoward. I wasn't a terrified little mouse, however; I wasn't going to live my life looking over my shoulder because I was worried about who was behind me. When it came to fight or flight, I no longer had an option. Besides, I figured wryly, if I truly were a phoenix, I should have nothing to fear.

I veered off, heading down the same narrow back road that Buffy had led me to the previous day. The crossbow was strapped to my back in a simple harness and I knew I could grab it within seconds if I needed to. For now I left it where it was, but it was comforting to know that it was there – and that I finally had the skill to use it properly. At least some of the time.

Walking casually, I kept moving until I was past the house I'd run into the day before. I strained my ears but, beyond the sounds of passing traffic from the streets further away and the occasional coo from a pigeon, there was nothing to be heard. I swung my arms, scratched absently at the side of my leg, and then whipped round.

Nothing. No-one was there. There wasn't so much as a flicker of a shadow. My eyes narrowed, searching the few obvious hiding places. It was possible I was being paranoid, though I doubted it, but with no-one to confront there was little I could do. At least I wasn't entirely helpless.

I unhooked the crossbow and held it loosely in front of me for a beat or two, then I slipped my foot into the stirrup and loaded it, thumbing off the safety and raising the bow. Sighting an old metal dustbin lid, I aimed and fired. The bolt zipped towards it with unerring speed, clanging loudly when it made contact. A crow nearby was startled into action, cawing and flapping into the air. I smiled, satisfied. As warning shots went, it could have been worse. At least it was loud enough to draw attention.

I didn't bother returning to retrieve the bolt. Assuming it was a werewolf that was following me, they would inspect it and realise it was silver tipped. That should be more than enough to tell them to back off.

I re-loaded the crossbow, just in case, and returned to my path. I stayed alert but it seemed I'd done enough. By the time I swung out onto the busy road at the end of the street, I was humming away quite happily. The grin remained on my face all the way to Lord Fairfax's club.

The same bouncer who'd been stationed outside the previous day was there. He'd been joined by three colleagues, who all glowered at me. None of them looked surprised by my appearance – and none of them looked remotely pleased by it, either. But it wasn't their identical expressions that interested me, it was the tags on their sleeves indicating they were highly placed selsas, all from separate clans. It was very unusual for a high-ranking wolf to do such a menial job – and it was as rare as a blue moon for four wolves from four separate clans to work together.

I tilted my head and gazed at them. 'Fairfax,' I said, pointing at the first wolf. 'Carr, McGuigan and Sullivan. Am I right?'

'You're not welcome here today,' the Fairfax bouncer said.

'And why is that?' I enquired.

'Go back to Supe Squad,' the Carr wolf growled. 'You're not wanted here.'

Interesting. My gaze swung from each one to the next. They might be from separate clans but they possessed the same air of stalwart immobility.

I tapped my mouth. 'There's only one reason why I'd be denied access today when I was so heavily involved yesterday. And that's because your alphas are expecting something illegal to take place.'

I couldn't be the only person who was suspicious about why Devereau Webb wouldn't say who he was nominating for turning. Likeable as he was, Webb was a career criminal. It would hardly be a shock if he wanted to circumvent the legal system by arranging for a criminal colleague to become a wolf and therefore elude justice. Werewolves were, after all, only subject to werewolf law.

'Let me speak to your alphas,' I demanded.

'They're busy,' the McGuigan wolf said.

'All of them?'

The Sullivan wolf folded his arms. 'All of them.'

Huh. They were playing with fire if they thought they could lock me out. 'In that case,' I said, as if it were of no consequence at all, 'please remind your alphas that it's illegal for any human to be turned into a werewolf when they've been charged with a crime or if they are suspected of committing a crime. If that happened, the entire clan would be held responsible.'

'Oooooh,' the Carr guy mocked. 'Now, I'm scared.'

'I can assure you,' I said calmly, 'that however desirable it might be to have exclusive use of the whole of Regent's Park to play in during the full moon, it's not worth the risk of turning someone illegally.'

'I don't know what she's talking about.' The Fairfax bouncer sniffed. 'You guys know?'

'Not a clue, man. Not a frigging clue.'

I was beginning to get irritated. 'Look,' I started.

'Fuck off, love.'

I could have raised my loaded crossbow and threatened them. I could have demanded to be allowed in. Legally, though, I had no standing here. Not only would forcing my way in damage Supe Squad's relations with the whole supernatural community, it would also result in my suspension.

I gritted my teeth. Then I noticed a flicker of movement out of the corner of my eye – and beyond the four wolves' vision.

'Very well.' I stalked past them, pretending not to hear the sniggers behind my back. I wasn't done yet. Not by a long shot.

I kept walking, aware that the bouncers were tracking my movements. When I reached the corner and turned left so I was out of their sight, I stopped dead.

'Oh good,' Buffy said. 'I wasn't sure if you'd noticed me.' She offered me a dazzling smile. 'How's things?'

'What do you want?' I asked flatly, toying with the trigger on the crossbow.

She continued to grin. 'I won't attack, if that's what you're thinking. I'm not your enemy, DC Bellamy.'

'You could have fooled me.'

Buffy flicked her hair. 'I was following orders. Besides, you won. You got away from me.' She shrugged. 'No hard feelings.'

That was easy for her to say. 'Were you following

me on the way here?'

Her smile stretched further. 'I was.'

I sighed and wondered if I was supposed to be grateful that she hadn't bothered to deny it. 'What do you want?'

'I am here on behalf of my alpha.'

Fine. 'What does Lady Sullivan want?'

'To make amends, of course.'

My eyes narrowed. That didn't sound likely. 'Go on.'

'Wait a minute.' She paused and tapped her temple. 'I want to make sure I've got the message right. I don't always have the best memory.' She giggled girlishly.

Buffy's routine wasn't fooling me in the slightest. She was strong enough to deny any compulsion, and she had no qualms about killing a police detective. She was one dangerous wolf. 'Get on with it,' I said.

Her smile vanished. 'If you insist.' She leaned towards me, displaying her sharp, lupine teeth. 'You displayed great nobility yesterday. You kept your end of the bargain and passed over your DNA sample when you had no reason to. We appreciate that. We also appreciate that you've not made a fuss about what occurred.'

I was running out of patience. 'And?'

'And Clan Sullivan would like to make amends.' She ran her tongue over her lips. 'Follow me and all will become clear.'

'If you seriously think I'm going to fall for that again—'

'My real name is Patricia. Patricia Sullivan.'

I blinked. She didn't look like a Patricia.

'Use it against me, if you wish. We both know you're capable of doing that.'

I wasn't so sure about that. 'I'll stick to Buffy.'

There was a flicker of relief in her yellow eyes and I suddenly realised she was more nervous than she was letting on. The revelation relaxed me slightly.

'As you wish, Detective. I promise you're not in any danger. You want to know what's going on with Devereau Webb. At Lady Sullivan's behest, I am in a position to help you.'

I cast a long glance at her then I swung the crossbow round and hooked it onto the straps at my back so it was out of the way. 'Go on.'

'There's a back entrance to Fairfax's club. I can let you in and take you to the security room. There you'll have eyes and ears on whatever happens in the meeting.'

'I don't get it.' I frowned. 'By doing this, Lady Sullivan could jeopardise your clan's chance of gaining full moon access to Regent's Park.'

Buffy didn't miss a beat. 'As desirable as that would be, we don't need to get into a squabble with the other clans. Devereau Webb wants to play the clans off against each other. As Sullivans, we're too smart to fall into such a trap. Plus, we owe you. This is our way of making up for what happened yesterday.'

I watched her for a moment or two. Lukas's black-eyed determination to come here with me flashed into my head. 'Let me guess,' I said, 'Lord Horvath has been making threats.'

Buffy didn't answer, but I knew I was right. This had nothing to do with making amends. Given a choice between a one-in-four chance of winning the Regent's Park rights and allowing a cold war to start between Clan Sullivan and the vamps, Lady Sullivan had plumped for the lesser of two evils. Whatever. If her machinations benefited me and Supe Squad in the long run, I could deal with them.

I gestured to Buffy. 'Lead the way.'

***

A fire door was wedged open at the rear of Fairfax's club. Buffy flashed me another of her brilliant grins and placed her finger to her lips, indicating that I should stay quiet. I nodded, wondering what fallout Clan Sullivan might incur if Lord Fairfax discovered they'd aided and abetted my intrusion into his club. Not my problem, I decided. You reap what you sow.

Buffy carefully pulled the door wide open and we padded inside. I followed her down a snaking corridor towards a narrow staircase. There, she turned to me. 'Up one flight and to the right,' she whispered. 'From here, you're on your own.'

That suited me. I nodded my thanks and pushed past her. When I glanced back, she'd already disappeared.

I continued upwards; hopefully I'd not already missed too much of the meeting.

At the top of the stairs I did as Buffy had instructed and located the door on the right. Holding my breath, I nudged it open to reveal a small room. It had an array of electronic equipment, walkie-talkies hanging on the wall – and a large two-way mirror looking out over the main floor of the club.

I peered through it. Seated at the same table as yesterday were the four werewolf alphas and Devereau Webb. Nobody else appeared to be in attendance. Webb's lips were moving but I couldn't hear what he was saying. I glanced round and found a set of headphones plugged into the complicated security system. I put them on. Bingo.

'I can assure you that the paperwork is in order. I'm not stupid enough to try to fool the entire werewolf population of London,' Webb was saying.

'My solicitors have checked it,' McGuigan said in an overly casual tone. 'We have no concerns on that front, even if Clan Carr do. Nobody is forcing you to be here,

Lady Carr. You're more than welcome to leave, if you wish to do so.'

Ah-ha. He was ingratiating himself with Webb to try and get the jump on the others, and trying to get rid of some of his competition at the same time. I doubted that would go down well with Lady Carr. I was right.

'You ridiculous excuse for a wolf!' she spat. 'You might be prepared to jump blindly into this agreement but I am more careful.'

'I'm not jumping blindly into anything,' McGuigan returned. 'I'm merely stating a fact.'

'Ladies, gentlemen.' Webb held up his hands, palms outward. 'There's no need to squabble. Lord McGuigan's solicitors are correct – but so is Lady Carr. This is purely *quid pro quo* and it is good to be cautious. I would be, if I were in your situation.'

Lady Sullivan, who must have known that I was watching from above, leaned forward. Her gaze didn't drift upwards for a moment. 'Then let's cut to the chase, shall we? Who is it that you're so desperate to turn? Who deserves to be made into one of our own?'

There was a heavy pause. Devereau Webb glanced from one wolf to another. Then he gave a small smile. 'You're right. We might as well cut to the chase. The person in question is my niece.'

I was startled. Niece?

Lord Fairfax rubbed his chin. 'She is ill?'

Webb nodded. 'Leukaemia. All other avenues of treatment have been exhausted. This is her last chance.'

'If she's ill,' Lady Carr said, 'she might not survive the transformation. Her immune system will already be compromised. This is not a certainty, Mr Webb.'

'I understand that. Her last course of chemotherapy was completed some months ago. Alice is dying, but she is also strong. It is a risk I'm prepared to take.'

'Is it a risk *she's* prepared to take?' Fairfax
questioned.

'I am her guardian,' Webb said. 'The final decision is
mine. And she understands that turning will be for the
best.'

Wait. What?

Lady Sullivan's back stiffened. 'What do you mean –
guardian?'

Webb crossed his legs. There was something robotic
about his movements. We were about to get to the crux of
the matter – and we all knew it.

'Alice is eleven years old.'

My shoulders dropped. It wasn't a criminal Webb
was trying to help; it was far worse than that.

For a moment, the four werewolf alphas were silent,
then they all exploded at once.

'A child? We can't turn a child!'

'It can't be done.'

'If word were to get out that…'

Webb cleared his throat. 'I understand your concerns.
I wouldn't have gone to such lengths to get your
attention, or have negotiated such a sweetener, if I didn't
realise how unorthodox this is.'

Lord McGuigan's voice, which had been saccharine
sweet seconds earlier, now dripped with ice. 'There are
many good reasons why we do not accept human
children, Mr Webb. It is not because of custom, but
necessity.'

Lady Carr nodded, finally in agreement with her
alpha counterpart. 'It is not only human law that prohibits
minors being turned. Puberty causes all sorts of issues
that can create havoc. They have been well documented.'

Fairfax got to his feet and started to pace up and
down. 'When was the last one? It was the boy back in the
fifties, right? The one taken into the Sullivan clan.'

'If that's a dig,' Lady Sullivan snapped, 'then remember that happened well before any of our time. As you well know.' Her jaw tightened. 'But yes, what happened with him was unfortunate. He killed three people, Mr Webb.'

'Forewarned is forearmed,' Webb returned. 'I'm sure you can put measures in place to avoid such unpleasantness again.'

Her eyebrows shot up. 'Unpleasantness?'

'We've fought hard for our independence,' Lord Fairfax said. 'Something like this has the potential to set us back decades.'

'She's not like other children. She's smart. Thoughtful. She—'

'She won't be able to control her own damned hormones!' Lady Carr interrupted.

Webb uncrossed his legs, stood up and strode towards the exit. For a second, I thought he was storming out – until he returned with a small figure in tow.

I stared at the short, pigtailed girl who'd screamed blue murder when she'd spotted me in the stairwell of Devereau Webb's tower block. My heart sank into my toes. Oh. Oh no.

'This is Alice,' Webb said simply.

Lady Sullivan shook her head. 'No.' She wouldn't look at the girl. 'No. We cannot do this. It was one thing when we thought it was a petty criminal you wanted to protect, but this child is another matter entirely. It can't be done.'

Alice rounded on Webb. 'See?' she said, her hands bunching up into fists. 'See? I told you! I don't even want to be a fucking werewolf!'

'Alice,' he chided sternly. 'Watch your language.' He looked up and appealed to the four alphas. 'Talk to her. You'll see she's special. I wouldn't be here if I didn't think it was worth it.'

'Of course you think it's worth it, Mr Webb,' Lady Carr said. 'She's your niece. But that doesn't change the facts. When she's eighteen—'

Webb's face contorted. 'She doesn't have that long!'

'Then there's nothing we can do.' Lady Carr rose to her feet. 'And if any of you suggest otherwise, I will do everything I can to stop you.'

'There is no need.' McGuigan's expression was blank. 'We're in agreement here. She cannot, and will not, be turned.'

Webb wasn't prepared to give up just yet. 'Regent's Park is—'

'It's not enough.' Fairfax glowered. He was obviously annoyed, although not at Webb or Alice; I reckoned he was simply pissed off with the entire situation. 'You should leave now. It's for the best.'

For the first time, Devereau Webb looked defeated. 'What will it take?' he asked. 'What else can I offer?'

'Nothing.' Lady Sullivan shook her head. 'We are done here.'

One by one, all four alphas strode out of the room. Webb's shoulders slumped. 'I'm sorry,' he whispered. 'I'm so sorry.'

Alice sniffed. Her bottom lip was quivering and her freckles were in stark relief across her pale skin. She put her arms round his waist and hugged him tight. 'It's okay.' She patted him on the back. 'Let's go home now, Uncle Dev.'

Chapter Twenty-One

I let myself out via the fire exit where I'd come in. There was no sign of Buffy but, before I'd taken five steps, a sleek car rounded the corner and pulled up beside me. The passenger door opened and a slender hand with bejewelled fingers beckoned to me. I sighed and got in, though I didn't close the door behind me. I wanted a fast exit if I needed it.

'I trust that your curiosity is satisfied, DC Bellamy,' Lady Sullivan said. Her expression didn't betray a trace of emotion.

'It is, if what I just witnessed was true,' I told her. 'Will you all stick to what you said in there? Or is someone likely to backtrack in order to gain the Regent's Park advantage?'

She didn't hesitate. 'None of us were lying. The risks created by turning a human child are far too great. It's not your laws which stop us, it is our own morals. We know the consequences, and we've learned from our history when others have tried to do the same. This is not something any of us are prepared to do. I can assure you of that.' She glanced down. 'Devereau Webb probably believes it is a lack of compassion on our part. The truth is quite the opposite.'

I felt sick with sympathy for both Webb and his niece. And I was desperately glad that I hadn't been forced to intervene in order to uphold the law. 'That poor girl,' I murmured.

'Yes.' Lady Sullivan sniffed. 'Poor girl, indeed.' She

raised her chin and looked me in the eye. 'I trust we are good now. You and I, I mean.'

'We are.' I hesitated. 'I kept my word. I didn't tell Lord Horvath what you did. He found out by himself.'

'I am aware of that. But please tell him that I have made restitution.'

I watched her for a moment, then I posed the question that I'd been dying to ask. 'Why are you afraid of him?'

She took a while before answering. 'There may be four werewolf clans and only one vampire group, and we might outnumber the vampires three to one, but they have the organisation and the strength,' she said finally. 'Not to mention the wealth. Until Horvath came along, the bloodsuckers were little more than a minor annoyance. Now they possess more money, more intelligence and more power than we do. I'm not being modest, I'm speaking the truth. You should be wary of getting too close to them, Detective. They seek only to enhance their own position, and they will stop at nothing to expand their reach. You might think you're starting to understand the supernatural community, but you've barely scratched the surface. And when it comes to the vampires, you probably never will.' She smiled humourlessly. 'Consider yourself warned. They are predators. And they love a chase.'

I absorbed her words then I nodded. 'Noted.'

'I hope so.' She twisted one of her rings. 'I will be in touch once I receive the results of the DNA testing.'

It was on the tip of my tongue to tell her what I'd learned from *Infernal Enchantments* but I managed to resist. True, vampires were predators – but so were werewolves. There was nothing to be gained by making their lives too easy for them. Instead, I murmured a brief farewell and left.

***

Angry rain clouds were darkening the sky by the time I reached St Erbin's. There was no sign of either the Reverend Knight or Lukas, but there was a solitary figure standing in the graveyard with her head bent.

I squinted and drew in a breath when I realised who it was. It was tempting to nip past her and hope she didn't see me, but that was the coward's way out. I could do better; I *was* better.

I swung open the iron gate and walked quietly along the path until I was a metre or so behind her. 'Mrs Clarke?' I asked. 'Is everything alright?'

Her head turned and her tear-wet eyes blinked at me. 'Yes. Yes. Everything is alright.' She pointed helplessly at Julian's gravestone. 'I know he's not there any more, but I don't know where he is and I have to come somewhere. Maybe he can still hear me. Maybe he knows I still care.'

'I'm sure he does know that.'

She gave me a grateful, watery smile. 'Are you any closer to finding him?' she asked. 'The woman I spoke to this morning said the investigation was ongoing, but she wouldn't tell me any more than that. Why did she ask me about Julian's necklace?'

'We're investigating every angle and ensuring we have all the details, relevant or otherwise.' I bit my lip. 'But I can tell you that we're close to identifying a suspect. There is also the possibility that Julian's death wasn't an accident.'

Mrs Clarke didn't gasp or cry; all she did was offer a small smile. 'I knew it,' she said, without a trace of triumph. 'I knew it all along. Who is it? Who killed my boy?'

'It's only conjecture at the moment. There's no proof.'

Her voice hardened. 'Tell me.'

'We believe it's a man called Edward Nappey. He's not a werewolf and he's not supernatural. He's human, through and through. We're trying to locate him. We *will* find him, Mrs Clarke. Hopefully then I'll be able to give you some answers.'

She turned away so I couldn't see her face. 'Did he steal Julian away? Did he take my son from his grave?'

'It's highly likely. He targeted this particular graveyard. We think that several werewolf graves were attacked over a number of years. We're waiting on further exhumations for confirmation.'

Her shoulders stiffened. 'Several graves?'

'I'm afraid so.'

A few raindrops started to fall, soaking the ground by our feet. Neither Mrs Clarke nor I made any move to take shelter.

'Thank you, Detective Bellamy,' Mrs Clarke said. She sounded distant. 'I appreciate your honesty and all the work you've put in on our behalf. You didn't have to do this for us, not after what we did to you. No matter what happens, you have my gratitude.'

I was only doing my job, but she didn't want to hear that. Not right now. 'I'll leave you in peace. I'll be in touch once I have some definite information.'

Mrs Clarke's head dipped further but she didn't speak. I hovered for another moment then stepped back and went into the church.

From the various buckets placed on the stone flagstones, it looked like it wasn't much drier inside than it was outside in the rain. I scanned the empty pews. Perhaps I'd missed Lukas and he'd been and gone. I hoped that in my absence he'd managed to be polite to

Reverend Knight. A vampire Lord and church vicar might not be natural friends, but I liked to think that the pair of them could be civil.

Then I heard a roar from somewhere beyond the altar and I froze. Uh-oh.

Worried now, I hastily located the small wooden door leading to the annexe at the side of the church. I marched over and opened it, just as there was a second loud roar. With my heart in my mouth, I jogged down the corridor. It looked like there was a small office at the far end. My hand twitched, already reaching for the crossbow which still lay across my back. When I reached the office and peered in, however, the sight that greeted my eyes was the last thing I could have expected.

Lukas and Reverend Knight were sitting side by side behind the vicar's messy desk. Knight's face was suffused with red – but not with anger. As far as I could tell, they were both struggling to contain their laughter.

'And then,' Lukas said, apparently delivering a punchline, 'the edge of his cassock caught one of the candle flames and … whoof!'

Knight couldn't stop himself. He roared again, doubling over as if in pain. Lukas glanced at me and winked. I didn't feel amusement, though; I just felt chilled.

'Having fun?' I enquired.

Reverend Knight jumped and, wiping his eyes, got up to his feet. 'DC Bellamy,' he said. 'You made it! Good to see you.' He reached forward and enveloped me in a tight and wholly unexpected hug. I stood stiffly until he released me. 'We were discussing old times,' he told me. 'Lord Horvath has some fascinating stories to tell about my many predecessors in this church.'

'Does he?' I murmured.

'Yes. Yes.' He nodded enthusiastically. 'Quite

extraordinary.' He looked at Lukas. 'I hope that we can have a better relationship.'

Lukas smiled. 'I'm sure that we can. You're a shrewd, intelligent man. I'm glad you're here.' He glanced round. 'Do you know, this is the first time I've ever been inside this church in all the time I've lived here. You are a true man of the people, Reverend Knight. I think that we can expect things to be much better, going forward.'

'Me too. Me too.' The reverend grabbed Lukas's hand and pumped it. 'This has been a most wonderful afternoon.' He grinned at me. 'Watch this, Detective.' He picked up a small wooden crucifix from his desk and gave it to Lukas. Lukas closed his fingers round it. 'See?' Knight crowed.

'Uh…'

'No burning!'

Lukas opened his palm.

'Not even a mark!' Knight beamed.

'Okay.' I scratched my head. 'Good.'

Lukas returned the crucifix to the desk. 'Now that you're here, D'Artagnan, why don't we examine the graveyard? It would be good to check the layout of the graves that have been disturbed and get an idea about how Nappey approached them.'

'Yeah,' I said slowly. 'Okay.'

The three of us trooped outside with Reverend Knight leading the way. Behind his back, Lukas raised a questioning eyebrow and I managed a tight smile in response. He frowned. He knew I was upset about something but he couldn't tell what.

There was no longer any sign of Mrs Clarke, which was definitely a good thing. I doubted that she would be comforted by the sight of a vampire wandering around what should have been her son's resting place.

It was raining a lot harder now, big fat droplets splashing into puddles. With the sky darkening as night drew in, the graveyard was becoming an even creepier place.

'Are you alright?' Lukas asked in a low voice. 'I know this is where you were killed the first time, Emma. If you'd prefer to wait outside the gate…'

'I'm fine.' I tucked my hair behind my ears and raised my chin. 'I've come to terms with what happened. No trauma.'

Lukas's expression didn't change. 'Okay. If you change your mind, say the word.'

I nodded tightly and put my hands in my pockets. Reverend Knight stopped at a grave at the far end, closest to the wrought-iron fence that closed off the churchyard on its northern side. The rain was plastering his hair to his skull and his expression was much more sombre. 'There have been two definite disturbances since I started my tenure. Here,' he pointed down, 'and over there.'

I followed his finger then turned and glanced at the spot where Julian Clarke's grave was.

'The other disturbances occurred before you were posted here?' Lukas asked.

'Yes. Reverend Baxter showed me where.'

'He was your immediate predecessor?'

Knight nodded.

'And what was his take on things?'

The Reverend's eyes slid away. 'He was an old-fashioned sort. He'd been here for decades. He didn't have many good things to say about the supernatural community.'

'Mm.' Lukas dipped his head grimly in acknowledgement. 'Our paths only crossed a few times and they were never pleasant encounters. It's a shame. You're obviously a different man. I think we can work together far more productively.'

Even through the rain, I could see that Knight was pleased. 'I hope so,' he murmured. 'I really do.'

My brow creased. 'If Baxter despised the supernatural community so much, why did he agree to werewolves being buried here?'

'He didn't want to agree but he didn't have much choice. The church authorities told him he couldn't deny the werewolves their one last shot at redemption. After all,' Knight added with a brief laugh, 'as you said yourself, DC Bellamy, we all have a capacity for evil. We are all sinners, each and every one of us.'

'Never was a truer word spoken.' Lukas swivelled round. He was only wearing a white shirt, and the rain was soaking it through and moulding it to his body. 'Stay here,' he instructed. 'I want to check something.' He strode out of the churchyard.

'He's not at all what I expected, you know,' the reverend said to me. 'Lord Horvath is very charming.'

'Yes,' I said distantly. 'He is.' I was keen to keep the conversation away from Lukas. 'Was it Reverend Baxter who told you that it was ghouls who were disturbing the graves?'

'Oh yes.' Knight nodded. 'He showed me all the records. He said that I should report it to the church but that I should be careful if I ever saw them.' He shuddered. 'They're dangerous creatures.'

I thought about Albert Finnegan; there was nothing remotely dangerous about him. Maybe I should take it as a fascinating exercise into how our misconceptions could shape not just our beliefs but our actions as well. Instead, I simply found it depressing.

Lukas called out from the other side of the church fence, 'Try walking forward. Move to Julian Clarke's grave. And then the others.'

Knight and I did as he asked. After a few moments watching us, Lukas returned. The rusty iron gate squeaked on its hinges as he pushed through it. 'It's raining and it's getting dark.' He frowned. 'The conditions are much like they were on the nights when the graves were attacked.'

'And?' I questioned. 'Could you see us from the street?'

'Barely. I think you were right before – it's conceivable that someone could dig down to the coffins without anyone noticing. It wouldn't be easy, and they'd need some way to transport the bodies out of here, but it is possible. They could park right at the entrance.'

'It would be risky, even in bad weather. We're still in the centre of London.' I shrugged. 'But I can't see any other explanation.'

'Edward Nappey got rid of his car,' Lukas said. 'I wonder if he has another vehicle hidden away somewhere – a van of some description.'

It would make sense, and it also gave us something to work with. At this stage, I'd take anything that might give us a clue about the bastard's whereabouts.

'I'll put Liza onto it,' I said. 'There's nothing registered in his name but we know where he's been. If he had a van when he went after Moira, it might have been captured on CCTV.' I looked round. 'And there's always the chance that there are some cameras near here that picked it up.' Frustration gnawed at me. I had no doubt that we'd catch up to Ted Nappey eventually but I needed it to be much sooner rather than later.

Lukas and I said our farewells to Reverend Knight and left the church. I walked absent-mindedly to Tallulah, pretending not to notice the hawk-eyed way Lukas was watching me.

'Was there any trouble with the werewolves?' he

asked.

An image of Devereau Webb hugging his niece flashed into my mind's eye. 'Not really.' I glanced at him. 'The minimum age for turning someone into a vampire is eighteen, right? Have you ever broken that rule?'

Lukas stiffened. 'Is that an accusation?'

I blinked. 'No. Just…' I searched for the right words. 'Call it curiosity. I'm not fishing for details of illegal activity, Lukas. If you don't want to tell me, you don't have to.'

His black eyes seared into me. 'We've not broken that rule for more than two hundred years. It exists for very good reasons.' He paused. 'Why do you ask? Because if the clans are thinking about turning someone below the minimum age, there are going to be problems.'

'They're not.'

'Then why ask the question?'

I sighed. 'It's a long story and it's not relevant to what's going on with Ted Nappey. Forget I asked.' I turned away but Lukas moved and barred my path, looming over me.

'What's happened?'

'Nothing's happened.'

He ground his teeth in frustration. 'Something is wrong. Since you walked into that damned church you've been looking at me strangely, like I've done something to offend you.'

My turbulent thoughts had been more obvious than I'd realised. 'It's nothing.'

'Clearly it's not nothing.' His gaze intensified. 'Tell me.'

I twisted uncomfortably under his scrutiny. There was value in being truthful; as a detective I knew that more than most. But there was also value in knowing when to stay quiet. In the end, however, I didn't need to answer because Lukas did it for me.

'Ah,' he said. He nodded. 'You weren't expecting me to get on with Knight. You asked me to talk to him, but it bothers you that we weren't at each other's throats. You think that because he's a man of God and I'm a vampire we should be natural enemies.'

The fact that I didn't say anything was answer enough.

'I didn't become Lord because of birth right, nor because of force. I'm good at what I do. The ability to charm is an important part of that.'

'Uh-huh. I get it. You're a vampire. Your charm is part of your nature. You use it to get what you want. It's a part of you, in the same way that a werewolf has claws. Charm someone enough, and they'll open their veins for you.'

He continued to watch me. 'Not everything is about blood, D'Artagnan. After all, I want to charm *you* and we both know that I've already had a brief taste of your blood and it wasn't to my liking.'

He was referring to several weeks earlier, when he'd used his tongue on my skin to heal some wounds. 'You want to charm me?' I folded my arms, feeling my hackles rise for no reason that I could adequately define.

'Not for the reasons you think.' His eyes glittered. 'In fact, my real motive might surprise you. I'm not using you because you happen to be in Supe Squad. I'm not using you at all. And I can assure you that my relationship with Tony, your predecessor, was nothing like,' he gestured between us, 'this.'

Whatever *this* was. 'People keep warning me off you.'

Momentary anger flashed across his face. 'Who? What people?'

'It doesn't matter.' I exhaled. 'I like you, Lukas. I trust you.' Up to a point, anyway. 'You've helped me before, and I know you're grieving for Moira. You want to catch her killer as much, if not more, than I do.'

'That much is true.' He didn't take his eyes off mine. 'I'm not an evil creature from the pages of a horror story, Emma. I might be the big bad vampire Lord but you're safe with me. I promise you that.' He stepped back. 'Perhaps some breathing space wouldn't go amiss,' he murmured, as much to himself as to me. 'Rain check until tomorrow?'

I shifted my weight from foot to foot. That was probably a good idea. I stared at him, wishing I knew what to say. Eventually I nodded dumbly. So much for Emma Bellamy, the ultra-confident detective with amazing truth-seeking skills.

'Stop fretting,' Lukas murmured. 'Sometimes you think too much.' He smiled faintly. 'Adieu.' He paused. 'For now.' A moment later, he whirled away into the darkening night.

Chapter Twenty-Two

I touched base with Fred and Liza before heading home for a rest. After the conversation with Lukas, my thoughts were in turmoil. I was indeed thinking far too much about everything he'd said.

I needed to focus on the case, but it didn't help that DSI Barnes had called several times, haranguing Liza for updates on the investigation. I didn't need reminding that this was the first real crime that Supe Squad had been responsible for solving in decades. In recent years, either the supes had taken charge or investigations had been passed to CID.

I knew without talking to Barnes that if I screwed this up and didn't find Ted Nappey soon, the same thing would happen again. Despite the inroads I'd made with the supes, failure to capture Nappey would have desperate ramifications. Unfortunately it felt like we were no further forward than we had been twelve hours earlier. Then again, a lot could change within a twelve-hour period. I knew that better than anyone. Anything could happen from here on in.

I had to clear my mind then come at everything from a new angle. I locked my door, headed straight for my bedroom and curled up on the bed without taking off my clothes. I closed my eyes and tried to relax. All I had to do was empty my mind.

The pillow was cool and comforting and it was good to lie down. I needed this.

Less than a minute later, my eyes snapped open

again.

I sprang off the bed and went into the bathroom. I splashed cold water on my face before dabbing it with a towel, then leaned my hands on the sink and gazed into the mirror. I had the beginnings of a spot flaring up in the centre of my forehead. As I stared at the angry red bump, my thoughts flitted around my skull like a cloud of nervous butterflies.

A moment later, I pushed myself back and whirled round, pausing only to grab my jacket to ward off the cool night air. I took three steps down the corridor and towards the stairs before turning back. It wasn't smart to be out and about at this hour without some sort of protection.

I'd finished strapping the crossbow to my back and was striding out again when I heard a set of heavy footsteps clumping up the stairs. My heart sank; there was no doubt who it was. When the slack face of Will, my neighbour, appeared, I did my best to smile. From the wafting smell of old beer, he'd been enjoying a night on the town.

He grunted when he saw me. 'Oh.' His lip curled. 'It's you.'

I was tempted to brush past him with a curt greeting but he *was* my neighbour. I wasn't moving to another flat any time soon – and neither was he. The least I could do was to try and improve our touchy relationship.

'Good evening,' I said, managing a sunny smile. 'Have been out enjoying yourself?'

From the range of emotions that flitted across his face, I could tell that Will wanted to tell me to piss off. Despite his slightly inebriated state, however, his inner public schoolboy won out and he forced himself to give me a polite nod. 'Just having a drink or two with some buddies from work.' He gave me a pointed look. 'Are you leaving now?' He made a show of raising his wrist to check the time. 'At this hour?'

'Unfortunately stopping crime isn't a nine-to-five kind of job.' I injected a wistful air into my voice. 'Perhaps I went into the wrong profession, but someone has to keep the streets safe.'

'They'd be a darned sight safer if there weren't supes around,' he muttered. The man couldn't help himself.

I deliberately pretended to mishear him. 'You're absolutely right, Will. You're a clever man, you know. We're very fortunate that the crime rates here are lower because of the supes in our community.'

He frowned. 'That's not what I—' He rolled his eyes. 'Whatever.'

Selective hearing, Emma, I reminded myself. 'I'm glad I bumped into you,' I told him. 'I wanted to say thank you and I never really got the chance before. You were very understanding over the whole mess with Tony—'

'You told me you were his niece.' His nose wrinkled with distaste. 'You lied.'

'I did,' I said honestly. 'And look at how well you dealt with that. You're a better man than most. And that's not to mention how well you dealt with bumping into Lord Horvath the other night.'

Will blinked. He hadn't realised who Lukas was when he'd created that song and dance about not inviting him inside.

'You know,' I continued, 'a lot of people would be scared of him. Not you. A lot of people would be tongue-tied but that wasn't you either. You know your own heart, and you don't take any shit from anyone, regardless of who they are. That takes guts and fortitude. I'm lucky to have you as my neighbour.'

Will's chest puffed out. He was far more mollified by

my compliments than I'd expected. 'Well,' he said, in an attempt at modesty, 'I deal with important people day in and day out in my job. I'm used to having to stand up to people.'

I offered him a small, admiring smile. 'Maybe one day I'll have your confident attitude.'

He pursed his lips as if that were doubtful. 'Maybe.' He dipped his head. 'Have a good night, Emma. And stay safe out there.'

'I will. Thank you.' I grinned to myself as I walked past him. That hadn't been so hard. If play-acting with Will would make my home life easier to manage, I'd do it more often.

As I jogged down the stairs, I paused briefly. What I'd done was turn on the charm to improve my circumstances – in much the same manner as I'd all but accused Lukas of doing. Hypocrisy, thy name is Emma.

***

Tallulah grumbled all the way, creaking and sighing at being forced out again in the dead of night. I drove slowly, easing up on the clutch with exaggerated care every time I changed gear, but it didn't seem to make much difference to the car. When I pulled up, her engine coughed and spluttered and I caught a belch of black smoke in the rear-view mirror.

'If you're having trouble with your exhaust again,' I told her, 'maybe we should schedule another trip to the garage.' She immediately subsided. I grinned, aware that any ideas of Tallulah's sentience were pure imagination on my part but enjoying them nonetheless.

I turned off her engine and pocketed the keys. A porch light in the grand house beside me flicked on and the door opened to reveal Albert Finnegan, dressed in the same dapper fashion that he'd been previously. I appreciated his consistency, even if I wasn't a fan of tweed.

I clambered ungracefully out of Tallulah and hailed him. 'Good evening!'

'Good evening, Detective,' he called. 'I'm surprised to see you here again. Are you about to take me into custody? Have you decided that we're breaking the law after all?' He eyed the crossbow but his expression remained friendly.

'Not at all, Mr Finnegan.' I walked up to him. 'I have a follow-up question that I was hoping you could help me to answer.'

He bowed. 'By all means. What would you like to know?'

'How old are you?'

He raised an eyebrow. 'That's your follow-up question?'

'What I really want to know,' I said, with a faint smile, 'is whether you're old enough to be one of those ghouls who stole bodies from the graves at St Erbin's.'

'If you're seeking to prosecute me for past crimes…'

I held up my hands. 'Nothing of the sort, I can assure you. Anything you say will not be used against you.'

'I should hope not.' He regarded me calmly. 'We were granted immunity for those deeds many decades ago. But yes, I am indeed old enough to remember those days.'

'How did you manage it without getting caught? I understand that if you worked around weather patterns, you could manage to do most of your … work without being noticed. But how could you move the bodies? Surely all it would have taken was a single passer-by to see what you were doing and raise the alarm. And in any case, it must have taken most of the night to dig down to the graves. I already know that sunlight is your enemy. Were your Halloween disguises enough to protect you?'

Finnegan's brow creased. I wondered if he was offended by my questions but, when he answered, I realised that was far from the truth. 'You're asking if we wandered around the streets carrying corpses?'

'I am.'

'In the centre of London?'

'Yes. I appreciate that pollution often meant that visibility was bad, but was the pea-souper smog that terrible? Did you have to wait until there was a storm so most people were already inside, and those who weren't couldn't see beyond their noses?'

Finnegan's eyes were troubled. 'I do apologise, DC Bellamy. I assumed you already knew. I thought the vicar would have told you.'

'Told me what?'

He watched me carefully. 'About the tunnel.'

I breathed in through my nose and waited.

'Ah,' he said. 'I see you didn't know.' He stepped back. 'I have an old map in here somewhere. Perhaps I can show you.'

'That would be good.'

I followed him and waited as he rummaged around in an old teak sideboard. 'It's here somewhere,' he muttered. 'Maybe … ah-ha.' He produced a tattered sheet of paper as wide as his arm span. It was stained yellow from years of use and there were several rips across it.

Taking care not to damage it further, Finnegan took it to a table and spread it out. 'We are here,' he said, jabbing to a point in the top left corner.

I squinted. Most of the streets were the same then as they were now. One or two had altered as the roads had been widened to accommodate cars rather than horses and pedestrians, but I still recognised most of the area.

'Initially,' Finnegan continued, 'we planned to develop a series of tunnels that would take us directly from the graveyard to this house. Such a network would have allowed us to avoid sunlight completely. There had been several unfortunate incidents where those of our kind were trapped outside when dawn broke and they were unwilling to abandon all the hard work they had undertaken at the church.'

His eyes lost focus as he remembered. 'It didn't end well for them,' he said quietly. He shook himself. 'In any case, those plans did not work out. There were proposals for a sewerage system that would have caused us considerable difficulties.' He smiled humourlessly. 'As it happened, the London sewers were not constructed until many years after we halted our underground tactics. The government wasn't very keen to spend money on such a project until they were forced into it.'

'*Plus ça change,*' I murmured.

Finnegan smiled. '*Plus c'est la meme chose.* Indeed.' He moved his finger across the old map. 'So we adapted. There was a single entry point.' He pointed at a mark a street away from St Erbin's. 'A trapdoor that led below ground. We purchased the property above it to avoid anyone noticing any suspicious activity. The tunnel was less than eighty metres long.' His finger traced along a slender blue line. 'From here to here. It leads directly underneath the graveyard and emerges at the small crypt in the south-east corner. The doorway is invisible from the churchyard end, and nobody had visited that crypt to mourn for more than two centuries. No-one would know the door was there unless they were told about it. It worked perfectly for us. Once a body had been retrieved, it could be transported underground regardless of the time of day.'

I absorbed this before pressing on with my next

question. 'Why did you think the vicar at St Erbin's would have told me about it? If you can't stumble across the entrance in the crypt, how would he know that the tunnel exists?'

Finnegan blinked at me. 'Because the tunnel's entrance starts at the manse.'

'The manse?'

'The church purchased the property from us not long after we changed our ways. At the time, I suspect they were afraid that we'd continue stealing from the graves despite our promises to the contrary. They wanted to ensure the graveyard was kept safe. They converted the building into a residential base for the incumbent at St Erbin's. The church still owns that building, DC Bellamy. And the current vicar, a Reverend Knight, I believe, lives there right now. The entry point for the tunnel is in his basement.'

Chapter Twenty-Three

I hammered on Knight's door. When he didn't answer immediately, I hammered some more. He kept late hours at the church in order to snag passers-by and try to dissuade them from venturing into vamp territory – but he didn't work this late. He was home. I was sure of it.

After a good two minutes, by which point I was on the verge of breaking his damned door down, there was the sound of a lock rattling. The door swung open and Knight, looking bleary and alarmed, and dressed in a striped dressing gown with tartan slippers, stared at me. 'DC Bellamy? What on earth do you want at this hour?' Suddenly, he seemed to remember who, or rather *what,* I was, and a flash of fear crossed his face.

I didn't care. I forced my way in and he stepped back hastily.

'The tunnel,' I snarled. 'Why didn't you mention it before?'

'I ... I...' he stuttered, his face pale. 'I have no idea what you're talking about.'

I reminded myself that I was a trained police detective, not a thug here to deliver threats. I exhaled and dropped my hands to my sides in a bid to appear less intimidating. It didn't matter that I was half the size of Knight; I was a supe – at least as far as we both knew. As far as Reverend Knight was concerned, that made me very dangerous and very threatening.

'There is a trapdoor in your basement,' I said. 'It leads to a tunnel. The tunnel comes out at a crypt in *your* graveyard. Two hundred years ago, the ghouls used that tunnel to gain access to the graveyard so they could transport the bodies buried there without anyone noticing.' I waited for a beat. 'Why, in the name of all that is holy, didn't you think to mention it before?' I met his eyes. 'Think very carefully before you answer.'

Knight's jaw worked uselessly and his eyes darted from side to side. If he was expecting someone to jump out from the shadows and help him, he was sorely mistaken. 'I haven't been into the basement, DC Bellamy,' he said, his voice quavering.

'You've lived here for almost a year. How on earth is that possible?'

He gestured helplessly towards me. 'It's locked and I don't have a key. I keep meaning to sort it out and get in a locksmith, but Reg told me there was nothing in there.'

'Reg?'

'Reginald Baxter. My predecessor.' Knight drew the cord of his dressing gown tighter around his mid-section. 'I'm telling you the truth. Why would I lie?'

'Show me.'

'Now? Can't it wait until morning?'

I ground my teeth. 'No, it can't wait. Show me the damned door.'

I reached for the crossbow at my back and Knight flinched. I unhooked it and dropped it to the floor, where it landed with a thud. The vicar jumped and I held up my palms and softened my voice. 'I carry the crossbow not because I'm legally entitled to as a Supernatural Squad detective, but because I am scared. In the last two months I've died three times. If that's not enough to scare someone, I don't know what is. The worst part is that my deaths are not the biggest thing I have to worry about right now. What truly worries me is that somewhere out there is a man who has killed at least twice. He's stolen werewolf corpses because of a gruesome recipe in an old book. He's a dangerous man. I'm scared what he might do next.' I shook my head. 'No. Not scared. I'm *terrified*. If he's been using your basement to sneak underneath your graveyard and take the bodies of people's loved ones, I need to know about it.'

Knight stared at me. 'I don't … he couldn't … there's no…' His shoulders slumped. 'It's this way.'

He led me down the hall. It was a large house for one person, and most of the rooms appeared to be sparsely furnished. I suspected it wasn't because Knight lived a particularly spartan life but rather because he hadn't given himself enough time to make the manse his home.

When we reached the door at the far end of the hallway, having passed several large boxes with labels marking their contents, I finally worked out the truth. 'You don't think you're going to stay here, do you? You've not finished unpacking, even though you've been here for months.'

Knight hesitated, his hand on the doorknob. 'You're not the only one who's terrified, Detective,' he whispered.

Shit. He was telling the truth about everything. 'I'm sorry.' I stopped moving. 'You're right. I should return in the morning. It's not fair on you to do this now. It can wait. You're not a criminal and you don't deserve to be roused out of your bed in the middle of the night. This was wrong of me.'

He turned and faced me. 'No, it wasn't. You're trying to protect this community and so am I, in my own way. It so happens that you're more successful than I am.'

'I'm not so sure about that.' My eyes met his and we shared a glance of mutual understanding. 'I'll go.'

'No.' Knight shook his head, his mouth set into a grim line. 'You're here now. I won't be able to go back to sleep after what you've told me. We have to do this.'

He was a stronger man than he gave himself credit for. 'Let's do it together.'

He managed a smile. 'Okay, Detective. Okay.'

Reverend Knight turned and opened the door. He reached across and flicked on a light switch. It took a moment or two for the electricity to buzz into life, then revealed a rickety wooden staircase leading downwards.

I swallowed. It was the dead of night and I was venturing into a dank basement with a vicar in a dressing gown. What could possibly go wrong?

The stairs creaked all the way down and the walls seemed to close in on us the further we went. At the foot of the staircase, Knight stopped. There was another door, and this one was firmly closed.

'Here it is,' he said. 'I've never been beyond this point.' He reached forward and rattled the doorknob. 'It won't open. There's a keyhole but,' he grimaced at me, 'no key.'

I stared at the door. It was made of wood and didn't appear to be reinforced. Much like the staircase itself, it looked like it had seen better days.

'Let me have a try,' I said. I crouched down and examined the lock. It didn't look particularly sturdy but I was no locksmith. Once upon a time, I'd never have dared to try something like this without the proper equipment but I was stronger now. There was a chance that I could force the door open.

'Stand back,' I ordered.

I stood up then, with as much as strength as I could muster, I slammed my shoulder against the door. It creaked and complained but it didn't give way. There was still hope, though. I pulled back and drew in a breath, then a moment later I tried again.

This time, the door frame started to splinter. The

wood was old and rotten in places, which helped considerably. I licked my lips. Third time lucky. I threw myself at the door again. The wood split some more and the door bulged where I'd hit it, but it didn't open. Okay, then. Fourth time lucky.

I sucked in my muscles, tensing before ramming the door yet again. Finally the rotting wood gave way. The door sprang open and I fell forward, stumbling onto stone flagstones.

I'd done it. I'd actually gone and done it.

'Are you alright, Detective?' Knight enquired anxiously.

I stood and dusted myself down. 'I'm fine,' I called. I glanced round and found another light switch on the wall. When I turned it on, it illuminated the basement – which was completely empty. There weren't even any mouldy old boxes stacked into corners, as one might expect in a long-abandoned room. There was, however, a trapdoor in the centre of the floor. Albert Finnegan had been right.

Knight joined me and we stared at it. It gave me the creeps and, judging by the way the reverend shuddered, I wasn't the only one.

'You didn't know this was here?' I questioned him. I already knew the answer but I felt the need to ask again.

He shook his head vehemently. 'No. I had no clue.' He averted his gaze from the trapdoor. 'Should we … should we open it?'

I wanted to; I wanted to see this damned tunnel with my own eyes. There was no telling what sort of clues might have been left in it. But venturing into it would only contaminate what was now a crime scene, and it would be smarter to leave it until a forensics team could investigate it properly. Besides, I suddenly had more pressing concerns.

'Mrs Clarke,' I said to myself.

Knight jerked. 'Pardon?'

I met his eyes. 'Mrs Clarke told me that Reverend Baxter was good to her. He counselled her and her husband after their son joined the werewolves. She also told me that they chose St Erbin's as the burial site because of Baxter's continued support.'

His brow furrowed. 'So?'

Reverend Knight wasn't being deliberately obtuse, he simply couldn't fathom what was right in front of his eyes. 'The graveyard has been disturbed twice since you started your tenure at St Erbin's, and it was disturbed several times before your arrival.' I raised my eyebrows. 'How do you suppose someone would gain access to this basement without you noticing?'

The vicar goggled at me as his face turned pale. 'You're not suggesting that Reginald Baxter is behind all this? That he's been taking bodies from their graves and … and…'

I sighed. 'No. He's not the main culprit.' Knight started to relax. My eyes hardened. 'But he colluded with the main culprit.'

Knight's mouth dropped open. 'He can't have.'

'You said it yourself. Baxter hated the werewolves being interred in his church. He used to live here. He presumably gave you the keys to this building?'

'Yes, but—'

'Did you change the locks when you moved in?'

'No. It never occurred to me.'

I scratched absently at my arm. 'Baxter must have made a copy of the front-door key and given it to Edward Nappey,' I said, as much to myself as to the hapless Reverend Knight. 'And he gave the only copy of the basement key to him at the same time. He wouldn't have wanted you to come down here, find the trapdoor and investigate it. He didn't want you to know that ghouls weren't the ones stealing corpses – he didn't want you to know that he was involved.'

'That's preposterous!'

'Why?' I asked. 'Because he's a vicar?'

Knight flapped his arms. 'Because it doesn't make any sense! Who is this Edward Nappey fellow, anyway?'

'He's the one who's ultimately responsible for all this mess,' I explained.

'How on earth would Reverend Baxter get involved with such a man?'

'I don't know,' I started, 'but—' I stopped. Maybe I *did* know.

I reached into my pocket and drew out my phone. It was almost two in the morning and Fred was almost certainly asleep, but this was important. I dialled his number and held the phone to my ear while Knight paced up and down the empty basement, muttering to himself.

It took several rings before Fred answered. When he spoke, however, it was clear that I hadn't woken him up. For one thing, there was thumping music in the background; for another, he sounded more than slightly tipsy and he was burbling with happiness. 'Boss! How's it going?'

'Where are you, Fred?'

'I'm dancing!' He let out a whoop. 'I've never danced before in my life, but you know what?' He continued before I could say anything. 'I'm really good at it. Better than good. I think I might have missed my calling. I shouldn't be in the police force at all. I should be on the dance floor!'

I passed a hand over my eyes. Unbelievable. 'Fred,' I snapped. 'Sober up. I need you.'

'Wh – what?'

'You heard me. Get out of Heart so we can talk properly.'

Confusion lit his voice. 'How did you know I was in Heart?'

'Lucky guess,' I muttered.

'I'm not doing anything wrong. It was a long day. I needed to blow off some steam.'

I drew in a deep breath. 'I didn't say you were doing anything wrong.' I had no doubt that Fred's presence in Lukas's club was Scarlett's doing. 'Right now, I don't care why you're in the vampire nightclub. I need you to go somewhere quiet. It's important.'

'Eh?'

'Get out of there so I can talk to you properly,' I repeated, doing my best not to snap.

For several seconds I couldn't hear anything but the music growing quieter. When Fred finally spoke again, he sounded considerably more sober. 'I'm outside,' he said. 'What is it that you need?'

I closed my eyes briefly. Fred was still with me; I could still count on him. 'Ted Nappey's grandfather,' I said. 'You were looking into him. What was his name? Was he also a Nappey?'

'No.' Fred's response was instant. 'Not Nappey. His surname was Collins. Sean Collins.'

I glanced at Knight. He was still pacing up and down. 'Is there a Sean Collins buried in St Erbin's?'

The vicar came to a stuttering halt. 'What? Sean Collins? Yes, but—'

Bingo. Ted Nappey had probably bonded with Reverend Baxter at his own grandfather's funeral.

'Anything else?' Fred asked anxiously.

Yes, there was. 'There's a heap of printouts from the Carlyle Library on my desk in the office. They are the names and addresses of everyone who's requested access to the Arcane Works room during the last ten years. I need you to look through them and find out whether

Reginald Baxter is one of those names.'

There was a brief pause. 'Now?'

'Yes, Fred. Now.'

'Okay.' Rather than sounding reluctant to curtail his drinking and dancing, Fred sounded eager. He wasn't daft; he knew by now that I was on to something. 'What's going on? What have you found out?'

I jabbed a finger at Knight. 'Do you know where Baxter lives now?'

He nodded. 'Travis Close. It's about a mile from here.'

'Good.' I addressed Fred again. 'Tell Scarlett to speak to Lukas – to Lord Horvath. He needs to meet us at Travis Close as soon as possible. Once you've checked through the list of names, you should head there too. I'll explain what's going on when you get there.'

'Yes, ma'am.' He disconnected without another word.

Knight watched me put the phone away. His mouth was turned down and it didn't take a genius to know he was upset about something.

'What is it?' I asked.

'It's two o'clock in the morning.'

'Yep.'

His mouth drooped further. 'No matter what you think Reverend Baxter might have done, he's an old man. You said yourself that he's not the main culprit. Can't you wait until morning before you bang on his door like you're the Gestapo? He's not going anywhere. I know you want to find this Nappey fellow, but surely it can wait until daylight. No-one's life is in immediate danger. Right?' Knight frowned. 'Right?' he repeated.

Oh no. My stomach dropped. I was a prize fucking idiot.

'Detective?' Knight asked in a small voice.

'I have to go.' I was already sprinting for the stairs. 'Get out of this room and don't enter it again. I'll make sure Forensics get here first thing in the morning.'

'What is it?' he called after me. 'What's wrong?'

I didn't answer him. I didn't have the time.

Chapter Twenty-Four

I took three wrong turns before I found Travis Close. Apparently even the satnav on my phone didn't know where to go. When I finally clocked the street sign, I didn't feel relief, however. The only emotion flooding my system was dread.

It wasn't a long road. I estimated there were only about thirty houses – and only one of them had lights on inside. There was a small car in the driveway and another parked directly outside. I pulled Tallulah up behind it and checked the number plate before radioing it through.

'I need ID on a car,' I said without preamble, relaying the number through to the switchboard.

It didn't take long. I'd barely unclipped my seatbelt and climbed out of the Mini to stride up to Baxter's front door when the answer came through. 'That vehicle is registered to a Vivienne Clarke,' the operator told me. 'Do you require her address?'

'No.' I grimaced. I knew where she was – and it wasn't at home tucked up in bed. 'Thank you.'

I marched to the door, leaving the crossbow I'd grabbed on my way out from the manse on Tallulah's worn backseat. It wouldn't do me any good here, not with two humans who needed a cool, calming touch. A weapon was far more likely to cause problems than solve them.

I wondered whether I should try to enter surreptitiously round the back, but I suspected that time was of the essence and that in the end it wouldn't matter how I got into Baxter's house. With that thought in mind, I rapped sharply on the door then twisted the doorknob and walked straight in.

'Police!' I yelled. 'Nobody move!'

I ran through to the living room. Television. Chair. Bookcase. Other than the furniture, it was empty. Then I heard a muffled shout from somewhere further inside. The kitchen – it had to be. I turned and darted towards the only other door.

Before I reached it, a voice called out. 'Don't come in, DC Bellamy! Don't come any closer!'

I kept my voice as gentle as I could. 'Mrs Clarke, whatever you're doing in there, I don't think it's a good idea.'

'Help me! Help me! Stop this woman!' No doubt that was Reverend Baxter.

I moved closer, hoping to peer through the tiny gap between the door and the jamb to see exactly what was going on. My priority was to calm things down and prevent Mrs Clarke from doing something she might regret. I prayed I had the wherewithal to manage it.

Unable to see anything more than flickering shadows, I carefully toed open the door. I didn't cross the threshold; I didn't want to alarm Mrs Clarke any more than I had to. It wasn't going to take much to provoke her into action and I needed to give her the space she needed to feel she was in control.

Her back was to me. I couldn't see Baxter's face, but I could tell he was seated on a kitchen chair in front of her. I licked my lips and spoke carefully. 'Mrs Clarke.'

'Go away. I told you not to come in here!' Her head swung round towards me. Her eyes were wild and her usually perfectly coiffed hair was unkempt and coming loose from its clips.

I held up my hands. 'I'm staying right here. I only want to talk to you.'

'This woman is crazy!' Baxter screeched. 'She's crazy! She—'

Mrs Clarke back-handed him. He yelped loudly then fell silent. Thank goodness for small mercies.

'Vivienne,' I said. 'I'm not coming in, not unless I have to. But I need you to move away from Reverend Baxter. We both know he's not going anywhere. Just take three steps back.'

Her body was stiff and rigid, but she wasn't so far gone that she didn't react to my command. She moved away, though only one step. For now, that would have to be enough.

I glanced at Baxter. He was tied to the chair with rope and he was bleeding in several places but, as far as I could tell, he wasn't in life-threatening danger.

I ignored his pleading eyes and focused on Mrs Clarke. I had to get through to her. 'This is because of what I said to you in the graveyard, isn't it?' I said softly.

She managed a tiny nod. 'I thought that Julian was the only one. I hadn't realised that more graves had been desecrated. I didn't known that St Erbin's had been targeted in that way.' She turned accusing eyes onto Baxter. 'You told us Julian should be buried in your church. You made us think that he would be looked after.'

'I had nothing to do with any of that,' Baxter blustered. 'I retired almost a year ago, remember! If you've got problems, you should talk to Knight. He's the one at fault here. Not me!'

'He's not the one who went out of his way to befriend us. He's not the one who manipulated Patrick and me into putting our poor son into that grave.' She stared at him. 'Was it you? Were you the one who ran him over?'

'Don't be ridiculous!' Baxter snapped. 'That was an accident. I don't know anything about your son's death beyond what you told me.'

'Tell him, DC Bellamy,' Vivienne Clarke said. 'Tell him what you found out.'

Perhaps a little self-awareness would help Reverend Reginald Baxter's cause. If he could show true contrition, Mrs Clarke might stand down. 'We have reason to believe,' I said carefully, 'that a man named Edward Nappey was responsible for the theft of Julian Clarke's body, not to mention several others. He was also the driver of the car that hit Julian and killed him.'

'Ted is not a violent person,' Baxter sneered. 'He wouldn't hurt a living being.' The old vicar glared smugly at us. He hadn't realised what he'd admitted to.

'Vivienne,' I said, alarmed. 'Wait—'

It was too late. She'd already rounded on him. 'You know him?' she whispered. 'You *know* this Nappey bastard?'

Baxter blinked as he realised his massive error. 'No,' he said. 'No. I made a mistake.'

'And here was me thinking that you knew what was going on at your church and didn't care,' Mrs Clarke said. 'It's worse than that though, isn't it? You *wanted* it to happen. You colluded with that man Nappey. You're a part of this as much as he is.'

Baxter's eyes narrowed. I'd thought he would continue with his denials but instead he threw caution to the wind. 'I don't know why you're getting so fucking upset,' he said in a low voice filled with irritation. 'You seem to forget all those hours I spent with you and your husband. You despised your son for what he did. You knew that by turning to the werewolves, he'd turned away from you. You hated everything he stood for. You can't backtrack on that simply because he's dead. You can tear your hair and gnash your teeth and wail all you like but, deep down, you're secretly thrilled that he's gone.'

Baxter had given me no choice and I stepped into the kitchen. 'I strongly advise you to keep your mouth shut from now on!' I turned to Mrs Clarke. 'Vivienne, you have to get out of here. I am ordering you to leave.'

She didn't glance at me. 'How dare you?' she breathed, her focus on Baxter. 'How dare you say such a thing to me?'

'Your son was an abomination,' Baxter said. 'You know it and I know it. So what if his body has gone? He never deserved to be buried there anyway. He—'

I saw the knife too late. Vivienne Clarke had probably been holding it all this time and I hadn't noticed it. With a loud war cry, she flung herself towards Baxter. Gritting my teeth, I threw myself between them. First her husband, now her.

'Enough!' I roared. I grabbed her wrist and wrenched hard. She dropped the knife almost instantly and it fell to the floor with a clatter.

'Why are you trying to stop me?' she shrieked. 'Why are you getting in my way? You know I've got nothing left now. Julian's gone. Patrick's gone. The least I can do is honour my son's memory by getting rid of the bastard who hurt him!'

'But,' came a calm, steady voice from the doorway, '*that* bastard isn't the one who hurt him.' Lukas, exuding calm strength, offered her a gentle smile. 'He is involved and he is culpable, but he's not the man who ran over your son. He's not the man who has your son's remains. He does, however, know where we can find them. Let DC Bellamy do her job. Your revenge is coming but, for now, you have to stand down.'

I occasionally had the power to command weaker supes using only my voice but that was nothing compared to the power that Lukas could exert. I knew he was deliberately twisting Vivienne Clarke's emotions to try and stop her harming Baxter, but his words were powerful enough to stop me in my tracks. Even Baxter seemed to relax.

'I want to kill him,' Mrs Clarke said, her features strained and her voice pleading. 'I want to reach inside and rip out his guts. I want to see him suffer.'

Lukas reached for her hands. 'I know. You're not the only one who feels that way. But your husband isn't gone. He needs you out here, still fighting for him. And we need Reverend Baxter to tell us where we can find Julian.'

'You *will* find him?' she asked.

'Detective Constable Bellamy will. I know she will.' Lukas's black eyes flitted to mine. 'There's no-one more capable, I can promise you that.'

Mrs Clarke nodded. She allowed Lukas to tug gently on her hands and lead her out to the waiting vampires in the hallway.

I breathed out. That had been close.

'That's Lord Horvath,' Baxter said.

'Yep. Where is Edward Nappey, Reverend?'

'Lord Horvath is a vampire.'

'Yep.' I gave him a hard look. 'Tell me where Ted is.'

Baxter's face started to suffuse with red. He struggled against his rope bonds.

'I will let you go,' I told him, 'but I need to know where I can find Ted. This will go easier on you if you tell me.'

Baxter didn't seem to hear me. 'A vampire in my house!' he yelled. 'How dare a vampire come into my house?'

'Mr Baxter,' I started.

'It's Reverend!' His voice was growing high pitched and whiny, increasing in decibels with every word. 'Just because I've retired doesn't mean that I'm not still Reverend!'

'Reverend Baxter, then.' I gave him a long look. 'You need to calm down.'

'A man's home is his castle! I can't have a vampire in here. I can't! He has to get out! *He has to get out!*' he all but screamed.

Baxter wasn't just red now; his skin had turned a distressing shade of purple. He started to choke and his fingers gripped the arms of the chair. Uh-oh. This didn't look good. His breath was coming in short, sharp gasps, and beads of sweat were breaking out all over his face. Either he was having a panic attack or a heart attack. Unfortunately, I suspected the latter.

I bounded over to him and scrabbled at the rope, untying him as quickly as I could. 'Lukas!' I shouted, as I lay Baxter on the floor. 'Call 999!'

'What is it?' he reappeared in the doorway. His expression contorted when he saw Baxter. 'Shit.'

Baxter moaned. 'I need you to stay calm,' I told him. 'Do you have any aspirin in the house?'

'Hurts,' he gasped. 'Hurts.' Then his eyes rolled back into his head and he stopped breathing.

I worked fast. Moving his arms out of the way, I knelt by his side and ensured his airway was clear. 'Reverend?' I tilted his head. 'Baxter?'

Nothing. Damn it. I linked my fingers together and started chest compressions. Baxter remained unresponsive. After a minute or two, Lukas took over.

'Tell me,' I grunted, 'that you have some magical vampire trick to help him.'

Lukas didn't look up. 'I've got nothing.'

My stomach clenched. We needed him; we needed Baxter in order to find Ted Nappey. I gripped my hands into tight fists as one of the other vamps called out, 'Paramedics are here.'

I exhaled. Praise be.

Chapter Twenty-Five

Lukas and I stood outside Reginald Baxter's house as the swirling blue lights of the ambulance disappeared around the corner and away from Travis Close. The old reverend's neighbours had switched on their lights, disturbed from their sleep by the commotion. Several were standing on their doorsteps and watching. Some looked anxious, but others were more stoic. I suspected that not everyone here liked Baxter very much.

At least I'd managed to get Vivienne Clarke removed to the nearest police station to cool off. Unlike her husband, she'd probably get off with a caution. I'd do my best to argue her case with the powers-that-be. That didn't alter the hopelessness of our search for Nappey, however.

'Fuck it,' I muttered. I shook my head in frustration. '*Fuck* it.'

Lukas reached for my hand and squeezed it. The touch of his skin on mine burnt into me. 'Are you okay?' he asked.

'I'm pissed off,' I told him. Very pissed off. 'But, yes.' I gritted my teeth. 'I'm okay.'

'Good.' He continued to watch me. 'I'm glad that you sent word to me about coming here. I appreciate that you're keeping me involved, even if you do have doubts about my intentions.'

'Sometimes I think *I* shouldn't be here,' I said. 'I've barely been a detective for five minutes, and I know next to nothing about supes.' I stared down the empty road. 'I feel like I'm making this up as I go along.'

'You're not giving yourself enough credit. You couldn't have known that Baxter would keel over like that. What happened to him isn't your fault. Besides, we all suffer from imposter syndrome sometimes.'

I let out a sharp bark of laughter. 'You don't.'

Lukas didn't smile. 'Of course I do.'

We stared at each other. I had the sudden sense that I was standing on the edge of a precipice, about to jump off into a deep, dark chasm. Except I wasn't scared of it. Not in the slightest. And I wasn't alone, either.

'Emma...'

A hooded vampire jogged up to us. 'Lord Horvath,' he said, bowing slightly. 'There is a vehicle approaching.'

We both stiffened. A second later, a pair of headlights appeared, moving closer towards us. It was only when the car stopped that I recognised it.

'What's happened?' Fred called, jumping out from the driver's side.

I frowned at him. 'You've been drinking. You shouldn't have been driving.'

He waved at me dismissively. 'I only had a couple of beers and that was hours ago.'

It had sounded like he'd had a hell of a lot more than a couple of beers when I'd spoken to him on the phone. Then he drew closer and I realised there was something on his neck. My eyes narrowed. A faint bruise? No. Two bruises. 'Where's Scarlett?'

She stepped out from the passenger seat, an easy smile on her lipsticked mouth. 'I'm here.'

I looked from Fred to Scarlett and back again. Lukas, who was still holding my hand, gently increased the pressure. His thumb stroked my palm and I pulled my hand away.

'Have you found him?' Fred asked eagerly, hope shining from his face. 'Have you found Ted Nappey?'

'No.' I shook my head. 'All we've found is another piece of the puzzle.'

Deflated, his shoulders dropped. 'Reginald Baxter?'

'Yes.'

Fred reached into the car for a piece of paper. 'Baxter requested access to the Arcane Works room at the Carlyle Library several times. As the resident vicar at St Erbin's, he was allowed in on every occasion.'

'Did he ask for any particular titles?' I asked.

'Unfortunately not,' Fred said. 'But the last time he gained entry to Arcane Works was four years ago.' He paused. 'I believe it was about three weeks before the first body at St Erbin's was stolen.'

Hmm. I doubted that was a coincidence. Then I remembered I'd seen a bookshelf in Baxter's living room. 'Hold that thought,' I said grimly. I ran back inside the house and made a beeline for the books.

Baxter had expensive tastes. Almost every volume was heavy and leather bound – there wasn't a single tatty paperback in sight. All the titles seemed to have religious overtones, apart from the odd one that related to the supernatural.

'I've got some of these books myself,' Lukas said softly at my shoulder.

I jumped, unaware that he'd come up behind me.

'You know,' he continued, 'Fred isn't a child. He must make his own decisions. Scarlett wouldn't have forced him to do anything he didn't want to.'

I didn't answer. Instead, I gave a small triumphant crow. 'Here,' I said. I crouched down and slid out a book with a gold-embossed cover and held it up. '*Infernal Enchantments.*' I opened the front page and gazed at the stamp. '*Property of the Carlyle Library.* It appears the good reverend isn't above petty theft when it suits his purposes.'

Lukas's expression darkened. 'I wonder if he approached Ted Nappey, or if it was the other way around,' he mused. 'Maybe Baxter manipulated Nappey for his own purposes.'

'Maybe,' I said. 'But even if he did, I suspect it's been a while since Ted was under Baxter's control.'

I stood up. 'I'm going to take this. We should search the rest of the house. There might be other clues as to where Ted Nappey is.' I doubted it – I was sure by now that Nappey had struck out on his own – but we couldn't afford to leave any stone unturned. The longer it took for us to locate him, the longer he had to plan his next move. I was certain he would still be looking for a vampire to kidnap.

'The vamps here with me are good,' Lukas told me. 'I'll get them onto it.'

I nodded distractedly.

'I was speaking to the next-door neighbours,' Fred said, appearing in the doorway and waving his hands excitedly. 'They didn't know Baxter well, and they don't think he has any family in the area. But they did say that until recently he received regular visits from a younger man. The reason they remember them so well is because they had to complain on several occasions when the visitor parked across their driveway and blocked them in.'

I stiffened. 'Can they describe the man?'

'Shaved head. Cold eyes.' Fred looked at me. 'It's Nappey. It has to be.'

'Was he driving a blue Ford Escort?'

'No.' He beamed. 'A white van. They never got a number plate and they didn't notice any markings on the side, but we did think Nappey might have another mode of transport. If he has a van, he might be sleeping in it.'

My shoulders sank. 'There must be thousands of unmarked white vans in London.'

'At least it's something.' Fred's hand went absently to the bruises on his neck and he rubbed them gently.

I looked away. 'Yeah.' It wasn't much. I sighed. Then another thought struck me. 'Did you see a phone?' I asked Lukas. 'Does Reginald Baxter have a mobile phone?'

A glimmer of optimism suddenly lit his face. 'There must be one.'

I straightened my back and addressed the room. 'We need to find Baxter's phone. Search this place from top to bottom.'

Everyone sprang into action; even Lukas's small assembly of vamps did as I asked without requiring further instruction from their lord and master. When there was a triumphant shout from upstairs, I knew one of them had hit pay dirt.

'Got it!' A blond vampire thundered down the stairs waving a phone. 'It was on charge in the bedroom.' He handed it to Lukas. Without a word, Lukas handed it to me.

I held my breath, thumbing the screen and praying that it wasn't password protected. When it immediately lit up and Baxter's apps flooded the screen, I exhaled with relief. I ignored most of the icons and went straight to the text messages. There had to be something here. There *had* to be.

I skipped past the texts from Reverend Baxter's bank and a couple from another vicar enquiring about his golf handicap. There was one message from an unknown number. I showed it to Lukas before I opened it up then we leant in close to read it.

New number. Had to lose old phone. If you need me,

reach me here. T.

'He's a man of few words,' Lukas muttered.

'And,' I added, 'he's not mentioned anything about the police or having to run. I reckon he doesn't trust Baxter with that information. Just like Maggie Tomkinson, Baxter was convinced that Nappey isn't violent. That might have been the case once, but it's certainly no longer true. Ted Nappey has told Baxter some of what he's up to, but not all of it.' I could feel my heart thudding with anticipation. 'It doesn't matter. With this phone and this number, we have what we need to draw Ted to us.'

'How do we play it?' Lukas asked..

'Softly, softly,' I said. 'Clear the street outside. Make sure all those nosy neighbours go inside their houses.'

Lukas clicked his fingers and half a dozen vamps left the room. I gave him a look and he shrugged. 'What? They do as they're told.' And then some.

'We know that the one thing Ted Nappey wants is a vampire, so all we have to do is give him one.' I mulled it over. 'Baxter was outraged at your presence in his home. We need to follow that theme.'

'Nappey might not have told him that he wants vampire blood,' Lukas warned.

'It doesn't matter. This is more about what we *don't* say than what we do.' I sat down on a chair and read through some of Baxter's other texts. I wanted to get the tone right. From what I could tell, the vicar used full punctuation, formal phrasing and self-righteous sentiment. Perfect.

'It's the middle of the night,' Fred said. 'Nappey might not see it until morning.'

'I can live with that,' I told him. I pointed at my gut. 'But something in here tells me our Ted is wide awake.' I licked my lips and started to compose my text.

What have you done? Thirty minutes ago, a vampire knocked on my door and forced me out of bed. He was asking about you. Why are these disgusting creatures coming to my home? What have you done to bring them to my place of sanctity?

I showed it to Lukas. 'Swap "disgusting" for "heathen",' he said.

I altered the sentence and nodded. 'It fits.'

I held the phone up for Fred to see and he grinned. 'We're going to get this bastard,' he said. 'He'll fall right into our laps.'

I crossed my fingers. 'Let's hope so,' I murmured. Then I pressed send.

We all stared at the phone, as if expecting an immediate response. Nothing happened. Fred expelled a whoosh of air. 'Well,' he said, 'that was an anti-climax. What do we do now?'

'We wait,' I said grimly.

One minute went by, then two. Lukas strode to the window and stared out at the darkness. I gazed at the copy of *Infernal Enchantments* lying on the table next to me, my fingers itching to turn to the section about the phoenix. I forced myself to look away. I could worry about me later; right now I had to worry about Edward Nappey. Answer, you bastard.

Scarlett strolled into the small living room and made a beeline for Fred. She reached up and started toying with the brown curls at the nape of his neck. My eyes narrowed and I opened my mouth to say something but, before I could, the phone dinged.

Lukas was by my side again in a second. I held the phone up so everyone could see.

What did you tell them?

Tense now, I glanced round me.

'Baxter would be furious,' Lukas said. 'How dare a

vampire darken his door at this hour of night?'

I started to tap out an answer. *What do you think I told him? How dare he come to my home? I am not going to be intimidated by one of those things!*

I sent it. The response came back faster this time. *Has he gone?*

I licked my lips.

Yes, I texted. *Although the vile creature said he would be back.*

Lukas raised an eyebrow. 'Vile creature?'

I was too nervous to grin. The phone chimed again. *I'm on my way.*

I placed Baxter's phone carefully on the table next to me, then I cleared my throat. 'We need to move the cars so they're out of sight, turn out most of the lights and get ready.' I finally managed a smile. 'Ted Nappey is coming.'

Chapter Twenty-Six

None of us had any idea how long it would take Nappey to get to Baxter's house. Presumably he was still in London, but this was a sprawling city. Even though the late hour meant that the streets would be free of traffic jams, he could be miles and miles away – or he could be around the corner. Either way, we had to make our preparations quickly.

Within five minutes, Travis Close looked exactly like it had when I'd driven here a couple of hours earlier. I'd moved Tallulah round the corner, out of sight of the house, and the vampires had done the same with their own vehicles. The only sound outside was the occasional hooting of a distant owl. To maintain a semblance of normality, and to avoid alerting Nappey, the thin curtains in the living room were drawn and only a single lamp remained lit.

Inside Baxter's house, the crowd of vampires, together with Fred and I, waited silently. In an ideal world, we'd have had people at strategic locations outside but this wasn't an ideal world and there was no cover or handy bushes to hide behind. Neither could we risk the neighbours growing anxious and inadvertently giving the game away.

'I know we're all here for the same reason,' I said quietly to Lukas, 'but this remains my investigation. No matter what he's done, Edward Nappey is human. You can't hurt him unless it's genuinely in self-defence, or it's to stop him getting away. And *I* have to take him into custody.'

'You worry too much, D'Artagnan.' Lukas's sense of humour had returned now that our quarry was near. 'I know you're in charge. You can be assured that neither I nor my vampires will impede the correct way of doing things.'

'I appreciate that.'

His black eyes glittered in the dim light. 'Once all this is over,' he said, 'perhaps we should take the time to get to know each other better so we can avoid further misunderstandings. Our last meal was curtailed because of our expedition to Nappey's house. We should try again. It would be a good opportunity to iron out any issues between Supe Squad and my vampires, and to air any grievances.'

He didn't look at Scarlett or Fred, who were standing together in the hallway. He didn't need to. 'I know an excellent Thai place not too far away from both our homes. Or,' he paused, 'you could come to me and I'll cook. It might surprise you to learn that I know some excellent vegetarian recipes. And my wine list is extensive.'

'You're being charming again,' I whispered.

'I can't help it,' Lukas ran his tongue over his lips. 'As I already said, I want to charm you. If that bothers you, you'll simply have to get over it.'

'It doesn't bother me.'

He smiled. 'Good. Let me be crystal clear, so that there are no illusions between us. It's not D'Artagnan the detective I want.' He dipped his head. 'It's Emma Bellamy the woman who truly interests me.'

My mouth was dry as my gaze flickered over his face. I wasn't good at any of this. Professional relationships were one thing but personal relationships were entirely different. And goodness knows, I had an appalling track record on that front. 'There's something I should tell you.'

Something about the note in my voice must have alerted him because he stilled. 'Go on.'

'The book,' I said. '*Infernal Enchantments*. When we were in the Carlyle Library, I flicked through to one of the later sections. There's information there about a supernatural species which—'

'Everything's ready, my Lord,' Scarlett interrupted. 'Four in the back garden. Three upstairs. Two in the hallway. The rest of us are here. Whichever way he approaches, we'll be ready for him.'

Lukas's expression darkened ominously. 'We are in the middle of a conversation here, Scarlett,' he bit out, every word laced with sharp, tempered steel.

She blinked and paled before glancing at me. 'I'm so sorry.' Her head and shoulders dropped. 'I didn't mean to interrupt. Are you talking about Devereau Webb?' Her eyes widened as she realised her mistake one question too late. 'Shit. Sorry, I…'

'Scarlett,' Lukas snapped. 'Fuck off.'

She whirled away as fast as her feet could carry her.

'Devereau Webb?' I asked. 'Why would we be discussing him?'

'Forget about it.'

I took a step back, suddenly wanting to put some distance between us. 'Actually,' I said slowly, 'I don't think I will. Why are you suddenly interested in Webb?'

A muscle jerked in Lukas's cheek. 'I was curious after what you told me about him. That curiosity was piqued when he visited all four clan alphas.' He nodded towards me. 'At the same time as you.'

'How do you know about that?'

'I told you before, D'Artagnan, I have my sources like you do. It's always a good idea to keep tabs on the wolves.' Lukas paused, his fists curling. 'After all, one never knows when they might decide to do something foolish, like trying to murder a Supe Squad detective in broad daylight.'

'I fixed that. As you know.'

'It doesn't matter.' His black eyes flashed. 'They stepped over the line.'

I folded my arms. 'That still doesn't explain why you're interested in Devereau Webb.' I had the distinct feeling there was more to this than he was telling me. This wasn't simply about what Lady Sullivan had tried to do.

'Another time.' He lifted his eyebrows. 'You were about to tell me about something you read in the book.'

I pointed to *Infernal Enchantments*. 'It's right there,' I said. 'You can read it for yourself.'

'Emma.' Lukas didn't take his gaze from mine. 'A moment ago we were having a lot more fun.'

'Yes,' I said sadly. 'We were.'

He continued to watch me. 'What happens between you and me has nothing to do with what happens between the clans and me. They are two separate issues.'

Mmm.

'Van,' the vampire by the front window called out. 'Approaching now.'

'We'll talk about this later,' I muttered and turned to the window. I couldn't see much through the curtains but the van's headlights were clear. Nobody moved a muscle but the atmosphere in the room altered considerably. The van pulled up directly outside Baxter's driveway. This was no late-night shift worker returning home. This was Edward Nappey. It had to be.

'Remember,' I cautioned, 'he's not to be hurt. He's to be taken into custody. Wait until he's away from the vehicle. Once he reaches the front door, I'll arrest him.'

The headlights were turned off and the juddering sound of the engine faded out. I held my breath, listening as the van door opened. Moving quietly, I stepped into the hallway until I was less than a foot from the front door. It was surprisingly reassuring to have so many vampires at my back. Come on, Ted. I smiled humourlessly. Your time is finally up.

Then there was another sound and I frowned. What was that? A second later there were voices. I froze. Was he not alone? Did Ted Nappey have an accomplice?

'What's going on?' I hissed.

'Neighbour,' called out one of the vamps who was positioned by a window. 'One of the neighbours has come out of their house.'

Lukas was already moving towards me, ready to yank open the door and go after Nappey. I shook my head urgently. 'No. Not while he has the opportunity to grab a hostage.'

Lukas's mouth twisted, but he held back.

I raised my chin. 'Can anyone hear what they're saying?'

There were various head shakes. Damn it.

'He's walking away,' the same vamp called quietly. 'The neighbour is still there, but Nappey is walking away. He's heading this way.'

I raised my eyes heavenward. Thank fuck for that. I straightened my shoulders and reached for the door handle. On a count of five. One. Two.

'Shit! He's gone for the van!'

I stiffened. 'What?'

A half second later, I heard the engine fire up. No, no, no, no, no. I yanked open the door and sprinted out, just in time to see the van wheels spin.

From the house opposite, a middle-aged man with a smug look on his face started to shout, 'That'll teach you to kick my dog! You and your vicar mate are screwed now! The vampires are here to get you!'

Unbelievable. I cursed. And then I ran.

Vampires piled out of the house after me. I didn't look back but I could tell they were going for Nappey's van, which was reversing to escape from Baxter's cul-de-sac. I didn't bother with that. I'd be delighted if they managed to stop the vehicle, but I took the longer view and pelted towards where Tallulah was parked out of sight.

There were shouts and yells from behind me and more than one pained scream. Then, as I reached Tallulah's door, the white van streaked past me and careened around the corner.

I jumped in and started the engine. Fortunately, Tallulah had decided that this wasn't the time to stall or grumble. I released the handbrake as the passenger door opened and Scarlett leapt in. I barely glanced at her, I was too busy flooring the accelerator.

Fumbling with one hand, I grabbed my police radio. 'In pursuit of subject. Male. White van.' I squinted through the darkness. I couldn't read his damned number plate; he was already too far away. 'Left from Travis Close. Back-up requested immediately.'

The radio crackled in response. 'No units are in your area but I'll dispatch several now.'

'Suspect may well be armed and dangerous,' I said. 'Noted.'

We veered round the next corner. The tail lights of Nappey's van pulled further away into the distance. I changed gears and gritted my teeth. Come on, Tallulah. Don't fail me now.

Scarlett clipped in her seatbelt and hung on for dear life. 'Get him,' she snarled. 'Get the bastard.'

My fingers tightened round the steering wheel. 'Why

did you come with me? Why not stay with your buddies?' I asked, zipping through the red lights at the crossroads and thanking my lucky stars that the roads were still deathly quiet. 'Or Fred?'

'Fred is a sweet boy. He has also served his usefulness. You seem to know what you're doing,' Scarlett replied, with considerably more calm than I felt. 'If anyone's going to run this fucker down, you are.' She paused as we screeched round to the right. 'And my Lord needs you safe. Anything I can do to help achieve that is a mark in my favour.'

I didn't have time to respond. The van was turning again. I followed it, Tallulah taking the corner at such speed that we were now only metres behind Nappey. I reached for the radio again, spitting out our latest position.

'Back-up is half a mile away,' the operator replied.

I exhaled. He wasn't getting away. I wouldn't let him.

We sped past a prowling cat who paused to stare after us. I narrowly avoided hitting a small baker's van that was parking in a loading bay at the side of the road. The driver banged on his horn, the long loud beep echoing down the empty street. The white van accelerated and started to pull away from us yet again.

A moment later, there were loud sirens and a police car pulled out of the next side street, taking up position between Nappey and me. The cavalry was here.

Nappey ignored both of us. He sped through the next set of lights and so did the cop car. I followed, only to be forced to slam on the brakes as a lorry came out of nowhere. Scarlett and I were thrown forward while the lorry driver gesticulated at us. Only the seatbelts saved us from being flung through Tallulah's windscreen.

I re-started the engine. The van and the police car had

disappeared. 'Shit,' I muttered.

'Turn left,' Scarlett urged.

'You sure?'

She shook her head. 'No.'

I tensed but did as she said, then I caught the flicker of blue lights barely visible on a distant street. There. They were there. I floored the accelerator yet again.

Tallulah screeched as we turned right. The shops and houses around us were giving way to warehouses. 'The river's right ahead,' Scarlett said. 'He's running out of places to hide.'

I managed a nod. We were catching up to him. Then there was an almighty crash and the sound of metal twisting and breaking. With my heart in my mouth, I rounded another corner. The van had rammed into the side of the police car and both vehicles had stopped in the middle of the road. The Thames lay ahead. There was nothing else visible in either direction except empty roads.

I pressed hard on the brakes. While Scarlett leapt out, I muttered an update into the radio. A second later, hauling the crossbow from the backseat where I'd left it earlier, I followed her.

The van's engine revved. Scarlett had already reached its rear doors and was trying to yank them open. I sprinted towards her, glancing into the police car as I passed. A flicker of recognition slowed my steps. The driver was the young police officer who'd asked about joining Supe Squad. His forehead had smacked against the windshield and a dribble of blood ran from his temple down to his cheek. He turned to me, blinking rapidly, his face twisted in pain.

Scarlett grunted and the van doors swung open, just as Nappey managed to get the van moving again and pull away. I put on a final spurt of energy and threw myself into the back of the van after the vampire.

I dropped the crossbow as I scrabbled for purchase to avoid falling out with the various boxes that were tumbling onto the road behind us. Scarlett had no such trouble. She was already locking her arms around Nappey.

The van jerked to a halt once again, while Scarlett flung herself forward to sink her teeth into Nappey's neck. I fell, planting myself face first against the cold metal floor of the van. I jumped up again – but it wasn't quickly enough.

Scarlett let out a small squeak, her eyes wide. She turned to face me, blood streaming from her mouth. At first I thought it was Nappey's blood, then I realised it was hers and that at least one of her fangs had snapped in half. Not only that, a syringe was sticking out of her neck. Her eyes rolled back into her head and her knees gave way.

Nappey heaved himself out of his seat and squeezed through the gap to join us. He didn't look upset; if anything, he looked rather pleased with himself. He glanced down at Scarlett's body and nodded. 'It's been so hard getting hold of a vampire,' he murmured. 'Finally.' He held his hands up as if thanking the gods. 'Finally!'

I snarled and Nappey's eyes snapped to mine. 'You,' he said. 'I remember you. You were with the other one, at the garage.' He tilted his head. 'But you're not a vamp.'

'Edward Nappey,' I said aloud. 'You are under arrest for the murder of a vampire and for the desecration of several werewolf graves.'

'Ohhh,' he nodded. 'So you're the police.' He pulled his hooded top away from his neck, revealing a metal cuff around his throat. On the CCTV footage from Moira's death it had looked like a tattoo, but I couldn't have been more wrong. No wonder Moira and Scarlett hadn't managed to bring him down with their bites – he was wearing his own bizarre vamp-protection gear.

'You do not have to say anything,' I continued, ignoring the lurch in my stomach, 'but it may harm your defence if you do not mention something which you later rely on in court.'

Nappey rubbed a hand over his shaved head. 'I guess you've got me bang to rights,' he said softly. 'Unless I can pull something out from my sleeve.' He reached under his right cuff and slid out a long knife. 'Well,' he purred. 'Look at that. I guess I do have something, after all.'

As his gaze flicked to a point over my shoulder, I glanced down. My crossbow was caught under Scarlett's body. If I could just get to it…

'Drop the weapon,' said a male voice.

I didn't need to turn to know that the policeman from the car was behind me. 'Stay back,' I warned him. 'I've got this.'

There was a thump as he climbed into the van. 'Drop the knife, sir,' he ordered. 'You're not going anywhere. More police officers are on their way.'

'I make it a rule not to harm humans,' Nappey said. 'We're special, you see.' His tone was earnest. 'Why should supes get all the power?'

'Ted—' I said.

He started to advance, brandishing the blade. 'However, I'm prepared to make an exception if I have to.' There was a crazed glint in his eyes. Suddenly I knew that if Ted Nappey had ever been going to listen to reason, that moment had long since passed.

'I've spent too long on this,' he went on. 'Too many years getting to this point. Both of you need to leave now if you want to get out of here alive.'

'You don't really think the elixir you're making will

work, do you?' I asked.

Nappey's cold eyes snapped to mine. 'How do you know about the elixir? Did Baxter tell you?' He stared at me, trying to fathom it out, then he shook himself. 'It doesn't matter. The old man never believed in it anyway, but now I have the vampire it will work. You just won't be around to see it.'

He leapt towards me with the knife held high. Like a martyr, the foolish policeman behind me rushed forward to meet him. I cursed. He was going to get himself killed. I muttered under my breath in irritation and, like a fool of another kind, blocked his approach as Nappey lunged.

Nappey side-swiped with the knife, slashing through my blouse and drawing a long bead of blood across my torso. The policeman drew his Taser, raised it and pulled the trigger. It missed Nappey by a good inch.

I stepped back, using my elbows to shove the policeman out of the van before Nappey could do him any real damage. As I did so, Nappey came at me again. This time, his blade found its mark, sinking into my chest with surprising ease.

I gasped, already feeling my life ebb away. 'Back-up is coming,' I croaked. 'Delay any longer and you're fucked.'

Nappey leaned into my face, a cloud of his stale breath adding insult to injury. 'Not as fucked as you are,' he said. He grabbed the knife by the hilt and pulled it out. Blood gushed forth.

I looked down. Strange. I could no longer feel any pain. I stumbled forward, knowing that I couldn't allow Nappey to throw out my dying body. There was no sign on Lukas and the other vamps, and no sign of any more police thundering to the rescue. I had to rely on my own bizarre powers.

I reached for the back of the passenger seat and

curled my hand round it. My foot caught on Scarlett's leg and I collapsed. I dimly heard the policeman shouting and other sirens cutting through the air.

Nappey muttered something and pushed past me, yanking the van doors closed. As my vision gave way to blackness, he returned to the front seat, standing on my body as he shoved his way past. Then the engine started and I felt the van shudder beneath me.

And then there was nothing.

Chapter Twenty-Seven

The familiar smell of sulphur was comforting, despite its eye-watering strength, but when I opened my eyes it wasn't Dr Laura Hawes' friendly gaze that greeted me. Neither was I in the morgue at the Fitzwilliam Manor Hospital.

I was more disorientated than usual, and initially I couldn't work out where I was. It was very dark, and several sharp, pointy objects seemed to be poking into my spine. The only good thing I could work out was that Ted hadn't decided to dispose of my body in an unpleasant manner. Apparently he'd decided that my corpse was low down his list of priorities. He would come to regret that decision.

As I got to my feet, I banged my head on the low roof. Still unable to see anything, I scrunched up my face and stretched out my arms. My fingertips scraped against cold metal. Ah-ha – I was still in his van. He'd left me where I'd died.

Now I had to cross my fingers and hope he hadn't abandoned the vehicle in barren, isolated scrubland. I needed some means to communicate and some clothes to wear. There wasn't any daylight coming in through the van windows, so I took that as a sign that the van had been left in a garage.

I felt around with my fingertips, searching for something to wrap round myself. Short of pulling a cardboard box over my head, there was nothing useful. Hey ho; worse things had happened.

On the plus side, although my clothes might have burned to cinders during my resurrection and there were no handy replacements in the van, I did find my crossbow. It was illegal to use it against a human, but desperate times called for desperate measures.

There was no sign of Scarlett. I knew it was twelve hours since Edward Nappey had slammed his knife into my heart, so that put the time at around four in the afternoon. Anything could have happened to her in the intervening hours.

I couldn't waste further time worrying about my state of undress or legal technicalities. I had to find Nappey and Scarlett and put a stop to whatever he was planning. It was all down to me.

I picked my way blindly to the back of the van and felt for the door handle. Relief flooded through me when my fingers curled round it and I tugged it down. I hopped out and planted my bare feet onto hard concrete. Definitely a garage, I decided.

I searched for an exit. I finally located a door with a push-button lock next to a particularly odorous wheelie bin. I pressed my ear against it for a few moments then, when I didn't hear any sounds from the other side, I twisted the handle. Locked. Well, that sucked. The door frame looked like it was in good nick, too; it wasn't rotting like the one in Reverend Knight's basement.

I jumped up and down on my toes a few times. I felt good. I felt *strong*. I shrugged then raised one leg experimentally – there was no harm in trying. A moment later my foot smashed against the door with all the power that I could muster. To my shock, there was a loud crack and the lock broke. Blimey. I flexed my leg in amazement. I really was getting stronger every time I died.

It occurred to me that if Nappey were nearby, he'd

have heard me. I quickly moved back in case he suddenly appeared. I was quite disappointed when he didn't.

More confident now, I peeked round the broken door. There was an immaculate beige carpet leading down a sun-filled hallway; it looked like the door linked the garage into someone's house. I could hear the thump of dance music. Ah-ha. So that was why he'd not come to investigate the noise. I stepped out. Ideally, the first thing I'd come across would be a telephone.

The room to my right was a small but tidy bedroom. I glanced inside at the smooth white duvet and plumped-up pillows. It was a far cry from Nappey's place. I took in the hairbrush on the bedside table and the lace-trimmed curtains. A woman's room, I realised. For a moment, I wondered whether Nappey had managed to make his way to his mother's without anyone realising. Then my gaze fell on the hospital scrubs hanging over the radiator. Shit. Maggie Tomkinson, Nappey's ex-girlfriend, was a nurse. My blood chilled.

Cursing silently for not checking on her again, I darted over, grabbed the blue scrubs and pulled them on. The beat-heavy music continued to throb, causing the walls to gently reverberate. I glanced out of the window and noted the quiet, leafy street outside and the other bungalows. There wasn't a living soul to be seen.

Go to a house nearby for help or continue alone? I considered it for only seconds. My death and subsequent resurrection were still fuelling my adrenaline and I wanted to see the look on Nappey's face when I rose up in front of him. Confronting him alone wasn't the smartest decision, but I wouldn't give him even the slimmest opportunity to escape again.

I left the bedroom and checked the room opposite. An empty bathroom. The smudged, bloody palm print on the edge of the bathtub gave me pause, and my grip on the crossbow tightened. If I'd had any doubt before that Ted Nappey was here, it had disappeared. Steeling myself for what was to come, I moved forward.

The living room was as still and silent as the rooms behind. That left only the kitchen ahead. The door was slightly ajar and I glimpsed the edge of patterned linoleum on the floor, as well as a flickering shadow. The music was coming from in there.

I edged as far forward as I dared. I wanted to be sure of the lay of the land before I proceeded. Holding my breath, I squinted through the narrow gap. There, with his back turned to me and his hips jiggling in time to the music, was the unmistakable figure of Edward Nappey. The bizarre ring of steel round his neck glinted in the afternoon sunlight that streamed in from the window. Scarlett was slumped at one side of the small wooden table in the corner. At the other side was a gagged and bound Maggie Tomkinson. My fingers twitched.

I angled my head to look round more of the room. At first it was difficult to tell what Nappey was doing. When he turned to address Maggie, however, and I spotted the glass bottles and schoolroom chemistry set, I realised that was he putting the finishing touches to his elixir. I gritted my teeth. All this for some daft concoction that was never going to work anyway.

Nappey's lips moved as he said something to Maggie. Her eyes were dazed. He frowned, then turned to the small radio and turned down the sound so she could hear him.

'You never did have much taste in music, Mags,' he said. 'Don't worry, though. Now that I've completed the elixir, you'll have plenty of time to learn to appreciate the merits of a good drum beat.' He grinned. He was very, very pleased with himself. I barely repressed a shudder.

'It's taken me so long to get to this point. It's harder

than you think to distil a liquid from werewolf bones. If you don't catch the corpse at exactly the right time, you miss your opportunity. It was harder than I thought it would be. Now that I've got the vampire blood I need to enhance the liquid, all that effort will be worth it – I promise you that.'

He beamed. 'In fact, it will be more than worth it. Just think of all the time you've spent in that grubby hospital hooking people up to IVs and pumping them full of drugs when one sip of this little darling and they'll be right as rain.'

He swung round proudly, holding up a narrow-necked flask. My eyes narrowed as I gazed at the murky red liquid it contained, and at the shark's tooth necklace hanging below his steel neck collar.

Maggie raised her head and stared dully at the elixir.

'No more cancer, Mags,' Nappey breathed. 'No more strokes. No more feeling inferior to supes and their disgusting ways. This,' he waved the flask, 'is the future. And I've created it. They'll be singing my name in the streets for decades to come.'

The man certainly had a god complex. I wrinkled my nose.

Maggie's eyes flicked towards me and she jerked in recognition. I shook my head urgently. Not yet. Don't give the game away yet. Fortunately, her ex-boyfriend was too enamoured of his supposed brilliance to notice.

'I'll drink it first,' he said. 'I'd give you some but I think you'd spit it out. You don't see what I've done yet but the book is right. What I've done will change everything. This little beauty here is how we reclaim our country.'

His lip curled in Scarlett's direction. 'It's a shame she's not awake to see it. Her blood has done what all the boiled wolf bones couldn't.'

Nausea rose up from my stomach. Enough already: I didn't need to hear any more. I stepped back, staying on the balls of my feet so that Nappey didn't hear me, then I raised the crossbow. I threw Maggie a meaningful look. From the slight tilt of her head, she understood perfectly.

I squinted and took aim. All he had to do was move slightly to the left. I held my breath, waiting – and then he shifted. A heartbeat later, the silver-tipped bolt left the crossbow and whistled through the air.

Maggie ducked and covered her head with her hands as the bolt smashed into the flask. The glass smashed, flying out in all directions, along with spatters of the disgusting liquid. For a second Nappey didn't move, too stunned by the destruction of what he'd achieved to react. Then he howled, a sound of anguished agony.

'No! No!' He whipped round and finally caught sight of me beyond the door. His mouth dropped open and he stuttered, 'You. But you're dead. What? How? I don't—'

I kicked the door open and calmly reloaded the crossbow. This time, I pointed it at his head. 'Get down onto the floor. Face down.' My voice hardened. 'Or I'll shoot.' It would have been nice if he'd done as I ordered, but it was never going to be that easy.

Nappey jumped to the side and grabbed a knife, the same one he'd been brandishing earlier. It was now stained with blood, which no doubt belonged to Scarlett. He might be psychotic but he was no fool. Rather than attacking me, he reached for Maggie and hauled her up by her hair.

 He held the knife to her throat. 'I'll kill her!' he yelled. 'Don't think I won't! Every great action needs a sacrifice. If that's to be Mags, so be it.' He pressed the blade into her skin. 'If you want her to live, you need to back off out of here. Now.'

'Drop the knife, Mr Nappey. You're not getting

away. Not now.'

'No fucking chance,' he snarled. 'I've come too far. I'm too close. I've *killed* for this. And not just you, either.'

'Yeah,' I said. 'You rammed your car into Julian Clarke.'

'Who?'

'The young werewolf,' I said calmly. 'You're wearing his necklace.'

'Him?' Nappey's voice was sneeringly nasal. 'He was a fucking wolf. I'm talking about human lives. Who cares about supe lives?'

'You think you're doing all this for the greater good. In truth, you're nothing more than a pathetic man with violent tendencies.'

'What I've created will save lives!'

'You're a killer, Ted. Plain and simple. Your elixir won't help anyone. It won't help you.'

He hawked up a ball of phlegm and spat it at me. Despite his best efforts, it didn't come close but splattered uselessly on the floor, where it mingled with the remnants of shattered glass and spilled elixir.

'You see?' I said softly. 'You can't even spit straight.'

Nappey roared. He jerked back and grabbed a large, bulbous, glass container. There was some red liquid still clinging to its sides. 'There's enough here. I can still drink this. Then you'll see! You'll all see! You'll realise what I've done.'

A fire sparked in Maggie's eyes. As Nappey had reached for the last dregs of his potion, he'd relaxed his hold on her. She raised her leg and stamped down on his foot. He screamed and released her. Still gagged, and bound by her wrists, she fell away from him and backed into the corner of the kitchen.

'You, you, you – bitch!'

I adjusted the aim of the crossbow as Nappey held the container to his lips. 'Watch out for flying glass,' I said softly. 'This might hurt.'

Panic flared in his expression. 'No!'

I dipped the crossbow an inch. 'Either you get down on the floor or I smash the last of your elixir to smithereens.' I raised my eyebrows. 'How much do you want it to work? How much do you believe in it, Ted?'

'I won't surrender.' He was getting desperate. 'I won't give in.'

Whatever. My expression didn't alter. 'Okay.' I lifted the crossbow and aimed again. And, amazingly, that was enough.

Nappey's shoulders dropped. 'No,' he whispered. He hugged the flask to his chest. 'You can't destroy it. This is all that's left. It will work. I know it will.'

'Then put it down,' I said. 'Get down on the floor.' I met his eyes. 'Do as I say and I won't shoot it.' I didn't smile but I knew I'd already won. 'On a count of three. One. Two. Thr—'

Nappey put the container on the table, next to Scarlett's head. Then he lowered himself. 'You'll see. You'll give it to someone and then you'll see. I'm not wrong. This is what the world's been waiting for.'

'No, it's not. The world doesn't care what you've done. In fact,' I walked into the kitchen and stood over him, 'the world will never know.' I gazed at him. 'I'll finish what I started twelve hours ago. Edward Nappey, I am arresting you for murder.'

Chapter Twenty-Eight

Joe was already waiting under the old oak tree in Trinity Square when I arrived. The expression on his face was sullen and petulant. Despite his obvious reluctance, though he was clearly a vampire of his word.

'Hey Joe,' I said. 'Whaddaya know?'

He scowled at me. 'Nothing. I know nothing. Can I go now?'

I tutted. 'I'd expected better. I thought you'd want to impress me and show me that you're more than merely a fanged grunt.'

'You're only trying to goad me.'

Yeah, I was. 'Then give me something useful and I'll stop.'

He put his hands in his pockets, every action designed to advertise his reluctance. 'After the boss hugged Scarlett and made sure she was alright, he bawled her out. Nobody knows why, but it had to be for something big. He never usually lets himself get angry like that. From what I heard, it was to do with a human she's been playing with.' He shrugged. 'I don't know why that would bother him.'

I blinked. 'Anything else?'

'He's set an entire team onto scouring old books for any mention of phonenixes. Phoenixi.' Joe blew air through his cheeks. 'Weird bloody birds that won't die.'

I swallowed. 'Okay.'

'And,' he continued without registering my expression, 'there's some big meeting coming up with the werewolf alphas. I dunno what it's about, but all the bigwigs are pretty excited about it.'

I absorbed this. 'I see.'

Joe smiled smugly. 'It's about time those furry fuckers were put in their place.'

'Is that it?'

'Isn't that enough?'

I supposed it was.

***

I parked Tallulah in the same spot as before. Devereau Webb's tower block cast a long shadow across the road in front of me. Fred glanced over from the passenger seat. 'Are you sure about this?'

'Not really,' I answered. 'But it feels right.'

He nodded half-heartedly. Scarlett had made a full recovery from her injuries at Ted Nappey's hands, but she'd lost a fang in the process and garnered herself several new nicknames. She was also no longer answering his calls. The bruises on the side of Fred's neck had long since faded but I suspected the bruises on his heart would take longer to heal.

'Liza messaged,' he said. 'Vivienne Clarke has been released with a warning. Her husband is being charged with attempted murder. Apparently he sent you a letter. It arrived in the post this morning.' He gave me a long look. 'It's a thank-you card, if you can believe that.'

I smiled sadly. In the end, the Clarkes had got what they wanted, even if the results weren't quite what they'd hoped for.

The details of Edward Nappey's mission to create the Elixir of Fortitude were not being advertised. He was being charged with killing Julian Clarke, but DSI Barnes had agreed that it would be wiser to leave any suggestion of a magical potion that could strengthen a person and cure them of any affliction out of the equation.

No doubt Nappey would continue to bawl his supposed achievements to anyone who'd listen. Fortunately, given his incarcerated status, no-one would be interested. Even his mother had declined to visit him so far. And Maggie Tomkinson was happily telling everyone she met that he was insane. Perhaps he was. Or perhaps there was a glimmer of truth behind the elixir. Either way, it was too dangerous to mention to the world at large. Edward Nappey was going to rot, and so were his ideas for creating a magical potion.

'Do you want me to come with you?' Fred asked.

I shook my head. 'No, it's alright,' I said. 'I've got this.' I patted him on the shoulder and opened the car door. 'I won't be long.'

Climbing out, I shielded my eyes from the sun and glanced up, offering a friendly wave to whoever might be watching from the windows above. Then I grabbed my bag and headed inside. Forget the stairs; this time I was definitely taking the lift.

The doors pinged open before I could press the button. Waiting inside was the familiar face of Gaz, one of Devereau Webb's loyal henchmen. 'You again,' he grunted. 'I've been told to take you right up.'

I smiled and stepped in to join him. 'I appreciate that.'

'Not my call.' He sniffed. The lift juddered and started to rise. 'But I suppose you're not all bad.'

'I suppose you're not either,' I said.

He grinned suddenly. 'Yes, I am.' He wagged a finger at me. 'I've got a reputation to maintain. And so does the boss.'

I glanced at him. 'We all have a capacity for evil,' I said. 'And for good.'

Gaz looked sceptical. 'If you say so.'

The lift stopped and Gaz escorted me out, unwilling to leave my side. I wasn't sure what he thought I was going to do without his watchful eye to stop me, but I didn't bother protesting. One day, Webb and Gaz and all the others would get their come-uppance. Today wasn't that day.

The door to Devereau Webb's flat was already open. I walked inside, giving Alice a friendly wave. She was curled up on the sofa with a blanket around her, her skin paler than the last time I'd seen her. She glared at me and hugged her knees. She knew where her loyalties lay.

'Detective.' Webb strode through from another room with an easy smile on his face.

I pretended not to notice the dark circles around his eyes and returned the smile. 'Mr Webb.'

'Are you here to charge me with a crime?' he enquired. 'Because I can assure you that I am wholly innocent.'

'Of course you are,' I murmured. I reached into my pocket and pulled out a small vial, setting it onto the table between us.

'What's that?' he stared at it. 'It looks disgusting.'

'It *is* disgusting.' I avoided looking at the bottle. 'I won't tell you what's in it. You don't want to know. But there is a slim possibility,' I said, with a quick glance towards the sofa and Alice's small body, 'that it might be what you're looking for. I can't vouch for its efficacy. It may do nothing at all. But there's a book hidden away in the Carlyle Library called *Infernal Enchantments* that suggests…' My voice trailed away. 'Well. It might work.'

Devereau Webb's hooded gaze flicked from me to Alice and back again. 'There's not very much in there.'

'No,' I said. 'And this is a one-time shot. There will be no more of what's in that vial. Ever.'

He scratched his chin. 'I really don't want to know what's in it, do I?'

'Nope.'

'What do you want in return? If you're going to ask me to leave my criminal ways behind me, I'm certainly willing to do so, but I can't speak for the people who follow me. I can control them to a certain extent, but only if they respect me. If I turn to the right side of the law, someone else will simply step into my shoes. Sometimes,' he said quietly, 'it's better the devil you know.'

'I won't ask you to go straight. I think you should, and I think your talents are wasted here, but I know that it wouldn't work.' I looked again at Alice. 'There are no guarantees this will do anything other than make her sicker, but it is given freely. There are no conditions attached.'

His clever eyes continued to watch me. 'But?'

I picked at a hangnail. 'But,' I said quietly, 'I would like to ask a favour.'

***

Fred looked relieved to see me return with all my body parts in place. 'Will she drink it?' he asked.

'I don't know.' I bit my lip. 'Probably.'

'Will it work?'

I sighed. 'Your guess is as good as mine.' I switched on Tallulah's engine. When my phone rang, I turned the ignition off again. I checked the screen before I answered and my stomach lurched. 'Hi,' I said.

'D'Artagnan.' Lukas's voice was clipped. 'I've just received a call from Devereau Webb. I had a deal with him. Unfortunately, that deal is now off. And apparently it's because of your intervention.'

The Shepherd hadn't wasted any time. I didn't play ignorant. This wasn't the time for games. I'd long since worked out what Lukas's deal with Devereau Webb had been about. As soon as Scarlett had mentioned Devereau Webb's name back in Baxter's house, I'd known what Lukas was up to. I also knew that putting a stop to the deal was the right choice.

'You approached him, didn't you? After his attempts to bribe the clan alphas, you decided to take matters into your own hands and for your own gains. You wanted to gain the rights to Regent's Park and you tried to get Devereau Webb to give them to you. What did you offer him for those rights? Money?'

'A great deal of money. He was happy with the arrangement. You should not have intervened, D'Artagnan.'

'Wielding such a thing over the clans would be dangerous. It would also give you more power than you have the right to possess.'

'That's not your call to make.'

I took a moment before answering. 'It's my job to ensure peace across the supernatural community.'

'I wasn't waging war. You should know me better than that.'

'What would you have demanded, Lukas? What would you have demanded from the clans in return for Regent's Park?'

His response was silky smooth. 'Does it matter?'

'You know it does.'

'I hadn't decided yet.' He paused. 'I'm not a bad man, D'Artagnan.'

'I don't think you are. And I didn't say you were.'

'But,' Lukas continued, 'I am the vampires' leader. I am their Lord, and I have to put our interests above those of the werewolves. I look after my own. For what it's worth, I would never have extended any offer to clan Sullivan. Not after what they tried to do to you.'

I drew in a ragged breath. 'Am I supposed to be grateful for that?'

'No. But I wanted you to know it anyway.' There was an edge of steel to his voice. 'And for what it's also worth, you can set that imposter syndrome to one side. By speaking to Devereau Webb behind my back, you've proved that you're as much a power player within the supe community as any of us.'

'I…' Shit. I wasn't sure what to say to that. Thank you?

'I would prefer it, however,' Lukas continued, 'if you didn't interfere in my business matters again.'

'That will depend on what those business matters happen to be.'

His response was immediate. 'And whether you find out about them or not. Joe will no longer be available to you.'

I'd already suspected as much. 'Don't hurt him.'

'I'm not a monster. It upsets me that you think I would harm him.'

'I'm sorry,' I said softly.

'Apology accepted.' There was a beat. 'How are you, Emma? You died again. And again I was not there when I should have been.'

'My death is not on you.'

'That's easy for you to say,' he murmured. 'Are you alright?'

'I'm fine.'

'Good. I still owe you dinner. How does next week sound?'

I blinked. 'I thought—' My voice drifted off.

'I've never mixed business with pleasure before. This is not a good time to start. Saturday night. My place. I will cook, as promised.'

'Uh…'

'I'll take that as a yes. Take care, my little phoenix.' He hung up before I could say anything else.

I stared at the phone. I suspected that Lukas was a lot more pissed off than he wanted me to know. And possibly impressed too. I scratched my head. I wasn't sure what to make of him. I tossed the phone to one side and turned on the engine.

'Come on then, old girl.' I gave Tallulah's steering wheel a pat. Then I allowed myself a smile and ignored Fred's curious – and slightly envious – glance. 'Let's go home.'

Thank you so much for reading Infernal Enchantment. *I truly hope that you've enjoyed it. If you can, please take the opportunity to review it – it makes a huge difference to small indie authors like me.*

Emma's story continues in Midnight Smoke, the third book in the Firebrand series which will be released on November 5th, 2020.

Helen x

Other titles by Helen Harper

The complete *Blood Destiny* series

"A spectacular and addictive series."

Mackenzie Smith has always known that she was different. Growing up as the only human in a pack of rural shapeshifters will do that to you, but then couple it with some mean fighting skills and a fiery temper and you end up with a woman that few will dare to cross. However, when the only father figure in her life is brutally murdered, and the dangerous Brethren with their predatory Lord Alpha come to investigate, Mack has to not only ensure the physical safety of her adopted family by hiding her apparent humanity, she also has to seek the blood-soaked vengeance that she craves.

Book One -   Bloodfire
Book Two -   Bloodmagic
Book Three - Bloodrage
Book Four - Blood Politics
Book Five - Bloodlust

Also
-      Corrigan Fire
-      Corrigan Magic

- Corrigan Rage
- Corrigan Politics
- Corrigan Lust

The complete *Bo Blackman* series

A half-dead daemon, a massacre at her London based PI firm and evidence that suggests she's the main suspect for both ... Bo Blackman is having a very bad week.

She might be naive and inexperienced but she's determined to get to the bottom of the crimes, even if it means involving herself with one of London's most powerful vampire Families and their enigmatic leader.

It's pretty much going to be impossible for Bo to ever escape unscathed.

Book One - Dire Straits

Book Two - New Order

Book Three - High Stakes

Book Four - Red Angel

Book Five - Vigilante Vampire

Book Six - Dark Tomorrow

The complete *Highland Magic* series

Integrity Taylor walked away from the Sidhe when she was a child. Orphaned and bullied, she simply had no reason to stay, especially not when the sins of her father were going to remain on her shoulders. She found a new family - a group of thieves who proved that blood was less important than loyalty and love.

But the Sidhe aren't going to let Integrity stay away forever. They need her more than anyone realises - besides, there are prophecies to be fulfilled, people to be saved and hearts to be won over. If anyone can do it, Integrity can.

Book One - Gifted Thief
Book Two - Honour Bound
Book Three - Veiled Threat
Book Four - Last Wish

The complete *Dreamweaver* series

"I have special coping mechanisms for the times I need to open the front door. They're even often successful..."

Zoe Lydon knows there's often nothing logical or rational about fear. It doesn't change the fact that she's too terrified to step outside her own house, however.

What Zoe doesn't realise is that she's also a dreamweaver - able to access other people's subconscious minds. When she finds herself in the Dreamlands and up against its sinister Mayor, she'll need to use all of her wits - and overcome all of her fears - if she's ever going to come out alive.

Book One - Night Shade

Book Two - Night Terrors

Book Three - Night Lights

Stand alone novels

Eros

As probably the last person in the world who'd appreciate hearts, flowers and romance, Coop is convinced that true love doesn't exist – which is rather unfortunate considering he's also known as Cupid, the God of Love. He'd rather spend his days drinking, womanising and generally having as much fun as he possible can. As far as he's concerned, shooting people with bolts of pure love is a waste of his time…but then his path crosses with that of shy and retiring Skye Sawyer and nothing will ever be quite the same again.

Wraith

Magic. Shadows. Adventure. Romance.

Saiya Buchanan is a wraith, able to detach her shadow from her body and send it off to do her bidding. But, unlike most of her kin, Saiya doesn't deal in death. Instead, she trades secrets - and in the goblin besieged city of Stirling in Scotland, they're a highly prized commodity. It might just be, however, that the goblins have been hiding the greatest secret of them all. When Gabriel de Florinville, a Dark Elf, is sent as royal envoy into Stirling and takes her prisoner, Saiya is not only going to uncover the sinister truth. She's also going to realise that sometimes the deepest secrets are the ones locked within your own heart.

The complete *Lazy Girl's Guide To Magic* series

Hard Work Will Pay Off Later. Laziness Pays Off Now.

Let's get one thing straight - Ivy Wilde is not a heroine. In fact, she's probably the last witch in the world who you'd call if you needed a magical helping hand. If it were down to Ivy, she'd spend all day every day on her sofa where she could watch TV, munch junk food and talk to her feline familiar to her heart's content.

However, when a bureaucratic disaster ends up with Ivy as the victim of a case of mistaken identity, she's yanked very unwillingly into Arcane Branch, the investigative department of the Hallowed Order of Magical Enlightenment. Her problems are quadrupled when a valuable object is stolen right from under the Order's noses.

It doesn't exactly help that she's been magically bound to Adeptus Exemptus Raphael Winter. He might have piercing sapphire eyes and a body which a cover model would be proud of but, as far as Ivy's concerned, he's a walking advertisement for the joyless perils of too much witch-work.

And if he makes her go to the gym again, she's definitely going to turn him into a frog.

Book One - Slouch Witch
Book Two - Star Witch
Book Three - Spirit Witch
Sparkle Witch (Christmas short story)

The complete *Fractured Faery* series

One corpse. Several bizarre looking attackers. Some very strange magical powers. And a severe bout of amnesia.

It's one thing to wake up outside in the middle of the night with a decapitated man for company. It's another to have no memory of how you got there - or who you are.

She might not know her own name but she knows that several people are out to get her. It could be because she has strange magical powers seemingly at her fingertips and is some kind of fabulous hero. But then why does she appear to inspire fear in so many? And who on earth is the sexy, green-eyed barman who apparently despises her? So many questions ... and so few answers.

At least one thing is for sure - the streets of Manchester have never met someone quite as mad as Madrona…

Book One - Box of Frogs
SHORTLISTED FOR THE KINDLE STORYTELLER AWARD 2018
Book Two - Quiver of Cobras
Book Three - Skulk of Foxes

The complete *City Of Magic* series

Charley is a cleaner by day and a professional gambler by
night. She might be haunted by her tragic past but she's
never thought of herself as anything or anyone special.
Until, that is, things start to go terribly wrong all across
the city of Manchester. Between plagues of rats,
firestorms and the gleaming blue eyes of a sexy Scottish
werewolf, she might just have landed herself in the
middle of a magical apocalypse. She might also be the
only person who has the ability to bring order to an
utterly chaotic new world.

Book One - Shrill Dusk
Book Two - Brittle Midnight
Book Three - Furtive Dawn

About the author

After teaching English literature in the UK, Japan and Malaysia, Helen Harper left behind the world of education following the worldwide success of her Blood Destiny series of books. She is a professional member of the Alliance of Independent Authors and writes full time, thanking her lucky stars every day that's she lucky enough to do so!

Helen has always been a book lover, devouring science fiction and fantasy tales when she was a child growing up in Scotland.

She currently lives in Devon in the UK with far too many cats – not to mention the dragons, fairies, demons, wizards and vampires that seem to keep appearing from nowhere.